George Ives loomed up against the light, his eyes slitted and a smile on his lips. He said, "I remember we had us an appointment, Reno. Let's see if you're man enough to stand up to me."

Ives had picked the moment well. He was not wearing a gun, and he had complete confidence in his skill as a roughhouse fighter.

"I don't like to fight, George," Reno said. He got to his feet and turned squarely to face the bulk of Ives. "Nobody wins in a fight."

Ives stripped off his coat, threw it to Haze Lyons, then came toward Reno, fists extended.

"I'm going to pound you into the ground, Reno. Get your hands up!"

THE VIGILANTE

GILBERT MORRIS

LIVING BOOKS
Tyndale House Publishers, Inc.
Wheaton, Illinois

First printing, January 1988
Library of Congress Catalog Card Number 87-51342
ISBN 0-8423-7811-1
Copyright 1987 by Gilbert Morris
Printed in the United States of America

To Monique, the third daughter,

who proves that there are some things

that sparkle in this dark world

ONE
Virginia City

Leaving the Hellgate River, Jim Reno traced his way through great dark gorges. The fierce blizzard that had torn the land like an angry beast had left huge drifts in the hollows, and he carefully skirted the crevasses. Peaks showed high above him in the early spring's sun, and creeks roared and tumbled white in the rocky beds. Everything seemed new and alive after the frozen silence of winter. As he paused on the crest of a jagged promontory and looked over a snug little valley, emerald green and rich with red and yellow flowers, he leaned back in the saddle and rested his eyes on the scene.

Riding had trimmed him, and there was a hollowness in his wedge-shaped face. His hair lay thick and black and ragged against his temples, and his eyes were sleepy under jet brows. A youthful look was countered by lines slanting out from his eyes across his tanned skin. Except for a slight break on the bridge of his straight nose and a small scar over his right temple, his face was unmarked. He wore a heavy dark wool coat, a fawn-colored shirt with bone buttons, and faded butternut breeches with a faint stripe down the side of the legs. A gray, low-crowned hat anchored by a leather lanyard was shoved back on his head, and a narrow black belt supported the gun at his side.

He looked at the scene before him, said, "Pretty," then urged his horse down the slope. All day he rode hard, then camped on the Beaverhead beside a stream. At dawn he was on the trail again. At noon he reached the Stinkingwater at the mouth of Alder Gulch. He followed the road upgrade, noting along the edges the potholes of prospectors. Camps clung to the edge of the Gulch, but he pushed his tired horse steadily along until he rode into Virginia City as the shadows were growing long.

Four thousand prospectors were scattered along Alder Creek with their sluices and pans and Long Toms gutting the hillside where once a river's channel had dropped its gold treasure. Virginia City, its streets and cross streets marked out by tents and brush wickiups and a few board houses, was beginning to wake up as Reno made his way down the muddy street. Like all boom camps, this one had been hurriedly thrown together with cheap lumber, canvas, and logs. Fully three-quarters of the camp was made up of saloons and dance halls. The rest of it consisted of stores, miners' supply houses, livery barns, and restaurants.

Reno was hungry, but, ignoring the pangs, he pulled up in front of a stable. A man with a steel hook instead of a left hand stepped out to meet him. "Help you?"

Reno handed him the reins and nodded. "Grain her good."

The one-armed man gave the horse a sharp look, then turned a pair of steady hazel eyes on Reno, and commented, "Pretty well used up, ain't she? You just come in?"

Reno nodded and pulled a pipe out of his pocket. As he packed it with tobacco from a worn leather pouch, he was aware of the stable man's interest. "Yes. From the Bitterroots."

"Pass's been closed for months. Must be clear now if you got through." He led the horse inside, removed the saddle and bridle expertly with his one hand, and said, "You want to leave the animal here for a spell?"

"Pulling out tomorrow morning," Reno said. "I need a couple of horses—or mules, if you know of any."

"Mules? None in camp. But I got a team you might look at." He dumped a bucket of feed in the box, turned, and put out his hand. "Sam Bible's my name."

"Jim Reno." The stable man had a hard, calloused hand with a grip like a vise. "Don't think I've ever met anybody with your name," Reno said.

"That's likely," Bible said with a grin. He had one tooth missing, and there was humorous expression on his moon face as he added, "Give me a pile of trouble, that name. Everybody expects a man with a name like mine to be a saint. Crimped my style considerable when I was chasin' the gals. But it has its advantages, Reno. Far as I can remember nobody ever forgot my name, like it was Smith or Jones. You wanna see that team?"

He led Reno to a corral, and after a quick

examination, Reno said, "They'll do. How much?"

"You better sit down afore I set the price," Bible said. "I got to get six hundred for the team." Reno's eyebrows shot up, and Sam Bible hurriedly added, "I know, I know—they ain't worth it. But things is different here at Virginia City. Gold's the cheapest thing there is! Why, I paid five dollars for a little apple this morning. Everything has to be freighted in, you see?"

"I'll take the team," Reno said. He pulled a black leather wallet from his coat pocket, removed a sheaf of bank notes, and counted out the money. Handing it to Bible, he said, "Like to rent a horse for a few days."

"That's a good bay," Bible murmured, motioning with his steel hook toward a rangy animal in the corral. He was holding the notes in his hand and there was an odd look in his hazel eyes. "Guess this is more bank money than I've seen in a spell." He lifted his eyes, then stuck the money in his shirt pocket and said, "I ain't much of a hand to meddle in other folks' business, Reno, but was I you, I'd keep that wad of bills tucked out of sight. This is a tough camp."

"Sure." Reno nodded, then he gave a smile and added, "I've been in the backwoods so long guess I've forgotten how to be careful." He added as he turned to leave, "I'll be around early to pick up the horses. You got a pack you can put on one of the team?"

"Sure." Bible almost asked a question as to the purpose, but he cut it off and added, "Creighton's is the best place for supplies, if you need any, Reno."

Leaving the stable, Reno made his way along the muddy street, which was already beginning to fill up with men coming in from their claims. Creighton's General Store was on the main street, a large unpainted board building between a blacksmith shop and a saloon. The interior was dimly lit by three lanterns, which cast their feeble glow over a jumble of wares. The floor was crowded with barrels, saddles, harnesses, boxes, crates, while along the walls canned goods, clothing, cooking utensils, and a hundred other items filled the rough shelves.

Several miners were inside, sitting around a pot-bellied stove, and two women with highly colored cheeks were handling bolts of material in the rear. A muscular blond man with sharp, good-looking features was looking at a repeating rifle at one end of the counter. He lifted a pair of pale blue eyes to Reno, bracketed him, then went back to working the lever on the rifle.

"Something for you?" A tall, stately man with white hair and a Vandyke beard moved away from the customer to stand before Reno.

"Need some supplies—bacon, beans, canned tomatoes . . . " As Reno named off the items, the tall man moved efficiently, pulling the food from the shelves.

"Creighton, you want to sell this gun or not?"

The blond man had moved up, rifle in his hand, and there was a steady arrogance in his pale eyes as he stared at Reno.

"Didn't know you were ready to take it, Lyons," the merchant said. "It's seventy-five."

"Take it out of this dust." The blond man reached into his pocket and tossed a bag on the counter, but did not take his eyes from Reno as Creighton moved to a pair of scales to weigh the dust. "Don't know you, do I?"

"Just came in," Reno said softly.

"From where?" The question came out sharply, and when Reno didn't answer at once, he said, "I'm Haze Lyons, deputy sheriff. What's your business in Virginia City?"

Reno turned to face him, aware of the silence that had spread out over the store. Lyons was a dandy in dress, but the foppish attire did not conceal the straight-grained nerve of the man. He would never rest, Reno realized, until he had tested his strength against a man.

"Just came in from the Bitterroots, Deputy. Left Oregon a spell back and got snowed in. Name's Jim Reno."

Lyons relaxed with a thin smile and said, "Yeah, it's been a bad winter. You stakin' a claim?"

"Thought I might try my luck."

"Here's your dust, Lyons," Creighton said. He handed the bag back to the deputy and said to Reno, "That all adds up to forty-three dollars."

The others in the store had turned away from the scene, but Lyons stood watching, and Reno had no other choice but to take his wallet out and pull a few notes out to pay the bill. He did not miss the look on Lyons's face, and he saw a frown on the face of Creighton at the sight of the thick wallet.

"Take this with you now?" the merchant asked.

"Like to leave it here until after I eat, if you've got room."

"I'll put it under the counter."

Haze Lyons nodded, said, "See you around, Reno," and left carrying the rifle.

"Appreciate your business," the tall merchant said, straightening up. "I'm John Creighton." He glanced toward the door the deputy had gone through, started to say something, but glanced at the men sitting around the stove and changed his mind. "Stop in any time."

Reno nodded. "Sure. Where's the hotel?"

"Two blocks down—the Royal. Food is pretty good, too."

The mention of food started Reno's juices flowing, and he made his way down the street to the hotel. A fat man with a beefy red face took his money and said, "Take number six."

The room could not have been much more primitive. A bed with a worn, dingy purple spread and a sagging mattress took up three-fourths of the space. The only other furniture was a table with a cracked pitcher and a washbowl. Reno dashed his face with water, dried on the thin towel, then went downstairs at once. The fat man motioned toward the door leading off to the left. "Get your eats in there."

The restaurant was a narrow room with two windows and a door on the wall facing the street. The place was half-filled, but men were coming in steadily, so Reno took a table, placing his back to the wall. There was a sign on the wall that read, "If you don't like our grub, don't eat here."

Most of the customers were roughly dressed miners who put their heads down and ate with the same intensity as they ripped the earth for the golden dust. At the back sat a couple, an older man with gold-rimmed glasses and a young woman in a dark dress. A waiter wearing a dirty apron came to stand before Reno. "We got steaks or stew, potatoes and onions."

Reno grinned at the simplicity of the menu, but he had been in mining camps before and was not surprised. "Bring me some of that steak—a double helping. And about a quart of hot coffee."

He at his meal slowly. The steak was tough, but the vegetables were well-cooked and seasoned, and the coffee was strong and black. He had learned to take the good moments and savor them. The waiter brought him a huge slice of apple pie, and he ate it slowly, washing it down with sips of black coffee.

Three men came in and went to a table in the rear near the couple Reno had noticed. One of them was Haze Lyons. He spotted Reno at once, and as the trio sat down, he leaned forward and said something to a tall, broad-shouldered man wearing two guns and a star on his shirt. The man turned a pair of dark eyes on Reno and nodded, then turned his back.

Reno got up, put on his hat, and caught the waiter near the door. He paid him, and as he turned to go, he collided with the couple.

"Sorry," he said with a smile. "Guess I'm getting clumsy in my old age."

"Well, it's pretty crowded in here," the man said. "I'm William Merritt. Don't believe we've met."

"Name's Reno. Just came in today."

Merritt was a slight man with hair going gray. He had light blue eyes behind the thick lenses and a gentlemanly air that seemed strange in a mining camp. "This is my daughter, Mrs. Warren."

The woman was fair with smooth skin and a round face. Her hair was honey-colored, and her eyes were so blue they seemed violet in the flickering lamplight. She nodded but did not speak when Reno said, "Glad to meet you."

There was a moment's silence and then Merritt said, "We're having a service tonight at our church, if you'd like to come."

Reno looked at him with interest. Ministry was the last profession to come to many mining camps. "Thanks for the invitation, Reverend. Probably not tonight, but I'll take you up later."

"Fine, fine!" Merritt's face lit up, and Reno suspected his invitations did not always find a welcome with the roughs in the camp. "Come along anytime. The church is at the north end of town." He looked at the young woman, but she said nothing, and there was a faint look of skepticism in her dark eyes that puzzled Reno. As they left the restaurant, Reno wondered about her husband. Women were scarce in any mining camp, and one as attractive as Merritt's daughter would be the center of hungry attention from the men of the camp.

For an hour he walked the streets, which were crowded with miners who had come in from their claims. They hit Virginia City like a wave, roaming the muddy streets in groups or individually, and the night air was loud with music from the hurdy-gurdy houses, accompanied by the shouts of customers and the calculated laughter of the dance hall girls.

Trail weariness was heavy on him, and he started back to the hotel to get a good night's sleep. Passing by a row of saloons, he heard someone call "Reno" and turned to see Sam Bible crossing the street. The steel hook glinted in the light of a lantern as he gestured toward the end of the street. "I was in Creighton's and he told me you bought some supplies. I figured you wanted them on that horse, so I had my hired man take 'em down with the stuff I bought and load on the pack. That all right?"

Reno grinned. "Thanks, Bible."

"Come on, let's have a drink." Bible pulled at Reno, drawing him to a saloon called the El Dorado. The bar was crowded two deep, and the two men had trouble making their way across the floor. Half of the room was filled with gambling tables, and two roulette wheels clinked as they spun. The middle of the saloon was cleared for dancing, and half a dozen highly painted saloon girls were spun around violently by heavy-booted miners. A mahogany bar ran half the length of the room, and in the back were several tables where men sat drinking and talking.

Bible shoved his way through the crowd to the back of the room and pulled up before a table. "Well, Reno, if you ain't too careful about the company you keep, guess this table will do as well as any." He grinned down at a short, bulky man wearing a heavy black overcoat and said, "Make a little room, X. This here is Jim Reno just come in from the Bitterroots. Reno, this is X. Beidler—Ringo Jukes—Nick Tbolt—Link McKeever. You already met Creighton."

Beidler peered up at Reno with sharp black eyes. "Passes clear at last, are they? We'll have two thousand more men in a month. Sit down."

"And most of 'em will leave here with less than they brought in." Ringo Jukes was a thick-shouldered fellow with dark eyes and black hair. He had the long arms and scarred knuckles of a brawler, and there was an angry light in his brown eyes as he added, "Fools expect gold to pop out of the ground like daisies!"

16

Link McKeever was the youngest man in the game, not over twenty. He lifted a pair of wide eyes and smiled at Jukes. "Well, Ringo, I came here pretty much the same way." He stared down at the palms of his calloused hands and murmured, "The stuff sure don't come easy, does it?"

"The only ones who get it easy are the crooks who take it from us." X. Beidler looked like a bulldog as he glowered around the room. "Did you hear about Jake Randall? A rough held him up in broad daylight yesterday. Jake didn't have much on him, and the scum said, 'Next time I brace you, have more money or I'll kill you!'"

"Looks like the law could do somethin'." Nick Tbolt was a young Dutchman with blue eyes and fair hair. "Seems like with four deputies they ought to be able to put a cap on this robbin'."

Ringo Jukes snorted and took a drink out of his glass, cursed and snapped, "Them yahoos? Why, they ain't no better'n the crooks they're supposed to be catchin'!"

"Be careful, Ringo." John Creighton spoke softly, but Reno noticed that the rest of them listened. "We all have our suspicions, but best keep them quiet for awhile."

Bible said at once, "That's good advice, John. Reno, what'll you have?"

Reno hated the taste of liquor, but said, "Well, I'd fancy a glass of wine if it's to be had."

"Most saloons serve only some sort of rotgut made the day before yesterday, but Saul Logan keeps a good stock," Creighton said. "Get us some of that French stuff, will you, X?"

Beidler got up and made his way to the bar, and

Reno was looking at Creighton carefully. The talk ran around the table until the stocky Beidler got back and poured each man a glass of wine, then Reno said, "I've seen you before, Mr. Creighton. Can't place you, though."

"You're from the South?"

"Yes."

"I was a colonel under Longstreet."

Reno snapped his fingers. "I remember—at Gettysburg!"

Creighton's eyes suddenly burned, and he asked quietly, "You were at the Round Top?"

"Third Arkansas, Colonel."

"I know the regiment. Not many left at the end, were there, Reno?"

"Not many." Reno took a sip of the wine and the moment came back—the long lines sweeping up the hill, falling like grain hit by a scythe as the Union fire cut them down. "I remember you now. You were on the right flank. I remember because it was the only time I ever saw General Longstreet. You were both mounted and talking. He was shaking his head and seemed to be mad about something."

Creighton's face grew sad, and he shook his head. "Dutch didn't want to charge the hill, but Lee insisted." He took a small sip of the wine and said softly, "For once General Lee was wrong. We had no chance at all that day. That was the day the Confederacy died, I think."

"It was a hard war," Reno remarked gently.

Ringo Jukes shifted rebelliously and declared, "Well, I tell you, I don't feel no safer here than I did in the army. At least I knew who was shootin' at me and who to shoot at." He rolled his heavy shoulders and stated harshly, "Look out there." He waved toward the crowded room. "Any one of them jaspers could be one of the Innocents!"

"Innocents?" Reno frowned. "What's that?"

"That the name for the outlaws who've got a stranglehold on this camp, Reno," Sam Bible explained. He gouged a track in the scarred table with his steel hook, and there was a smoldering fire in his hazel eyes as he looked over the room. "Ringo is right, though. Anybody here could be one of them."

Reno sat in his chair loosely, hating to leave the warmth of the saloon for the cold hotel room. The talk was mostly of mining—new claims, new methods, old camps that had played out and new ones cropping up. Creighton and Bible were, he noted, watching him carefully, but he could not fathom why. He joined in a penny-ante poker game, lost ten dollars, and grew familiar with the men at the table. He had known men, good and bad, and it was his quick judgment that these men, especially John Creighton and X. Beidler, were leaders of some sort in the camp. Ringo Jukes was a bruiser and probably could influence the rough miners, but the two older men had a steadiness Reno had seen in good officers during the war.

Finally he sighed and forced himself to stand. "Guess I'll turn in. Enjoyed the game."

He left and made his way along the crowded room, and Nick Tbolt said, "How come he couldn't be one of the Innocents, Sam? You don't know nothing about him."

"Why, I just *know*, Nick!" Bible said, tapping the table with his hook.

"I've seen his kind before," Creighton said. "He's

the sort who always got killed off quick in the war because he was always quick to run to the guns. But he's got cunning as well as courage."

"He ain't very big, though," Jukes said doubtfully. "Can't be no more'n one-sixty."

"You big ox!" Bible glared at Jukes and spat. "If muscles was the test of a man, a mule's hind leg would be the best man in the world."

"Hey, look at that!" Link McKeever said, and as they all turned to look toward the door, he said, "Haze Lyons is bracin' him!"

Reno had been threading his way through the crowd when a hand gripped his arm and pulled him around. He turned quickly to face Haze Lyons, seeing at once that the man had been drinking heavily.

"Well, my old friend Reno!" Lyons said loudly. He kept his grip on Reno's arm and winked at the other deputy Reno had seen at the restaurant. "Hey, Jack, this is Jim Reno. Jack Gallagher. Have a drink with us, Reno!"

Lyons's eyes were gleaming, and his grip was harder than it should have been. He was not as drunk as he appeared, and Reno knew at once that Lyons was on the prowl for a brawl.

Reno said evenly, "Glad to meet you, Gallagher. Don't guess I'll have another drink, Lyons. Some other time."

He tried to pull away, but Lyons tightened his grip, and there was a wicked smile on his full lips as he said loudly, "Why, blast your eyes, Reno! You're not gonna insult a man are you?"

The sounds of the room washed away, and Haze Lyons looked around, satisfied that he had everyone's attention. He picked up a glass of liquor with his free hand and shoved it toward Reno, saying, "Now, you just drink that down and it'll be all right."

Time flowed over him, and Reno thought, *Nothing ever changes. Always something like this.* He thought of the many times he'd stood before some man and had to decide whether to stand or fold. And he knew that if he were to survive in Virginia City, he had to meet the challenge.

A smile touched his broad lips, and he spoke so gently that at first Lyons failed to catch the words. "Haze, if you don't take your hand off me, I'm going to tear your face off."

A quick thrill ran around the room, and men started shifting to get out of the line of fire.

Lyons was a dandy, but he was three inches taller and twenty pounds heavier than Reno, and he was solid muscle. He stared at Reno, and his fair skin flushed with pleasure at the prospect of a fight.

With a sigh he looked around and said, "Well, you all heard it. A man can't listen to talk like that, can he now?" He unpinned his badge and laid it on the bar, then carefully lifted his .44 and laid it beside the badge. "Just put your gun right there, Reno, and we'll have our fun."

"There's no fun in fighting, Haze," Reno remarked, pulling his gun free and placing it beside that of Lyons.

"Not for you, maybe," Lyons said with a smirk. "Back up there, let's have a little room! Give this joker room enough to fall down."

Gallagher said, "You ought not to fight this man, being as you're a lawman, Haze."

"I'm a lawman, but that don't give this—" Lyons glanced toward Gallagher, but it was a ruse to catch

Reno off guard. He threw a powerful right at Reno, which would have ended the fight if it had landed. But it missed, as Reno, expecting something tricky, pulled back. The force of the effort caused Lyons to fall against Reno.

Quick as a cat, Reno grabbed Lyons by the shoulders and sent him crashing into a table, overturning chairs. He did not attempt to follow up, but stood there, a tough shape in the light, as Lyons kicked at the chairs and came to his feet, face blazing with anger. "You'll be dead meat, you sucker!"

The long left of Lyons flicked out, but Reno moved aside. In a lightning motion, he slashed Lyons's mouth with a blow that did not travel more than six inches. It stopped the advance of the large man as if he'd run into a railroad tie.

Lyons was driven back by the force of that single blow, and it was obvious to every man that he was stunned. They expected to see Reno charge in and beat him to the floor, but Reno dropped his hands and said quietly, "I told you there was no fun in it, Lyons."

For one instant Reno hoped that Lyons would call it off, but as the man's eyes cleared and he reached up to touch the blood running down his chin, several of his supporters said, "Get him, Lyons!" and he drove at Reno with a yell of rage.

The force of the charge drove Reno back against the bar, and he caught a wild blow on the temple. Lyons felt him going down, and Reno twisted just in time to parry the knee that would have crippled him. He held on as Lyons battered at his head and tried to shake free.

With a surge of power, Reno wrested loose, and

his head cleared as Lyons came at him with both hands pounding. Reno backed away, catching most of the blows on his arms and shoulders. They had a numbing force, but he had learned to endure an enemy's attack. *Let him wear himself out, then one good blow will take him out. That had been Old Blue Light's way. Put everything you have in one blow that will destroy the enemy's confidence.* So he backed away, dodging and parrying, and finally Lyons's blows grew weaker and his breathing began to rasp in the smoke-filled air. Suddenly Lyons stepped back and yelled, "Fight, you louse!"

It was what Reno had been waiting for. He planted his feet and drove a right into the face of his opponent with every ounce of his weight. The blow exploded like a mortar in the face of Haze Lyons, smashing his nose and flattening his lips against his teeth. He was driven backward, and there was a looseness as he collapsed. Every man knew he was out.

Reno stood there for one instant, then whirled to get his gun and get out, but a fist caught him in the neck and he fell to his knees hearing a coarse voice yelling, "You ain't goin' to get away with it, sucker! I'll bust you up myself!"

Reno came to his feet to find a huge man glaring at him. Another man, smaller but broad and muscular, moved in, saying, "Yeah, Boone, let's put him down."

"Brunton, you and Helm ain't gonna do nothin' to nobody!"

Ringo Jukes burst out of the crowd and stood there, as big a man as the hulking Boone, and added,

"If you want a little action, Boone, why, you just let me call the tune!"

"Back off, Jukes!" Jack Gallagher drew his gun and waved it toward Jukes, adding, "This ain't your fight."

"It's not theirs either, Gallagher." Sam Bible advanced, his face flushed, as he said, "You can't let these two loose on the man!"

"Why can't I?" Gallagher said with a smile. He turned to the two men and said, "You fellers fight fair, you hear me?"

Boone Helm was a hulk of a man with blunt features and pale eyes. "I'll bust you to pieces!" he hissed, advancing on Reno.

Sam Brunton was shorter, but broad and thick through the shoulders. He had the face of a heavy drinker, and there was a light of pleasure in his eyes as he came at Reno from the left.

As they closed in, Reno knew that two of them would get him down and kick him to pieces if he didn't stop them. They had him wedged in, and there would be no help, not with Gallagher holding a gun on the crowd.

A thought struck him, and he remembered what a sergeant had said just before they had made the attack at Franklin. "We got to hit 'em where they don't think we will in a way they won't never think we'll do."

In that moment, Reno knew that Helm would expect him to go for the smaller man, so he did just the opposite—but not with his fists as the huge man expected. He made a pass with his right, which drew the big man's hands up, then he pivoted and swung his right boot forward in a tremendous kick that caught Helm on the left kneecap.

There was a loud thudding sound as his sharp pointed boot struck the knee, driving the leg from under Helm, who dropped suddenly with a shrill cry of pain.

Without pausing, Reno swept up a half-filled bottle of whiskey and in one smooth motion brought it down on the unprotected head of Sam Brunton. The force of the blow split the scalp and drove the man to the floor, where he lay with one leg kicking the floor in a reflex action.

The wild eruption of violence had taken only a few seconds, and the miners, accustomed to fights that went on for much longer, were hushed, staring at the two men on the floor.

Then Jukes let out a yelp. "Well, you son-of-a-gun!" But as a swarm of men rushed over to pound his shoulder, Reno heard Gallagher say, "Stand back! You hear me!" He cursed and waved his gun at the crowd. "This man is under arrest!"

"Under arrest?" Bible cried. "For what?"

"For disturbing the peace!"

A yell of laughter swept the room. Every night there were fights and Gallagher had never arrested anyone. But the laughter angered him, and he looked down at Haze Lyons, who was getting to his feet slowly, his mouth a ruin. "Haze, you all right? Let's get this man to the jail."

Reno took one look at the raging anger in the two men and knew that he would not live through a night in their jail, but there was no hope of making a getaway.

They were moving toward the door, Gallagher pulling Reno and covering the crowd. The irate miners were yelling, but they did not dare to do more.

Then a voice cut across the air: "What's going on, Jack?"

Reno turned quickly to meet the eyes of a tall, thin man with a star on his vest. He was about forty, and there was a smile on his lips as he looked across the room and said, "Hello, Jim. Still in a jam, I see."

"Hello, Jay." Reno remembered the last time he'd seen Jay Dillingham, the man who'd been his lieutenant for most of the war. He'd seen him last just outside of Appomattox. Reno's squad, or what was left of it, had been pinned down by Yankee artillery, and Jay had said, "See can you hold 'em, Jim, while I go for help."

He had not seen Dillingham from that time until now, but he remembered suddenly how many times the tall man had helped him in those days.

"What's going on, Jack?" Dillingham asked again.

"This bird is under arrest!"

"On what charge?"

Gallagher turned red as he said, "Disturbin' the peace."

A shout went up and someone said, "He sure disturbed Haze Lyons's peace!"

"Who started this brawl?" Dillingham asked, looking curiously at the ruined mouth of Lyons and the two men on the floor.

"Lyons!" a dozen voices called out. Then John Creighton stepped forward and said, "I'll testify to that in court if necessary, Dillingham."

"No arrest, Jack," Dillingham said.

The room grew still, and Reno saw the two men locked in a struggle. Though they both wore the star there was enmity between them, and for one brief moment, Reno thought that Gallagher would push the issue.

Then with a forced smile, Gallagher said, "All right. Come on, Haze."

The two men walked out of the room, followed by several others, and there was a shout from Jukes as he said, "Done!"

Reno felt a dozen hands pounding his shoulders. He made his way to Jay Dillingham and said, "You still got that habit of pulling me out of trouble, Lieutenant!"

Jay Dillingham settled back on his heels, and there was a mock severity in his gray eyes. "Jim, are you ever gonna grow up and stop fighting wars?"

Reno shook his head. "I'm trying to quit, Jay. But every time we get a good war started, peace keeps breaking out, don't it now?"

Dillingham stared at Reno, then smiled and said, "It's good to see you, Jim. I've thought about you many times." Then he looked at the men who were crowded around.

"If I'd been here when those three tried to tree this coon, I'd have told them that the whole Union army had a heap of trouble doing that little chore. Come on, Jim, we've got some catching up to do!"

TWO
Wash's Claim

The heavy-bodied black woman picked up the iron pot from the top of the potbellied stove and stared down at the meager portion of grits in the bottom. Shaking her head, she moved to a battered table in front of the room's single window, put the pot down beside the platter of bacon, and muttered in disgust, "Mistah Jim bettuh gits hisself back today 'fore we starves to death!"

Walking to the door, she opened it and called out, "Come on an' git it!"

A tall girl dressed in men's pants and a red-and-blue checked man's shirt entered at once. She was followed by a bean pole of a boy, no more than fifteen, with fair hair and light blue eyes. The boy reached out to pick up a piece of bacon and had his hand sharply rapped by the black woman. "You keeps yo' paws to yo'self, Lee Morgan!"

"Ow!" Lee put the finger stung by the large spoon in his mouth and said in an injured tone,

"Well, shoot, Leah! Looks like if a fellow's goin' to get enough to eat off *this* table, he's got to get an early start!"

"Ain't dat de truf!" A thin black man had come through the door to stare down at the food. "Woman, is dis whut you calls a meal?"

"Say, Jackson, you best leave Leah alone." A bandy-legged rider named Easy, not over five-six and wiry as a snake, had brought up the rear, and, shutting the door against the cold, had come to stand beside the table. He had tow-colored hair and a huge prow of a nose, and his ears stuck out wildly from his head. In the bleakness of the rough cabin, his garish clothes seemed to glow: a hideous yellow shirt, a high-crowned white hat with a snakeskin band and an eagle feather, sharp pointed boots with high heels, and a bloodred neckerchief. "Don't aggravate the cook," he said with a grin, and plopped down on a wooden crate.

The rest of them took their places and Leah glared at Jackson. "If you knows of a bettuh place to eat, why, you jest up and go there! It ain't much, but it's more'n we'll have fo' suppah, I reckon—'less Mistuh Jim gits hisself back today."

The girl looked out the window, then sighed and looked down at the grits, cold water cornbread, and the plate of bacon and salt meat. "I guess we ought to bless this food, but it's been blessed about ten times already, and I just can't seem to be very grateful."

"Why, shoot, Dooley," the puncher said with a wide grin. "You just stand back and let me do the honors." He gave the black man a sly wink, saying, "Jackson, keep your eye on them johnnycakes whilst I say grace." Then he shut his eyes and said loudly,

"Bless this meat,
Dang the skin!
Pull back yore ears
And cram it in!"

"Easy, you fool!" Dooley laughed and shook her mane of glossy auburn hair. "You don't have any more religion than a stick!"

The little puncher grinned as he speared a piece of salt meat with his knife. "Well, I ain't exactly been took with salvation, but I guess for a sawmill lunch like this, I can handle the 'Thank you.'"

There was little conversation as they ate. The cabin was one room, no more than ten feet square. Poles running across half the meager space created a small loft for sleeping, and through the rough shakes portions of blue sky were evident. This cubicle with the rude furniture—a small stove, a table and two chairs, a cupboard built of wooden boxes, a double bunk built of poles against one end of the room—had been their home for over a month.

Lee finished his grits, swallowed the last of the bitter coffee, then rose and picked up his rifle. "I'm goin' huntin'."

Jackson got up to go with him, but Leah said, "You ain't goin'—not till you fills dat wood box!"

"Aw, woman, Mis' Jim be back today. I ain't choppin' no wood dat ain't fo' my own usin'!"

Easy and Dooley, accustomed to the minor skirmishes of the black couple, got up and left the cabin. "Might as well go to the pass and watch for him," Easy murmured.

"All right."

They walked through the thin layer of snow

toward a path that led through scrub oak, and Easy kept the conversation going, pointing out some patches of green grass breaking through the whiteness. "Another week and it'll be plumb purty in these mountains," he said.

"I guess, but I'm worried about Jim. Shouldn't he have been back before now?"

Easy touched the wide mouth with stubby fingers, wiping away a quick grin. "Not unless he sprouted wings, Dooley. That Cherry hoss of his was in bad shape, and it's pretty rough country to Virginia City. He may have had to walk in."

They passed through the thickets, emerging onto a flat, open space that began to drop downward. The land fell away sharply, broken with irregular outcroppings of granite, and far off Dooley could see a range of mountains rolling across the horizon.

Dooley picked up a stick, broke it, then threw the pieces away. "I wish that blizzard hadn't caught us, Easy. We came so close!"

Easy squatted down on his heels, stared off at the mountains, then back to the girl. "Speakin' personal, Dooley, I figure we come out right well. If we hadn't come on that ol' minin' shack when that blizzard hit, we'd be froze stiff! That was a real sockdologer, Dooley!" He shook his head and there was a look of wonder on his ugly face as he added, "I ain't been so nervous since I was a porch child!"

Dooley frowned, then asked, "A porch child? What in the world is that, Easy?"

He gave her a pitying look, shook his head sadly, and exclaimed, "You shore did get neglected in your education, Dooley, I swear." He stood up and stared more closely at the horizon, saying, "Why, shucks, an arm youngun is one toted in his mama's arms. A lap baby's one too small to quit the lap. A knee baby, now, that's one able to toddle. A porch child's old enough to play on the porch by hisself."

Dooley laughed and asked, "Any more categories, Easy?" She was fascinated by the rich language of the diminutive cowboy, and it was mostly his cheerful attitude and endless store of tall tales that had made the weeks inside the cabin bearable.

"Why, shore they is! They's a yard child—able to git off the porch and play in the yard, and then there's a set-along child. That's a little tad who stays put on a quilt whilst you pick cotton to the end of the row."

She listened while he went on from one yarn to another, but he saw the troubled lines on her smooth face. Finally he rubbed his chin, looked at her and said, "You worried about something, Dooley?"

"Well . . ." She stirred her shoulders restlessly and tried to give him a smile. She had olive skin, smooth and clear, set off by a wide mouth with a full lower lip. He admired the straight nose, the even teeth, and, most of all, the almond-shaped gray-green eyes shaded by long lashes that brushed her cheeks. She was seventeen years old and the most beautiful thing that Easy Jones had ever seen. But despite the fact that they had been thrown close together for weeks, he had never let his admiration show. He was only twenty-six, but he was wise enough to know that she would never think of him in any way except as a good companion.

"Not worried about Jake Skinner?"

"Easy, he's never going to give up on finding me!"

Jake Skinner was her legal guardian, her mother's second husband. After her mother had died, Skinner had begun behaving in a way that had frightened her, and when he told her bluntly that he was going to marry her, she had run away from home. With Jackson and Leah, the old family servants, she had fled to Jefferson City, Missouri, planning to join a wagon train bound for Oregon. Jim Reno was a distant relative of hers, and he had made the crossing with the train. Reno had led a hard life, but his courage and resourcefulness had saved the train from disaster, and by the end of the trip she had half-fallen in love with him.

But almost as soon as they arrived in Oregon, Dooley had been arrested as a fugitive as a result of a reward notice posted by Skinner. Reno, Lee, and Easy had broken her out of jail and left in the dead of winter for the mining camps of Montana. Getting snowed in by a blizzard, they had begun to fear starvation. Then the pass cleared, and Reno took the best horse to go for help.

"Oh, Easy, I thought when you and Jim got me out of that awful jail and we got to Montana, everything would be all right," Dooley said. She wound a tress of auburn hair around her finger in an intensely feminine gesture, then added, "But it's no use. Skinner sent all the way to Oregon for me. He'll find me no matter where I go!"

"Well, two things you ain't thinkin' about, Dooley." Easy put his hand on her shoulder and gave it a comforting squeeze. "One thing is you're gettin' older. All you got to do is stay away from that hombre for another year or so, and you'll be full growed in the eyes of the law."

"I've prayed for that," Dooley said. "What's the other?"

"Why, the other is right out there." He raised his arm pointing at something in the distance. He grinned at her and said, "Mr. James Reno—he's the reason you ain't got no reason for being afraid of Jake Skinner."

Dooley whirled and stared across the glistening whiteness, shading her eyes. "Jim? Where, Easy? I can't see him!"

He got behind her, and being shorter, stepped up on a flat rock and laid a pointing arm across her shoulder. "Right there, to the left of that deep V in the pass."

"I can't see!"

"Look for little black dots, squiggling along the snow."

She stared hard, then clapped her hands and cried with delight, "I see him!"

Dooley's eyes were wide, and there was a smile on her lips. Easy watched her, moving with excitement along the crest of the bluff, then when she came back, he said, "I'm tellin' you, Dooley, right there's the reason you ain't got no reason to lose sleep over Jake Skinner. I ain't never met the skunk, but if he locks horns with James, he'll find out he's done overwound his watch!"

"But the law's on his side, Easy. What could Jim—?"

"Honey," Easy interrupted with a wave of his hand, "I'm tellin' you that Jim Reno is one of them fellers that can pack a saw log to Hades and back before breakfast!" He spread his hands and pronounced strongly, "Why, Dooley, he stacked muskets at Appomattox!"

She stared at him. "What does that mean, Easy?

Didn't all the Southern men do that?"

He laughed grimly. "Dooley, some of them didn't *have* no muskets. Lots of them was jest stragglers. But them what *stacked their muskets*, why, they was the ones who not only had stood it all, but carried their weapons and was in a fightin' trim!"

Dooley stared at the moving dots across the distance, then nodded. She smiled then and put her hand on Easy's arm. "I'll bet you stacked your musket, too, didn't you, Easy?"

He grew flustered, turned red, then said, "Ah, I just sorta hung around till the fun was over, Dooley."

The pass was still icy over rocks, and it was four hours later before Reno arrived. Easy had gone back to the shack to announce his return, but Dooley waited, watching the figures of the horses grow larger as the sun rose. A line of trees cut across the pass, forcing Reno to lead the horses toward the south. He dropped out of sight, and Dooley walked nervously back and forth, watching the slash in the canyon where the trail reappeared. When Reno rode out leading two other horses, Dooley forced herself to sit down on large outcropping of granite where the snow had melted. As she heard the sound of his approach, she pulled at her hair and glanced down with distaste at the worn jeans and bulky shirt. "I look like a miner!" she murmured grumpily.

Then Reno swung out of the thicket and, seeing her, waved and made for where she sat.

His face was reddish with the new sun, and as he pulled up and stepped to the ground, teeth white and gleaming, she thought not for the first time, *He doesn't know how good-looking he is.* There was a smoothness in his action, an ease that was partly natural to him and partly the result of a lifetime in the saddle.

"Hello, Jim." Dooley concealed the agitation that stirred her. She had not known how much she missed him until he came to stand before her.

"Give up on me?"

"No. I've been a little worried, though."

He stamped his feet to get the circulation going and grinned at her, looking boyish in the fresh morning air. "Was it me you were worried about—or the grub I was bringing?"

"Oh, the food!" She laughed suddenly and stepped closer to him, putting her hand on his arm. He smiled at her and there was a sudden wish that he might put his arms around her. But he did not, and she stepped back, stung by her own desires. She had never felt so strong an attraction for a man, and yet she knew he did not think of her as a woman.

Then he suddenly put his arm around her and gave her a vigorous hug, and he said, "Well, I've missed you, Dooley!"

She looked up at him, the pressure of his arm stirring her, but it was over. He squeezed her again, then said, "Well, I guess we'd better get this food to the shack."

It was that fool business of dressing like a boy! she thought with a sudden anger. *He'll always think of me like that—never as a woman!* When she had met Reno, she had been disguised as a young man to throw off pursuit, and it had not been until almost the end of the overland journey to Oregon that Reno had discovered she was a girl. That, and the fact that they were kinfolks—fourth cousins or something like that—kept her in Reno's eyes a boyish figure—one to be protected as he did Lee.

She turned and did not see the hooded look of admiration that Reno gave her as he pulled up beside her leading the three horses.

"Everything all right?" he asked.

"Oh, we're pretty hungry, and all ready to get to town."

"Trail's fine now. We can leave first thing in the morning and get to Virginia City in maybe three days."

He told her a little about his trip, then they reached the cabin where the others stood ready to greet him.

"If you ain't got no grub, Jim," Easy hooted, "I aim to eat one of them horses!"

Reno pulled the pack from behind his saddle. Handing it to Leah, he said, "Reckon you can do something with this, Leah?"

"Anybody can cook if they got somethin' to work with." Leah looked at him, then said with a smile, "Sho' am glad you got back safe." Then she turned and disappeared into the cabin.

"Did you see any gold, Jim?" Lee piped up. He had been wild to get to the mines, convinced that he would find nuggets lying on the ground.

Reno laughed and gave the boy a short jab in the ribs. "Saw the holes it came out of, Lee. I think we'll have to dig our own, though."

They laughed, and while Leah cooked a big meal they listened as he told them about his trip. He didn't mention the fight, however. They sat down an hour later to a big meal, and after that Easy asked, "Reckon we can shake the dust off our feet purty soon, Jim?"

"We're ready for sunup," Reno nodded. "That team

may need a little handling, Easy. They're about half-broke."

"I'll jerk a knot in the suckers if they give me any sass!" Easy snorted. "I've got me a bad case of cabin fever, and anything that stands in my way of gettin' to the fleshpot had better watch out!"

They went to bed early that night and pulled out at first light. Easy drove the team, Dooley rode in the wagon with Jackson and Leah, and Jim and Lee led the way.

They moved slowly, tracing the same journey Reno had made earlier. The weather was breaking fast, spring flowing across the land with warm breezes. The birds that had fled south from the chilling blizzard were stirring in the skies and in the fields. Lee brought down an eight-point buck that came dashing out of a thicket, and they gorged on the fresh meat.

They pulled into Alder Gulch on Tuesday at noon. As they passed through, Ringo Jukes spotted them and came running up to say, "Hey, Jim, where you been?"

"Had to get my folks, Ringo. We hit a blizzard in the hills and it killed our horses." He introduced the group to Jukes, who looked closely at Dooley.

"Well, pile out and we'll give you a real Gulch welcome, Jim."

"Thanks, Ringo. We better get to Virginia City and get settled."

"You got a place?"

"Not yet, but Jay Dillingham is on the prowl. Said he'd find something."

"Yeah, well, soon as you get settled get back here, Jim."

"Be back soon as I can, Ringo."

They rolled on through the line of camps and into Virginia City late that afternoon. Jay Dillingham was coming out of the jail as they threaded their way down the middle of the street, and he hailed them at once.

"Reno! You made it in good time."

"Hello, Jay." Reno dismounted and said, "This is Jay Dillingham. Jay this is Easy Jones, Lee Morgan, that's Leah and Jackson, and this is Dooley."

Dillingham studied each face with the practice of a lifetime, nodded to each, then smiled at Dooley. "This your wife, Jim?"

Reno was taken off guard. "Why, no, Jay. This is Dooley Wade. She's my cousin."

"Fourth cousin," Dooley said instantly.

"I see." Something in the scene amused Dillingham, and only a sly light in his eyes revealed it. "You'll be popular in Virginia City, Miss Wade. Only a handful of women and four thousand men."

The statement displeased Reno, and he said curtly, "She's a little young for that kind of attention, Jay. Did you find any place for us?"

Dillingham rubbed his chin thoughtfully, then shook his head. "Got one possibility, Jim, but it depends on Sam Bible. He's gone to Bannack for a couple of days. But you can put Miss Wade up at my place. Just a rough bachelor's shack, Miss Wade, but it won't be for long, I hope."

There was a courteous air in Dillingham, one that Dooley recognized at once as that inborn gentility she had seen in some men in the South. "Thank you, Mr. Dillingham. I'm sorry to put you out."

He studied her face, and smiled. "No trouble at all. Come along and I'll show you the place."

Dillingham had spoken the truth, for his shack was a mere box thrown together from old lumber and covered with tar paper. But it had a small iron stove and could offer some protection for Dooley, since it was the house of a lawman.

"Jay, it's handsome of you, but it's like you." Reno smiled at the tall lawman, and then frowned. "I'd like to go the Gulch and see Jukes. Would you keep an eye on Dooley until tomorrow?"

"Glad to."

Reno said, "Dooley, I want to get a line on a claim as soon as I can. Jay will look out for you, and Easy can stay—"

"I been nursemaidin' that filly long enough," Easy snorted. "I'm headed for one of the palaces of sin and that's all she wrote."

Dooley frowned at Reno. "Don't think you have to babysit me, Jim Reno. You just get right on with your rat-killing!"

Reno stared at her, then grinned. "You been picking up worldly talk from Easy. I'll start giving you lessons right off, Dooley, soon as we have time."

Dooley sniffed and took Jay Dillingham by the arm. "Jay, do you mind taking me to one of the mercantile stores to pick up a few things?" She smiled up at the tall man, fluttered her eyes, and said sweetly, "I know you're a busy man, but it would be such a help!"

Dillingham swallowed, then turned to lead her off toward the main street.

"Like a lamb to the slaughter!" Easy laughed. "Whoooo, child, that gal is gonna cause problems right here!"

Reno said, "I'll take her in hand soon as I get time.

Maybe have to explain a few things to her. She's just a kid, Easy."

The eyes of Easy Jones sparkled wickedly as he nodded. "Oh, sure, James, *I* know she's a kid, and *you* know she's just a yonker, but you're going to have to explain that real careful to about four thousand woman-hungry miners!"

Reno and Lee found Ringo Jukes leaving his claim at dusk, and they joined him in a thrown-together meal of beans and stew. They were just finishing up when a knock at the door sounded. Without a pause a group of men entered.

"These suckers come round every once in a while to let me take their money at poker," Ringo said with a grin. Jukes dragged an old blanket off his bunk, spread it over the small table, brought out a deck of cards, and introduced his gambling buddies.

"You know Link McKeever. That's Charley Rixie." He motioned to a pale-faced man around thirty who gave Reno and Lee a quick nod. "Charley used to teach school in Illinois. Gave it up to win the war for the Union."

"Was in the quartermaster corps the whole time," Rixie said with a smile. "Never heard a shot fired. Glad to know you both."

"That's Ivo Morgan—Ed Rachaner—Beans Melton. This here is Jim Reno and this young feller is Lee Morgan."

A mutter of greetings went around the room, and Ivo Morgan said at once, "Heard about your fight with Lyons. Wish I'd been there to see it." Morgan was a compact Welshman with a cheerful face.

"Ivo likes two things, Jim," Jukes said as he grinned at the group. "Fightin' and singin' in church."

"Not brawling!" Ivo Morgan said instantly. "Professional. I did a little of that sort of thing myself in England."

As they fell to the game, Link McKeever asked innocently, "How do you get by with that, Ivo, singin' in church and fightin'? Seems like they're kind of opposed, you know?"

"The Lord is a man of war," Morgan said. "And I'd say that if Reno here put Haze Lyons down—not to mention Sam Brunton and Boone Helm—why, that's as much glory as singing a good hymn!"

Ed Rachaner was an old-time mountain man, dressed in old-fashioned buckskins. He had a long beard, untrimmed hair falling to his shoulders, a set of restless eyes, and a hawk nose. Looking at his cards, he muttered, "Can't open." Then he stared at Reno and said, "Only thing you done wrong, Reno, was to let the sons live. I made that mistake once with a Cheyenne, and he come back and put an arrow in my back. Should have kilt 'em."

Reno grinned, recognizing the iron in the old man. "The law might have something to say about that, Ed."

"Law? What law?" Rachaner scoffed. "You mean them scum that Henry Plummer pins a star on, like Haze Lyons? Like Buck Stinson? Why, they ain't no better'n lots of outlaws I seen strung up!"

"Who's Plummer?" Reno asked.

"Sheriff at Bannack—that's the only organized county in the territory."

Ringo Jukes stared at his cards, then raised the bet before saying, "Don't know much about Plummer, but them Ed mentions is crooked."

"Jay Dillingham's no crook," Reno said, looking around the circle.

"That's right," Beans Melton nodded. He was even older than Rachaner, and there was an unhealthy pallor in his withered cheeks. "Only time Plummer ever sent a good lawman this way."

"He's a good man, but he won't stay," Ivo Morgan said. "Either he'll give up or the Innocents will take him out."

"They wouldn't do that," Melton protested.

"They killed Rob Simkins, didn't they?" Ivo Morgan asked. "He was too honest for this camp. And they'll get Dillingham, too, you mark it down."

Link McKeever threw his cards down, his young face angry. "That bunch is gettin' too bold! Sooner or later we'll have to do somethin'!"

"Do what?" Rixie asked mildly.

"Why, hang a few of 'em, Charley!" Link said.

"I could pick some good candidates for a rope right now!" Morgan said.

"Who'll kick the box from under 'em?" Rachaner asked, and a silence fell over the circle. "You boys are just talkin'."

"Maybe we can organize some law, like they did in California," Charley Rixie murmured. He leaned forward, his thin face serious. "There's not over a hundred of the Innocents, and there's four thousand honest men. Stands to reason that if we team up—"

"Just talk, Rixie," the mountain man snapped. "Them crooks is in the saddle 'cause there ain't nobody in this camp tough enough to stand in front of 'em. Likely to stay that way."

Rixie stared at Rachaner, his face red. "We won a revolution in this country over this sort of thing, Ed.

When men got sick and tired of being pushed around, why, they ganged up and fought."

Rachaner stared at Rixie, his hawk eyes glittering. "You're the teacher, Charley, but I seen a few things in my life that ain't in no books. One of them is that a crowd's got to have a man to follow—a real he-coon, one that ain't afraid to die. They're just a mob till they get a feller like that."

Rixie nodded slowly. "In that, you'd be right, Ed. And there was a Washington there that men would follow straight to hell."

Link McKeever bit his lip. "Well, somethin's got to be done. They been comin' around me and Beans again."

"George Ives?" Jukes asked.

"Yes. And he pushed Beans down last time. Said it'd be worse if we didn't sign our claim over to the Syndicate."

"Syndicate!" Jukes snorted. "That's Saul Logan's pocket."

"Yeah, we all know that, but who's goin' up against George Ives?" Ed Rachaner spat out. "He's smelled plenty of powder in his day—already killed two men in this camp."

The argument went on for over an hour, the cards forgotten on the table. A bottle came out, and two hours later the men all left.

"They come over here to do that, not to play cards," Ringo said. He stretched his thick arms high over his head and stared up at the ceiling. He was a cheerful man, but there was no joy in him as he leaned forward and stared at his fists. "If it was just a fight with hands, why, it would be different, Jim. But it's not like that. Every time a man tries to stand up against Logan and Ives, he winds up dead with his claim in their pockets."

Reno nodded. "Seen it before, Ringo. Tough."

Jukes looks up, taking in the figure of Reno, his mind busy. He said slowly, "You want a claim, Jim?"

"Sure, Ringo. It's what we came for."

"Well, most of the good ones is taken, but there's one you could maybe take a lot of dust out of."

"What's wrong with it?"

Ringo lifted his head and laughed. "You ain't slow, Jim. Well, there *is* a catch. It belongs to a fellow named Wash Tatum. Old Wash was here from the first, and he's made a pile. Nobody knows how much. But the roughs have been pushin' hard at him, and he wants out."

"Why don't the crooks just buy it?"

"They'll get it for nothin'," Ringo said. "And everybody here knows what to expect if they buy Wash's claim. They'll get beat up or worse."

Reno leaned back slowly, his dark eyes hooded and a stillness in his face. Lee, who had sat back against the wall all evening, taking it all in, had seen him look like that many times. He knew that it was a deceptive thing, that Reno, despite his sleepy appearance, had a brain that was running like a machine, thinking, weighing possibilities, considering alternatives. Finally Lee said, "Whatcha say, Jim?"

Reno turned, gave a sudden grin, and said softly, "Why, I say we go for it."

Jukes slapped the table with a hard hand. "I was hopin' you'd say that, Jim. Maybe we can get somethin' goin'."

Reno shrugged, and there was a trace of the sober fatalism Lee had seen at times as he said, "Don't expect too much, Ringo. I got all I can say grace over without taking on anything else."

"Sure, Jim," Ringo said, but there was a new life in his voice as he slapped his hands together and said, "You go into town tomorrow and look Wash up. He's about quit workin' his claim and spends most of his time playin' blackjack."

The three went to bed, rising early the next morning, and Ringo left to work his claim as Reno and Lee made the trip back to Virginia City.

"Maybe we better check with Jay," Reno remarked as they made their way through town. They found him eating a late breakfast, and he greeted them with a smile.

"Stake a claim yet?"

"Not yet, Jay." Reno and Lee joined him, pitching into a stack of buckwheat cakes and syrup. "Seen Easy this morning?"

Dillingham chuckled, saying, "He had himself a pretty large night, Jim. Got thrown out of a couple of saloons, and I finally had to pilot him to my place. But I've got a good word about the place I mentioned. Bible came in early and I took him over to meet Miss Wade. They hit it off real good. Soon as we finish, I'll take you to the place."

They finished, and Dillingham led them to a side street where they stopped before a small frame building. "This is the place," Dillingham said. "I reckon they're inside."

They found Dooley, Jackson, and Leah cleaning. Sam Bible came through a door in the rear as they entered.

"What's going, Sam?" Reno asked. He looked at Dooley, whose face was covered with dust, and smiled. "He hire you as a charmaid, Dooley?"

47

"Oh, Jim, Mr. Bible's been just great! This is our new business!" She waved an arm around the room, and her face was alive with excitement.

"Business?" Reno asked curiously. "What kind of business?"

"Laundry business, Mis' Jim!" Jackson piped up. His white teeth gleamed, and he added, "And there's a nice room in the back fo' me and Leah!"

Bible grinned, saying, "Town ain't got but one laundry, and it's always two weeks behind. So I put up the place and the tubs and they do the work."

"Sounds great, Sam, but we still need a place for Dooley."

"Oh, there's a nice place over my stable," Bible said. "Take a little fancyin' up, but it'll be a safe place. I'm always around, and it'll be close to the laundry."

Reno grinned and gave Lee a wink. "Guess you and me ought to go out of town more often, Lee. Things get done better. Well, guess we'll be on our way."

"No you don't, Jim Reno!" Dooley said sharply. "We've got a lot of work here and my place needs a good cleaning, too. So you just grab a broom and start in!"

They all pitched in, even Bible and Dillingham. All morning they worked on getting benches, tubs, a stove, a mangle, and enough furniture to fix up a room for Leah and Jackson. Then after a brief lunch they started on Dooley's room.

It was a large room with two large windows that looked down on the street. It had a flimsy bed and a battered dresser, but Bible had them take the old things out and some good things from a place across town brought up. Wrestling the furniture up the narrow stairs was a mean chore.

They were in the middle of the move when William

48

Merritt and his daughter came up the stairs.

"Well, the preacher has come to make his pitch," Bible said.

"Well, that's about the way, I'm afraid." Merritt smiled at Dooley. "I'm William Merritt, Miss Wade, and this is my daughter, Mrs. Warren."

Dooley smiled at him, then looked down at her filthy clothes. "I'm not very presentable, Reverend Merritt."

"Oh, moving is a dirty job," he said quickly. "But we're glad you're here, aren't we, Rachel?"

"Of course." Rachel stepped forward and extended her hand to Dooley. "There are so few women here, it'll be good to have an addition. Do you sing?"

"Oh, a little."

Rachel Warren smiled then, and the warmth that broke across her still features changed her completely. "I hope you'll consider being in our little choir at church. We're just about to perish."

"I'm not much, Mrs. Warren, but I'll be there to try. You'll come too, won't you, Jim?" She turned and put a hand on Reno's arm, saying with a mischievous smile, "Jim won't admit it, but he's got a good baritone."

A change went over Rachel Warren as she looked at Reno. The smile disappeared, and her classic features turned smooth and cold as she said evenly, "We'll be happy to have Mr. Reno, of course."

There was a small silence, the woman's obvious dislike of Reno being noted by everyone present.

"Well," Merritt said quickly, "can we help you with this moving, Miss Wade?"

"We're about finished, Reverend," Dooley said. She did not take her eyes off Rachel. "Thank you for coming. I'll be in church Sunday."

"Fine, fine! And of course, the rest of you are coming as well? You, Sam?"

"Well, preacher, like I been tellin' you for quite a spell, I sure do mean to come. It's just a matter of time."

The pair left, and Lee, who had been watching the whole thing, said, "Gosh, Jim, what'd you ever do to *her*?"

Reno had a quizzical look in his face, and he smiled gently, saying, "Well, I reckon you could say that I didn't exactly overwhelm the lady with my fatal charm, did I, Lee?"

Dooley went to the window and watched the pair leave, then turned with a frown on her face. "She's so beautiful!"

Bible shot a swift look at Dillingham and said, "Well, the preacher, he likes everybody, but Mrs. Warren—she don't take to some folks."

"Guess all of us could say that, Sam." Reno shrugged his shoulders and went back to moving furniture, but Dooley kept thinking of it, her face intense.

"You find out anything about a claim, Jim?" Sam asked as they finished up.

"Ringo put me onto something. Said a fellow named Wash Tatum wants to sell his claim."

"Don't do that, Jim," Bible said at once. "Word is out on that one. Man that gets it will have to fight Ives and his bunch to hold it."

"That's right," Dillingham said. "I'd do what I could, Jim, but there's lots of places to ambush a man in this camp."

Reno leaned against the wall, a still shape in the strong afternoon sun that came in golden bars through the window.

"This camp is full of bad ones, Jim, and George Ives

is the worst," Dillingham said quickly. "Oh, he puts up a smooth front, but he's a cold-blooded killer, and he's not particular whether he comes at you from the front or the back."

Dooley came to stand beside Reno, and fear was in her eyes as she said, "Maybe there's another way, Jim."

Reno looked up and all of them wondered at the smile on his broad lips. It was as if he were seeing something he had seen many times before, something that was an old game that had to be played again. He let the silence run on so long it seemed that he had forgotten they were there, then he said in a summer-soft voice:

"You let the bullies of this world start calling the tune, pretty soon there's no place to hide. We'll just see what this hole card is that he's so proud of!"

THREE
George Ives
Meets a Man

Saul Logan descended the stairs leading from his office over the El Dorado, his hand running over the polished mahogany railing. He was a man given to self-analysis, and his thin lips curled in a bitter smile as he suddenly thought that most men would have never given a thought to the action. He prided himself on his clear vision of the world—seeing it as a vicious dog-eat-dog struggle for survival where only the strongest won the battle—and also in his honesty with himself. At the same time his small brown eyes were counting the paying customers that packed the saloon, not forgetting to give one searching look at McClure, the blackjack dealer he suspected of cheating the house.

I'm running my hand down this mahogany rail because it's expensive and cost me a fortune to get it freighted in from Frisco. He looked again over the rich fixtures of the saloon, which was the fanciest place in Virginia City, and his handsome face was stirred in an unusual manner by his pride—almost love, one might say—for what he had built.

Then the thin lips curled, and he thought with the harsh honesty he imposed upon himself: *You hold on to that railing because you're a cripple.* Then he reached the lower level and brought the rosewood cane in his right hand forward. He did not need to push his way through the crowd, for a path opened up for him at once. As always, he had to force himself to ignore the looks he got as he limped heavily across the crowded room to seat himself at a small, round walnut table at the side. It was his personal table, never used by anyone else, a carved and polished piece, rich and expensive as were all his personal things.

"Bring me some of that good brandy, Earl." He broke the seal on a deck of cards, and for the next half hour sat there playing solitaire and drinking alone. Nobody offered to stop at his table. He sat there like a monarch on a throne, cold and withdrawn in the midst of the laughter and cacophonous music that surged around him.

Finally he saw something that brought a light into his dark eyes, and he said to the bartender who was passing with a tray of glasses, "Earl, get George."

"Sure, Mr. Logan."

The bartender threaded his way with practiced ease through the dancers, stopped beside a table against the wall, and said, "George, Mr. Logan wants to see you."

George Ives looked up with a flash of irritation on his handsome face, but covered it quickly. "Play this hand without me, gents," he grunted. He got to his feet and walked directly to Logan's table. He was a tall, broad-shouldered man with reddish hair brushed smoothly back. His eyes were wide-set, and there was a recklessness in them that was reflected in the way he simply pushed men out of his way rather than go around them. It was a tough crowd, but nobody thought of protesting. There was a feline quality in his good looks that in no way detracted from his intense masculinity. He walked lightly for all his weight, catlike and balanced on the balls of his feet, a man hard to get off-balance.

"Hello, Saul." He took a chair and poured himself a drink from the bottle, tossed it off, then grinned suddenly, white teeth gleaming under his trim moustache. "What's going on?"

"You been on a vacation, George?" Logan asked smoothly.

Ives recognized the tone, hard despite the smooth demeanor of the saloon owner. He was surprised, but came right back, "If you've got a complaint, Saul, don't dance around. Not with me."

"All right. I told you that kid and the old man were ready to fold. That was three weeks ago. You've sat around on your duff and nothing's done. If you can't cut it, George, I can get somebody who can."

A flicker of anger ruffled Ives's face, but he shrugged it off. "McKeever and Melton? It's no problem. I been squeezing them some, and they're about ready to take."

Saul stared at him silently, then nodded. "All right. But I want them bought out right away. Take care of it."

"All right." Ives got up to go but sat back down at a wave from Logan.

"There'll be a meeting of the boys at Dempsey's

tomorrow. Plummer will be there, so pass the word."

"That all?"

"No. It's time to put some weight on Tatum. He's going to find some way to sell out and skip with all his dust."

"You want me to take him, Saul?"

Logan stirred slightly, frowned, and said, "He's pretty well liked in the camp. But he's been coming in every night for a week. Always plays poker with Simms because he thinks he's a straight gambler. See, there he is."

Ives looked across the room and noted Wash Tatum, a thick-set middle-aged man with a balding head and large ears. "What's the play?"

"Tatum's a pretty sharp card player. He'd spot it in a minute if Simms pulled something. But you get in that game and Simms will feed you the right cards. The sky's the limit. Build the pot up big enough, and I think Tatum will put up his claim."

"Simms know what to do?"

"Yes. Don't fall down on this one, George. Tatum's claim is probably the best in Alder Gulch."

"Don't worry, Saul," Ives said. "He'll need to borrow his fare to get out of Virginia City."

The laundry had been a success from the moment it opened. At the end of the first day Dooley found herself standing in the midst of small mountains of filthy overalls and shirts, a little dazed by it.

Reno had stepped inside to find her trying to shift the bundles around and make more room, and outside Leah and Jackson were singing "Go Down, Moses" as they worked.

"Looks like you got enough to say grace over,

Dooley." He helped her pick up a huge bundle and put it on a long table against the wall.

"Isn't it great?" she said. Her eyes were alive, and her lips curved in a smile as she brushed her hair away from her forehead. She was only a couple of inches shorter than he, but he never thought of her as a large girl, probably because her figure was trim and she moved lightly as a breeze.

Now she laughed and said, "You want a job? I don't see how we'll ever get this work done. Most of this is miners', of course, but some of the ladies from town came by and they're happy to get rid of the clothes washing chore."

"You'll be rich when I'm an old worn-out prospector, Dooley," he said with a smile.

A shadow crossed her face, and she moved toward him. He had put on a clean white shirt and was wearing a string tie. She reached up and straightened it, and then looked at him with fear in her greenish eyes. "Jim, I wish you'd forget about buying Tatum's claim. I've been talking to Sam, and he says nobody ever gets anything away from the wild bunch here."

"Maybe I'll start a tradition."

He smiled at her, and she thought again how young it made him look. There was an ease about him, almost an indolence as he stood there, head turned to one side as he watched her. There was nothing pale about him. His appetites were sound, his urges very strong. There was a solid thickness that rounded his chest, and his arms and legs were corded with pads of muscle. She had seen him when the easy manner turned to a catlike explosion of fury, but she believed the odds were too great this time.

"You'll do what you want to do, Jim," she said with a shrug.

"Guess that's right," he murmured. "Had to learn early about that." He reached out and put a strand of her auburn hair back in place with a gentleness that surprised her. "I'll see you tomorrow."

She watched him leave, then going to the door stood there until he disappeared around the corner, then with a sigh turned to her work.

Reno made his way down the street, avoiding the puddles of mud that spotted the street. The shills were already standing outside the gambling houses, calling out their endless invitations: "Come on, gents, give us a game now!" A board sidewalk had been built down part of the main street, but it was so packed with groups of men that Reno kept to the street. As he passed by a store, he was greeted by a short, bulky man carrying a shotgun longer than he was.

"Reno, how are you?"

"All right. I can't recall your name."

"X. Beidler."

Reno grinned and said, "Don't see how I could forget a name like that. What's it stand for?"

"Xavier," Beidler said with a small smile. "Let's have a drink."

"Got to find a man, X. Wash Tatum."

"He'll be in Logan's place. You know him?"

"No. Ringo Jukes said he had a claim he might sell."

The stocky Dutchman turned and plodded beside Reno. "Trouble goes with that claim, you know that, Reno?"

"I'll take that, too."

The simple reply seemed to please Beidler, and he said, "I believe you will."

They entered the El Dorado, and Beidler pointed to a table along the back wall. "That's Tatum—the one with the bald head." But when Reno moved forward, he said in a lower voice, "See that big man in the game? That's George Ives."

"Heard he's the big noise around here," Reno murmured, then moved forward.

He noted that Haze Lyons was standing at the bar watching him, the scars of their battle standing out rawly on his face. Reno met his eyes, then moved to stand at the table. Besides Tatum and Ives there was a tall, thin house man and one other man, a miner with hard hands and sullen features. Most of the chips were in front of Ives, Reno noticed, and Tatum's face was sweaty, his hands not too steady as he picked up a card dealt by the house man.

A crowd had collected around the table, and Reno pushed against a man, getting a hard look, but paid no heed. He brushed against the table as he came to stand beside Tatum, but before he could speak, George Ives looked up and said with a loud curse, "Get away from the table, you!"

Reno lifted his eyes and caught the reckless gaze of Ives. He was a tough one, proud of his strength and not accustomed to resistance.

"Like to see you when you get through, Tatum," Reno said quietly.

Ives cursed and said, "Didn't you hear me? I said for you to get away."

Tatum looked at Reno and asked, "What you want with me?"

"Heard you had a claim to sell. I'll buy it if the price is right."

The piano music tinkled down the room and the

dancers were stomping the wood floor, but a silence spread out around the table.

Tatum said, "Wait till I win this hand and we'll talk." He waved at a piece of paper on top of the stakes in the middle of the table. "I just put it up for this hand."

"How much you put it up for, Tatum?" Reno asked quickly.

"Why, two thousand, but—"

"I'll give you three for it right now."

"You don't hear very well." George Ives laid his cards down and sat up straighter in his chair. The saloon grew quieter as he said, "I've told you once to get away from this table. This is a private game."

Tatum stared at Ives hard, then turned to Reno. "You got the cash?"

Reno had bought his stake. He pulled his wallet out, took out the bills, and said, "There's your money."

Tatum reached out and took the money, and Reno at once swept up the claim paper and put it in his inside coat pocket.

It happened so quickly that the men at the table were stunned. Ives's face, which had been deeply flushed with anger, turned pale, and his mouth dropped open. A mutter of amazement went around the room, and Ives knocked his chair backward, leaping to his feet. Men behind Reno jumped to get out of the line of fire, and there was a wild scramble as Ives stepped clear of the table, his eyes squeezed tight by the fury that ran through him. He wore a .44 in a hand-tooled holster, and he brushed the tail of his coat clear in a smooth motion.

"You're going to take a bad fall, friend!" he said

through clenched teeth. "I don't let any man interfere with my game."

Reno did not answer. He turned to face Ives, and there was, despite the ease of his movement, something rocklike in the way he stood there. His face was unlined, and his dark eyes were locked onto those of Ives.

Ives hesitated, and his eyes left Reno's face, seeking something to his right. He seemed to find it, and Reno knew he was in a bad spot. This was Ives's ground, and he had friends in the crowd. But there was no way to watch the crowd, so Reno concentrated on Ives, holding his gaze.

Ives grinned, and said, "Give that paper back and you can walk out of this thing." He was a bold man, sure of his skill, sure of his luck, and he laughed loudly, saying, "You got no luck in here; you'll be dead meat."

"I'll keep the paper."

The stark statement brought a flush of anger to Ives's cheeks. He cursed, and with a quick glance again toward his right, he said, "All right, if you got to have it—!"

Then the sound of a gun being put on cock struck against Reno's nerves, and on Ives's as well. The dandy looked to his right and his eyes opened wide. Reno risked a quick glance and saw the indomitable form of X. Beidler at one end of the room, his shotgun aimed along the bar where Haze Lyons and another man were standing, their hands on their guns.

"Haze, you and Red scratch for it." The two men at once dropped their hands, and Beidler looked across the room. "Get on with it, Ives," he mocked loudly.

"Beidler, this is not your fight."

"You got to have a crowd, George?" X. Beidler asked. "There's your man right in front of you."

Ives glared at him, his handsome face twisted with rage, but then he turned back to Reno and said, "You're buzzard meat!"

"Any time you're ready, Ives, let 'er flicker."

Ives made a small movement toward his gun, then paused. He was reckless and proud of his strength, but there was a streak of animal cunning in him. He knew his own skill, but there was something in the readiness of Reno that signaled a danger. Most of the men he'd faced had manifested some trace of fear, but this one stood there as if he were mildly interested in some pleasant game. He glanced down at the gun at Reno's side, then expelled his breath. There would be another time for this one.

"Get out of here," he said, letting the moment go, and turned back to the table, but the voice of Reno caught him before he completed the turn.

"You're yellow, George."

Ives whirled, his lips drawn back. He had no choice now, for he kept his power in the town only because he was strong. He had seen it happen to other men like himself who lived by their strength. If they backed down from a challenge, it gave courage to another.

"All right, then." Ives stiffened his back and his right hand almost streaked for his gun.

"That's enough."

Saul Logan had risen from his table, and now he crossed the room, the tapping sound of his cane echoing faintly. He stepped in front of Ives, then said softly, "Not in here. Take your quarrels someplace else."

"Stand aside, Saul," Ives gritted out. "I'll kill this—"

"You heard me, George!" Logan did not raise his voice, but he whirled and shot a look at Ives that caused the big man to clamp his lips together. Then he turned to Reno. "Sorry about this. I don't like trouble in my place. Have a drink with me and forget it."

Reno was not deceived by the smooth talk. He knew that beneath the suave exterior of Saul Logan lurked a carnivore. "Thanks, maybe some other time."

He turned and left the saloon, and Ives stared at his back with a hatred that boiled. Then he followed Logan back to his table, and in a low, furious voice said, "Why'd you do that?"

"Two reasons," Logan said evenly. "In the first place, you should have nailed him earlier before all that talk. Once he got the paper it was too late. You're not bright, George. In the second place, I'm not sure you can take the man. He's smelled powder somewhere. Didn't you see him standing there smiling at you? Like to have a man like that on our side. There's a thought."

"I never saw the man I'd take water from, Saul!" Ives snarled.

"You keep that in mind, George, because you may have to pull on him yet." Then the streak of cruelty that ran through Logan surfaced. "But you won't face him, George. You had your chance and you curled your toes and backed off. You may get him from an alley in the dark, but not face to face."

Ives stared at the saloon owner, his face red with anger, but then he forced himself to laugh. "Easy for you to talk, Saul. You never have to look down the barrel of a .44."

"No, that's your business, George." Logan shrugged, then before he left he nodded and said, "It would look pretty raw if you got him now. Let it lay. He can take some dust out of that claim, but don't let him live long enough to spend it."

Outside Reno found X. Beidler beside him as he moved down the street.

"Thanks, Beidler. That was a little tight in there."

"Forget it, Jim. Don't think this is all of it, though. Logan is smart. He called Ives off, but that was just a play for the crowd. They've got your number now, and you'll have to watch your back."

Reno gave him a quick grin. "Habit of mine."

Beidler examined him, saying, "I thought you were in that way a little." Then he added as he turned to go his own way, "There's a new grave every day out in the cemetery, Jim. I don't want to see you in one of them."

FOUR
The Frolic

"Jim, when do we start diggin' for gold?" Lee panted.
"We ain't gonna get rich foolin' around with all this
other stuff!"

Reno rested his axe against his boot, looked over
at Lee with a grin, and said, "You want to sleep
under a toadstool? Gets mighty wet with these
spring rains."

"Shoot, *I* wouldn't care!"

Reno laughed and straightened his back as he
looked over the work the two of them had put in
during the week. It didn't look like much, he admit-
ted, but they had to have shelter.

Tatum had built a cabin at another claim that had
petered out, choosing to make the three-mile walk
twice a day rather than building again, but despite
Lee's burning anxiety to begin the operation, Reno
had insisted on building a shelter.

They had cut alders from the top of the bluff and
rolled them downhill to make the hut walls. Brush

had been laid over the wall, layer on layer interlaced. A tarp served as the roof. They had made two bunks with poles, using grass and stems for mattresses. Two old windows contributed by Sam Bible, a hand-built door, and a small stove with pipe sticking through the roof finished the shack.

"Not much, but it'll keep the rain out," Reno said with satisfaction. "I guess we can start getting rich, Lee."

"Where do we dig, Jim?" Lee grabbed a shovel and followed Reno to a new location, the old digging being pretty well exhausted, according to Tatum.

Reno let the boy dig away a small section of top earth, then into the coarser subsoil. Filling a bucket with this, they moved to the creek that ran lower in the gully. Squatting in the water, Reno swung and spilled the gravel from the edges of a pan, working the residue down to black sand.

"Gold!" Lee yelled excitedly, his eyes flashing. "There's gold, Jim!"

"Sure is, but not enough to retire on." He probed at the pea-sized nugget and a scatter of colors, saying, "Worth maybe a dollar."

Lee's face fell. "Is that all?"

"There a lot of luck in prospecting, Lee. Lots of men can make more working for wages." He laughed at the look on the boy's face. "Well, as we go deeper, it'll get better. Looks like the river might have made a turn here, maybe laid down a deposit. Sometimes you find a pocket like that—about a foot square and yellow as a coon dog's belly."

They worked hard for four days, digging holes in a line across the claim. Reno made little dumps beside each hole and worked the dumps one at a time. They paused long enough to make a wheelbarrow, one load of dirt in it saving many trips to the creek.

Easy rode in late in the afternoon on Thursday, his face pale, and he walked carefully as though afraid to move too quickly.

"You look awful!" Lee stated. "You been sick, Easy?"

"No, I been sinful," the little rider said. "Which is worse! You got a drink of water?"

Reno handed him a dipper, asking with a wicked grin, "You get the town treed, Easy?"

"Son," Easy said after sloshing water into his throat and down the front of his mustard yellow shirt, "I'm gonna give you some good advice. Trust the Lord, write your mother, vote the Democratic ticket—and stay outta gin mills and gamblin' dens."

"Well, if you got your celebrating done," Reno said, "you can put in with us here."

Easy looked around at the shack and shook his head. "I promised my mama I wouldn't put no mules outta work, Jim, and that's about what minin' amounts to. Bible's got so many irons in the fire he can't tend to all of 'em, so he hired me to run the livery stable."

"Dooley all right?"

A broad grin spread across Easy's homely face. "All right? Why, son, I wish to my never if that gal ain't set the Gulch on its ear! Why, when word got around that a pretty gal was runnin' a laundry, them miners started foggin' in like bees to clover!" He gave Reno a sly look and added innocently, "Guess you gonna have the burden of raisin' a girl chile took off yore hands, Jim."

Reno frowned and moved his shoulders impatiently. "She's too young for all that attention."

"Well, I couldn't say as to that," Easy shrugged. "But I come out to give you a message from her. She says you and Lee got to come to Virginia City fer the big frolic Saturday night."

"What's a frolic?" Lee piped up.

"Why, boy, you don't know that? Why a frolic's a party to celebrate the end of workin'," Easy said. "Usually it's associated with log splittin's, corn shuckin's, molasses bilin's, nut crackin's, quiltin's, peanut poppin's, and cotton seed pickin's." He rolled his eyes upward and said sadly, "But jes' as often frolics constitute mayhem, shootin's, cuttin's, eye-gougin's, hair-pullin's, tooth-loosenin's, rat-killin's, and other bucolic divertissements. Always somebody accommodatin' to provide the trouble."

"You going to attend the festivities, Easy?" Reno asked.

Easy pulled his high-crowned Stetson off, stroked the eagle feather stuck in the band, then looked up with devilment in his blue eyes. "Why, I purt near *got* to do it, Jim. Got me a leetle gal named Rosy Birdwell, see? Took her off the hands of a gent named Jack Weese, and he's got idees of gettin' her back." He put the hat on and went to his horse. Swinging up with an ease that Lee envied, he said, "Want me to tell Dooley you'll be in to take her to the trouble?"

Reno bit his lip, then nodded. "Tell her I'll be there."

As Easy spurred his horse away from the claim, Lee was watching Reno. There was a line of worry on the man's brow, and he worked silently for so long that finally the boy asked, "You worried about Dooley, Jim?"

"I guess I am a little, Lee. This is a rough camp.

Lots of bad customers floating around."

"You in love with her?"

The sudden question brought a flush to Reno's neck, and he gave Lee a look of sharp irritation. "No!"

"She's in love with you." Lee cocked his head, and there was a wise light in his youthful eyes. He nodded and insisted, "She *is*, Jim. I seen it myself a long time ago."

"Let's get started building that flume," Reno snapped, and Lee knew him well enough not to pursue the issue.

They spent the next two days building a flume from the head of the creek to their claim, a hard job that wore them both out.

It was nearly three o'clock Saturday before they finished. They stood there watching the water rush through the small pipe with a gust of satisfaction.

"*Now* we'll really get some diggin' done, won't we?" Lee said.

"Be lots easier than toting the earth to the creek," Reno said. He tossed his hammer aside and said, "We better get going."

"You goin' to the frolic?"

"No. I'm too shaggy for that. We'll have to go tell Dooley, though."

They cleaned up and rode to Virginia City, noting that most of the miners had already forsaken their claims, which was unusual. "Be a big crowd there tonight," Lee said. "Most of them are shaggy, too. Can't see why you have to be so particular."

Reno didn't answer, but led the way to the assayers office, where he left several samples with a man named Ron Tilden. As they were leaving, the assayer asked, "You're not going past the preacher's house are you?"

"Where is it?"

"Just past the blacksmith shop."

"Sure."

"Tell him that Bill Landers's wife is bad sick and he wants him to come and pray over her, will you? He knows where to go."

"All right."

They made their way down the crowded streets, and Reno noted that most of the miners had on their best clothes for the frolic. They found Merritt at home.

"Well, Jim, come on inside, and you, too, young fellow!"

Reno took the hand Merritt extended, saying, "Can't stop now, Preacher. Tilden asked me to pass the word that Mrs. Landers is sick and wants to see you."

A frown creased Merritt's high forehead and he shook his head sadly. "She's in poor shape. Won't make it without a miracle."

"And I guess that crop has been sort of rare around here?"

"I guess miracles are scarce enough in most places, Jim." The eyes of the preacher touched on those of Reno, and he said quietly, "There *are* precedents, though."

"Sure. Well, guess we'll—"

"You're going to the celebration, aren't you?"

Lee kicked at a clod saying, "Aw, he says we can't go 'cause he needs a haircut."

Merritt took Reno's arm and pulled him toward the door, saying with a smile, "Why, that won't be hard to fix. I've cut some hair in my time."

Reno started to protest, but Lee urged him. "Well, get this boy here trimmed, first. He looks like a buffalo."

Merritt turned out to be a pretty rough-hewn barber. He led them to the kitchen, put Lee on a straight chair, and hacked away at his hair. Lee winced several times as the preacher pulled at his scalp, but said nothing.

Merritt finished the job, and Reno had just sat down with a wry grin at the rough job on Lee's hair when the door opened and Rachel Warren came in. She nodded briefly and said, "Dad, they need you over at the Landers' home." There was an urgency in her voice and a faint pallor tinted her cheeks. "I think she's dying."

Merritt paused, looked down, and said, "I was afraid of that." He half-turned, then stared at Reno in the chair before him. Then he handed the scissors to the woman, saying, "Here, Rachel, finish up this job, will you? I better go at once."

Reno did not miss the frown that creased her brow, and he started to rise. "No need for that, Reverend—"

"Oh, sit down, Jim!" Merritt pressured him, shoving him down. "Rachel is really the barber around here. Why, she cuts hair for every stray lamb in Virginia City. Here, Rachel, straighten up this mess."

He left hurriedly, and Reno had seldom felt more uncomfortable as when she began to trim his hair. Her dislike of him was almost palpable in the room, and Lee was watching carefully, his sharp blue eyes missing none of the scene.

"Lee, go tell Dooley I'll be along soon as I get through here."

"All right."

After he left, the only sound for some time was the ticking of the clock on the wall and the snip of her shears.

Finally he said, "Hate to put you to the trouble."

"It's no trouble."

She was working on his right side, and he suddenly turned his face to meet her gaze. She had the most beautiful eyes Reno had ever seen—purple as the haze on a concord grape, but there was a hardness in them.

He studied her, noting her strong femininity. A faint scent of lilac came to him, and faint hungers stirred him. He said quietly, "You don't like me, do you, Mrs. Warren?"

"My husband died in Belle Isle," she said at once in a hard voice. "Not killed in battle, but starved and left to die in the mud like an animal."

Reno had heard of the horrors of Belle Isle, a Confederate prison camp. "That's a bad one."

She was breathing shortly, her breast lifting as she stared at him. "Yes, you could say that."

She pulled his head around with a sudden move, and he sat there as she finished the job. Finally she stepped back and said, "That's the best I can do."

He rose, picked up his hat, and started to leave. Then he paused and wheeled to face her, stepping close. "You plan to go on hating every Southerner you meet the rest of your life?"

She caught her breath, his directness striking her composure. She bit her lower lip, then said, "Why shouldn't I?"

"Hate to see a woman get hard—it's worse than for a man."

She stared at him, and there was a sudden vulnerability in her face, as though he had touched something deep inside she'd kept hidden. He made a tough shape as he stood there, regarding her with his dark eyes. He was hard, she knew, had taken his beatings from the world. But there was a gentleness in his face and in his tone as he stood there, and the seething anger she kept under control seemed to fade.

"What would you have me do?" she cried. "Forget him?"

He tapped his hat against his thigh and said evenly, "Two kinds of casualties in war. Some die on the battlefield. Others live but can't stop hating when the last gun is fired." This was a wisdom that she could not combat. "The last kind is the worst. I've seen a lot of it, and what it amounts to is dying over and over. Hate is worse than any minié ball, I reckon, Mrs. Warren." Then he nodded and slipped his hat on. "Didn't mean to preach."

She stood there, her face swept by a sudden flood of thoughts as she stared down at the raven locks on the floor, then she walked quickly to the window and watched him as he made his way down Front Street. When he was gone, she began cleaning the floor, and once she held a lock of black, glossy hair in her fingers and stared at it for a long time.

He made his way to the livery stable, climbed the steps to Dooley's room, and knocked on the door. When it opened, she stood there framed by the last light that filtered through the window. He was so accustomed to seeing her in rough man's dress that the picture she made halted him in his tracks.

She was wearing a simple blue dress with a low-cut white bodice and fragile yellow lace around the hem. The contours of her body were molded by the dress, and she seemed like a stranger. There was a maturity in her face that disturbed Reno, and he had to force himself to say, "You ready, Dooley?"

"Do you like my dress?"

He looked at her, then muttered, "It's too old for you."

She had caught his look at the low cut of the dress, and an impish grin touched her full lips. She picked up a coat, handed it to him, and as she slipped her arms into the sleeves she asked innocently, "Did you and Widow Warren get along all right?"

She whirled to face him, studying his face, and he felt awkward. "I suppose so."

As they went down the steps, Dooley held onto his arm, and she pursued her question. "She's a much better barber than her father." She laughed lightly, a tinkling sound on the dusky air. "Lee looks awful!" They reached the foot of the stair and she stopped, pulled his hat off, and touched his hair. "But she did a good job on you."

"I've had worse," he said.

"She hates Rebels. Sam Bible said so. But maybe she sees some extra quality in you, Jim."

"Don't know. Just plain Christian charity, I guess."

"I doubt it." She continued to probe at him, but he said nothing more about Rachel.

The celebration was already in full swing when they got there. A large new tent destined to be a saloon was being used, and lanterns cast their pale glow over the crowd of people that moved restlessly under the canvas. A platform occupied one end, and on it a band was already pumping away, drowning out conversation in its vicinity. Along one side, tables filled with food and drinks were being raided by hungry miners, and the center was filling up with dancers.

"Looks like everyone in town is here," Reno said. John Creighton, Sam Bible, and other businessmen had already found their niche and were watching the dancing. Freshly shaved miners with clothes so new they still bore creases danced with the few women in the place, and the haze of tobacco smoke already dimmed the interior.

Creighton greeted him warmly, looking down in surprise at Dooley, "Reno, introduce me to this young woman." Then with a courtly bow he said, "On the other hand, I'll do it myself. I'm John Creighton, and you'll be Miss Julie Wade, I take it?"

"Yes. It's good to meet you, Mr. Creighton."

Creighton said, "I'm stealing your girl, Jim," and led her off to introduce her to the other women, who were clustered near the tables.

X. Beidler came to stand by Reno, accompanied by Dr. W. L. Steele and a tall, well-built man in his thirties.

"Reno, this is Dr. Steele. And this is Jim Williams."

Williams had a droopy moustache and sad brown eyes. He said in a soft voice, "You made a considerable splash in certain quarters, Reno." He paused, gave Reno a careful look, then added, "Heard George Ives has been makin' remarks about what he intends for you."

Reno shrugged, saying only, "George will probably make a try, I guess."

Beidler said, "You're not taking him serious enough, Jim. He's a wolf. Don't let his smooth way or his fancy clothes fool you."

"He's that all right," Reno murmured, but Beidler

saw that he was not really listening. Reno spotted Lee over by the door and said, "Excuse me."

He skirted the crowd, made his way to the boy, and said, "You seen Easy?"

Lee swallowed a huge bite of cake and pointed to the dancers. "There he is."

Easy was dancing with a pretty, plump young woman wearing a red dress. She was laughing at something Easy had said, her head thrown back and her eyes dancing.

"Gonna be a fight, Jim," Lee said. "Jack Weese has been tellin' how he's goin' to take that girl back away from Easy."

"Think he can do it?"

"Naw, Easy can take him!"

Reno smiled, and for the next half hour he kept to the fringes of the dance floor, talking with several men. His fight with Ives had made him a marked man, and everybody knew him.

He was leaning against one of the poles supporting the tent when Ives came in, flanked by Gallagher and Haze Lyons. Ives grabbed a young woman from the arms of a tall miner and whipped her out onto the dance floor. His momentum carried him around the floor and he lifted his eyes and met Reno's gaze. His smile broke and a hard sheen came into his eyes, but he swung his partner around with a vigorous action.

"Dance with me, Jim?"

Reno looked around to find Dooley at his side. She touched his arm, and there was an innocence in her face that caught at him.

"Well, I don't see any harm in it," he said with a grin, "as long as no women or children are present."

He led her to the floor and put his arm around her. Then they moved together to the music. "You're the belle of the ball, Dooley," he said with a quick smile. "Don't see why you want to waste yourself on an old man like me when there's lots of young bucks would give their right arm to dance with the prettiest girl in Virginia City."

She missed a step, and her face changed. She moved in closer to him, and there was a softness in her voice as she said, "That's the nicest thing you ever said to me, Jim. Mean it?"

"Think I go around spouting compliments I don't mean?"

"No," she said. "You're the most honest man I ever met, Jim." Then she leaned back and there was a humorous look in her fine eyes as she said, "And you are *not* an old man! You'll be twenty-eight years old on May 24."

"You make me feel like an old man with a long white beard, Dooley," Reno smiled at her. "You're seventeen years old and we're kissing cousins, aren't we?"

She gave him a searching glance, then said, "You're blind, Jim Reno! What I am is—"

"Jim, Easy is about to lock horns with Jack Weese."

Reno turned around to see Lee, his eyes big with excitement. "Excuse me, Dooley."

"Never mind that," she said, firmly taking his arm. "I'm going too."

They followed the crowd outside to find Easy and a thick-muscled young man in the center of a group of spectators. The talking had been done, and Reno pulled Dooley into the inner circle in time to hear

Easy say loudly, "All right, Weese, I aim to tan your hide till it won't hold shucks!"

Easy looked like a reed against the body of Weese, the town blacksmith. He lowered his head and ran straight into the rocklike torso of Weese and bounced off like a rubber ball. He fell on the seat of his pants, and a roar of laughter ran through the crowd.

Easy shot up and stared at Weese, then said, "That hold you, do you think? Or do I gotta turn my wolf loose?"

"Rosy is my girl," Weese said, and would have continued, but Easy leapt forward and gave him a hard right in the mouth.

It rocked the head of Weese back, and a trickle of blood appeared on his lower lip. Then as Easy drew back to hit him again, Weese's huge fist shot out and caught the small puncher in the forehead. Easy fell like a pole-axed steer, his body loose and boneless.

Reno moved forward, knelt beside Easy, and then looked up at Weese. "You win, looks like."

Weese's face had a trace of alarm. "I didn't want to fight him."

"Sure. He'll be all right. Lee, help me get him over against the tent until he wakes up."

They started to move the unconscious man, and suddenly George Ives loomed up against the light, his eyes slitted and a smile on his lips. He said, "I remember we had us an appointment, Reno. Let's see if you're man enough to stand up to me."

Reno saw that Ives had picked the moment well. He was not wearing a gun, and he had complete confidence in his skill as a roughhouse fighter.

"I don't like to fight, George," Reno said. He got

to his feet and turned squarely to face the bulk of Ives. "Nobody wins in a fight."

Ives stripped off his coat, threw it to Haze Lyons, then came toward Reno fists extended.

"I'm going to pound you into the ground, Reno. Get your hands up!"

As Ives advanced, Beidler said in a low voice, "Jim ought to take a gun to him. He can't whip Ives with his fists!"

As the crowd moved closer, the two men met in the middle of the circle.

FIVE
Death at
Midnight

Ives came in on the balls of his feet, fists held high in a professional manner. The memory of his encounter in the El Dorado with Reno had festered in him like hot coals. Reno could have left Ives alone forever, but as the big man moved toward him with the will to destroy burning in his eyes, Reno knew there would be no rules: *If he gets me down, he'll kick me to death—got to stay away from him.*

He moved to one side, avoiding a vicious right hand that would have ended the fight, but Ives was even faster than he had thought. Off-balance as he was, he threw a left that caught Reno in the temple and drove him back. Only by instinct did Reno manage to lift his arms, catching the lightning blows that Ives rained at him. He knocked the blows aside, then caught a sweeping right hand that Ives threw, holding on until his head cleared.

"Bust 'im up, George!" Haze Lyons shouted.

Beidler shook his head, saying to Creighton, "He's too big for Reno!"

Reno kept backing away, catching Ives's blows on his forearms and shoulders, and several of them stung his face. The world had narrowed for him; the crowd faded. All that existed was the big man who kept coming forward inexorably, fists pounding and slashing. He thought of the many times in the army when his regiment had been outnumbered and they'd had to feint and retreat, taking their shots as they fell back. And more than once they'd drawn the Yanks into a trap and cut them to pieces.

He began to fall back even more rapidly, bumping into men who didn't retreat fast enough, and his blows at Ives were mere tokens. He had to draw the larger man in, convince him there was nothing to fear. Outweighed by twenty-five pounds against a fast, skillful brawler, he had no other chance.

He found himself in front of the opening to the tent, and he allowed one of Ives's jabs to catch him high on the head, then back-peddled into the tent. Ives came barreling after him, a wide grin on his face.

Reno heard the groans from his friends as Ives beat him back, but he paid no heed, concentrating on wearing the man down. His face was bleeding, but he was breathing strongly, and he saw, finally, that Ives's chest was beginning to heave and his face was flushed with effort. Ives stopped, dropped his hands, and cried, "Fight, you yellow—"

It was the moment Reno had waited for. He threw himself forward, forgetting caution, and smashed the hardest right hand he'd ever thrown against Ives's mouth. It drove him backward, and Reno was after him like a cat, driving blow after blow into the face and body of Ives. He took some punishment, not feeling it as Ives reeled backward.

He hit Ives in the stomach, driving the big man's breath out instantly. Ives grabbed him, and threw him spinning, then gave a yell as Reno hit the floor. With a yell Ives fell on him, and Reno raised his foot, kicked out, and caught him full in the face with his sharp heel.

It snapped Ives's head back, and his eyes were glazed as he rolled over and came to his knees, one raw strip hanging down from his upper lip. The shock of the blow had dulled his senses, but he struggled to his feet.

Reno caught him with a driving lunge, and they careened backward until the back of Ives's legs collided with the pot-bellied stove. They fell against it, and as the stove collapsed, Ives let out a strangled scream.

Reno rolled off at once, and Ives thrashed on the floor moaning, the smell of burning flesh beginning to fill the room.

Reno stood back, his chest heaving as the big man stood up. Ives held his fists up weakly, but he was whipped. His eyes wandered, and then he focused on Reno.

"I told you nobody wins a fight, George."

Ives stood there, swaying back and forth, trying to concentrate. He drew himself up, and through his ruined mouth said in a slurred voice, "You'll never use your hands on me again." Then he turned and stumbled out of the tent, shaking off the help of Haze Lyons.

Pain began to roll over Reno, his nerves crying out over the punishment he had taken. He looked down at his knuckles, which were furrowed into ridges of raw flesh, and the nerves in his arms began to scream. He knew he wouldn't be able to lift his arms without pain for a long time.

The crowd exploded with shouts, and the excited talk swept over him. He felt hands patting his shoulders, but the sickness deep in his stomach that always took him after a battle was coming fast.

"Sam, help me get him out of here."

Dooley was speaking, and he was dimly conscious of her cold hand taking his and followed as the crowd broke aside to let them pass. Lee was at his right side, looking up at him with enormous eyes, and as they left the tent, Doctor Steele said, "I better put a stitch or two in that eyebrow, Reno. Let's take him to your place, Reverend."

In five minutes, Reno was sitting on the same chair where Rachel Warren had cut his hair. "Better get me some hot water, Rachel," Doc Steele said. "Let me see that hand."

Beidler and Ringo Jukes had come along, and there was a tense air in the room. Looking down at his hand, Reno gave a faint smile. "Look at that hand shake." He shook his head and looked up, saying, "Not as young as I used to be. I can remember when a little fracas like that wouldn't have done that."

"He'll kill you, Jim," Ringo Jukes said. "You've put him down twice, and he's got to get you or he's out with Logan."

Beidler nodded, his sharp black eyes bright with anger. "He's killed men for less. You'll have to leave Virginia City."

The two men knew the ways of the camp, and they weren't quitters, but Dooley saw that in their minds Reno was a dead man already. Fear raked her nerves, and she moved to stand beside Reno as Rachel brought a pan of hot water. "I'll clean the hand out," Rachel said quietly. Taking Reno's hand, she began to wipe the grime and blood from it. Her hands were steady and sure as she worked, and Dooley watched closely, noting the look that Reno gave her as she bent over his hand.

"This'll hurt some," Doc Steele said as he picked up the needle and thread. He was a rough-and-tumble surgeon, but Reno did not flinch as he drew the skin together, put in a few stitches, then snipped off the loose ends. "That ought to hold." He fished a roll of bandages out of his bag, wrapped Reno's hand with it, then collected his tools and snapped the bag shut. "Try to stay out of fights for a whole day at a time, will you, Jim?"

Reno got up and smiled at the doctor. "How much do I owe you for the advice and the patching up, Doc?"

Steele was a burly man with thick, blunt features. He was the only doctor in Virginia City, but he was into the politics of the place up to his ears, and he said in a voice heavy with experience, "You better listen to Jukes and Beidler. I've been in some pretty tough places, but this is the worst. Most of the time the wild ones are lone wolves, and the law can get 'em one at a time. But it's different here. Somebody is pretty smart, and the Innocents are well-organized. They know everything that goes on, they stand up for one another, and if a man gets in their way, they get him one way or another."

"I guess I'll have to take my chances," Reno said.

Steele looked at Beidler and then back to Reno. "Some of us have been tryin' to come up with a way to stop the organized crime here. We've got about the same problem they had in San Francisco a time back, and I think we'll have to go at it like they did."

"Vigilantes!" Beidler said grimly. "There's no law here, so until we make our own, we're like sheep to these toughs!"

"We need some good men," Steele said. He stared at Reno, and asked, "You want in on it?"

Reno shook his head. "I don't reckon so, Doc. If a man comes at me with a gun, I'll take care of it myself."

"That's what men have been doing, and it won't work here," Beidler answered. "You were in the war, Jim, and you ought to know that a lone man can't stand against an organized force. And you've got friends here already. Can you stand by and see them butchered by the Innocents?"

Reno faced him, and there was a sadness in his dark eyes as he remarked, "I joined up in a losing war once, Beidler. After that, I swore I'd never tie myself to another one."

Steele shook his head sadly, then as he turned to go, said quietly, "You won't survive by that code, Reno. You'll die alone and bitter."

Reno didn't answer, but there was a stubbornness in the set of his jaw that Dooley and Lee recognized.

They filed out of Merritt's house, and Reno went to pick up his horse at the stable.

"Don't go back tonight, Jim," Dooley pleaded. "Wait till tomorrow."

He shook his head. "Don't feel much like company, Dooley. I'll come back in a week or two."

"Let Lee stay with me, then."

"No. I'm goin' back with Jim!" Lee shook his head stubbornly, and nothing she could say would change them. They rode out of Virginia City, down Front Street and past the cemetery, neither of them saying much.

Lee asked, "You think they'll try to get you, Jim?"

Reno shrugged and said, "They'll probably have a try, Lee." He glanced over at the thin form of the boy and said, "Good thing I've got a partner like you to watch my back." He knew what to say to a boy. Lee's face flushed with pleasure, and he drew himself up straighter in the saddle as the two rode slowly out of town.

Dr. Steele threw his instruments into his bag and gave George Ives a final bit of advice. "Keep those burns covered with that ointment for a week."

Ives was lying on his face on the bed in his room over the El Dorado. His torn lip was drawn together with stitches that drew the right side of his mouth up. He got up and stared in the mirror. Saul Logan stood against the wall watching carefully, and Haze Lyons stared out the window.

"Will it heal like this?" Ives asked.

"Probably leave a scar," Steele said. He left the room, and the three men listened as his steps echoed down the stairs.

"Haze, get Plummer in here."

Lyons left the room, and Ives stared at his face in the mirror. He turned to face Saul Logan, and there was a haggard look on his face, but his eyes were alive with hatred. "I'll kill him for what he did tonight, Saul."

Logan slowly took a cigar from his pocket, bit the end off and lit it with a match from a silver box. Staring at the glowing end of the cigar, he seemed to be in a deep study. His silence made Ives nervous. "You hear me, Saul?"

"I heard you, George." There was a flat quality in the voice of Logan that caught at Ives, and a faint flush rose in his cheeks.

"You don't believe me?"

"I think you'll try."

Ives winced with pain as he moved, then looked at the other man. "Listen, he's just one man, Saul." He went to the table, poured himself a drink from a bottle, and after tossing it off, said, "No man's tough enough to stay alive if we want him bad enough. I can pot him from an alley, have him gut-shot from ambush. You know that, Saul."

Logan stared at Ives, then said, "The man's tough, as you say, George, but I also think he's got luck."

The door opened, and a middle-sized man wearing a dark suit walked into the room. He wore a star on the lapel of his coat, and there was an air of confidence in every move he made.

"Hello, Saul—George."

"Hello, Henry," Logan said. "Anybody see you come into my place?"

Henry Plummer had sharp eyes, and there was a sly gleam in them as he looked at Logan. "Not likely, Saul." He turned his gaze on Ives and asked smoothly, "Had a little trouble, did you, George?"

Ives shrugged but said nothing, and Plummer said, "Heard about this Reno all the way over at Bannack. A pretty tough boy, eh?"

"I'll take care of Reno, Plummer," Ives snapped. "He had luck, but his luck is due to run out."

Plummer nodded. "I leave it to you, George."

Then he added in a soft voice that had a veiled threat, "I'd take care of it pretty soon, George. Let a man like that loose in the camp, he'll draw others. First thing you know, he'll collect a crowd. We've had it easy because there's been nobody for them to rally around. Let's see to it that it stays that way."

"He's dead!" Ives said flatly.

Plummer stared at him, then nodded, "All right, George. Now, what about those three claims we've been waiting for?"

Logan said, "You know about Tatum's claim, the one Reno got."

"Leave that for now," Plummer said quickly. "This Reno is no Tatum. What about Rachaner and McKeever?"

"A little more pressure and they'll fold," Ives said. "I'll see they get it."

"All right." Plummer talked rapidly then, and fifteen minutes later he put his hat on. "We'll need another meeting next week. By the way, you know a man named Dodge?"

"He's been in my place a few times," Logan said.

"He's loaded, so I hear," Plummer said. "I got word he's decided to leave Bannack and go back east. He's a real greenhorn, so it ought to be easy. Word I got is he'll pull out next week. I'll send you word when he's ripe. Ought to be good for four thousand, I think."

"I'll take him, Henry," Ives said. Plummer left and Logan moved to follow him. When they had left, Ives said to Lyons, "Haze, you take Red and Boone and ride out to McKeever's place. He's soft. I want the papers on that claim of his."

"All right." Lyons stared at Ives, then asked, "You

want me to get a bunch and punch Reno's ticket?"

Ives took another drink, then shook his head. His voice was tight with anger as he replied, "No. That's a little fun I've promised myself, Haze. Just take care of McKeever."

Dooley had been helping Leah sort through the heaps of dirty clothes, and Jackson was singing so loudly that she did not hear the door open.

"Can you do these things for me, Miss Wade?"

Dooley looked up to find Rachel Warren standing before her, holding a muslin bag. "Of course, Mrs. Warren." She took the bag saying, "You can just call me 'Dooley'."

"I'm Rachel, then." She looked around the room filled with steam from the tubs and said, "You work very hard. I hate to add to your load."

Dooley opened the bag and poured the clothes onto a table. She picked up a delicately made underskirt and rubbed her hand along the smooth satin. "I'll wash this myself. It wouldn't do to throw it in with overalls stiff with mud." Then she said, "That was a terrible fight Jim had with that man last Saturday."

"Yes." Rachel's face clouded. "Always something like that around here."

Dooley idly drew a series of circles on the tabletop, then lifted her eyes. "You do much nursing, Rachel?"

Rachel considered the question, and there was a smile on her lips. "Actually, quite a bit. We have no nurse, so I help Doctor Steele at times." She added with a straight face, "I'm making rounds with him this afternoon. He said we'd stop at Jim's claim and take those stitches out."

Dooley lifted her head, and there was a short silence as she thought about that. "Everyone says you don't like Southerners. It doesn't seem like it, the way you've treated Jim, cutting his hair and fixing his hand."

Rachel reached out and touched Dooley's face with an impulsive gesture that was rare with her. There was an innocence in the girl's beauty that once had been hers, and Dooley's infatuation with Reno was so obvious it was almost painful.

"Why don't you come with us, Dooley?" she asked gently. "If you can get away from the work here."

Dooley's face lit up, and she cried out, "Oh, that's no problem, Rachel. Leah and Jackson do most of the work. What time will we leave?"

"In about an hour. I'll have Doctor Steele stop by here on our way out."

She left, and Dooley whirled and ran to the large room in the rear where Leah was arguing with Jackson.

"Leah," she said with a beaming smile, "I'm going out to see Jim—if you can do without me, I mean."

"No mo' work than we gets outta you, Dooley, that ain't no problem." Leah straightened up and listened while Dooley told her about going with Doctor Steele. With a sly grin, Jackson said, "You better stays here, Miss Dooley. Give Mistuh Jim a chance to court that purty widow lady."

Dooley shot him an indignant stare. "He's not interested in *her!*" she said, then flushed as both of them stared at her. "She's a Yankee." That was the final answer for her, and she whirled and dashed out, slamming the door as she went.

Jackson stared at her, then reached up to rub his gray hair. "Dat youngun is pitiful in love with Mistuh Jim."

Leah nodded, and a sadness filled her deep-set dark eyes. She shook her head and went back to work saying, "Po' chile ain't had no luck—and she plumb set fo' anothuh fall!"

Doc Steele and Rachel pulled up in front of the stable at one o'clock, and for the next five hours they picked their way along the rutted roads, stopping at half a dozen places. It was isolated country, and everyone welcomed them, glad of the chance to find out any news. By the time they arrived at Alder Gulch it was growing dark.

Reno and Lee were still working, but they stopped and Reno said, "Lee, guess we'll have to feed these strays."

"Too late to get back to Virginia City tonight, Reno," Doc Steele grumbled. "Can you put these womenfolk up? I'm so tired I could sleep in a thorn patch."

Reno said at once, "They can have our shack. You can bunk with Lee and me over there at Ivo Morgan's place. He's all alone with plenty of room."

Lee grabbed Dooley's hand saying, "Come on, Dooley, you can help me fix supper."

"Maybe I'd better—in self-defense!"

"I need to take some books over to Charley Rixie, Jim," Rachel said. "Can you tell me where he lives?"

"I'll show you, Rachel. It's just around the bend of the creek." He got the bundle of books, and the two of them walked off in the fast-falling dusk.

Doc Steele said, "I'll be going over to take some tonic to Waylon Ord. Be back in time to eat."

Lee and Dooley went inside, Lee talking like a machine as they threw a hasty meal together. He was filled with excitement about mining gold, but he soon saw that Dooley wasn't really paying attention. Stirring a pot of chili and beans, he asked, "What's wrong, Dooley?"

"Why, nothing, Lee." She began to pull the few plates out of the rough shelves and put them out. She paused, looking out the window into the falling darkness, and said, "Shouldn't they be back by now?"

Lee opened his mouth, then shut it again. He shrugged and said, "It's a pretty good walk, I reckon." But he did not miss the lines that marred the clear forehead of Dooley, and he tried to entertain her by telling her about the miners in the Gulch.

Doc Steele came back in about an hour, but it was fully an hour after that when Reno and Rachel came in. The others were sitting at the table eating, and Rachel said, "Oh, I'm sorry we're late. We got to talking to Charley Rixie about books, and the poor man is so hungry for somebody to talk to who's read anything, he just wouldn't let us go."

They sat down and ate the meal. Dooley was quiet, saying nothing except when she was asked a question, and even Doc Steele, who was not sensitive to such things, threw a sharp look at Dooley, then at Rachel and Reno. He shook his head but said nothing.

After supper the men were leaving for Ivo Morgan's cabin when Reno suddenly straightened up. "Was that a shot?" Lee asked.

"Over at Link's place," Reno said. He grabbed a

rifle from a rack and said, "Stay here!" then plunged into the darkness.

He ran as fast as he could, sliding down the incline recklessly. At the foot of the hill was a well-worn path, and he ran along it, his eyes getting accustomed to the darkness. Link McKeever and Beans Melton had a small cabin off the main diggings, the nearest one to Reno's claim.

He heard horses snorting, and then there was another shot, loud and ringing in the black silence. He levered a shell into the chamber and pushed forward.

As he approached the clearing, he saw a light in the cabin, and even in the darkness he saw the forms of several horses.

He slipped forward carefully. A loud voice said, "Let's git!" and there was a scuffling sound of riders mounting. As they pulled around, Reno threw a shot over their heads, causing the horses to rear. Someone cursed loudly.

"Hold it right there!" he called out, but at once the night was starred with flashes of gunfire as they opened up on him. He drew down and winged one of them with a single shot, but the flash of his rifle had been seen, and he was forced to drop behind a tree to avoid the hail of shots that sliced the air around him.

He emptied his rifle then, but they rode around the corner of the shack, and he knew they were taking the old Indian trail that led back to the Gulch.

He drew his six-gun and ran forward. The door was open, and he called out, "Link?" then stepped inside.

Link McKeever was on the floor, face up, the blood bright beneath his head in the yellow lamplight. He was shot in the heart.

Reno turned, and what he saw made him pause. Beans Melton was in a chair, tied, and his feet were bare. A litter of kitchen matches lay scattered close by, and there was the smell of burning flesh in the air. He had been shot in the forehead, point-blank.

"Tortured him to get him to sell, then Link probably made a break, and they killed them both," Reno murmured. He'd seen many dead men during the war and after, but something about the fragile look of old Beans Melton and the youthful look on Link McKeever's dead face made a wild surge of anger cut through him, and he patted Link's arms, then went to get Doc Steele.

SIX
End of a Man

Over twenty horses were tethered in front of the murdered men's cabin, and Reno saw that there was a mixture of anger and fear in the faces of those gathered there. Everybody had liked McKeever and Melton, but as the bodies were brought out and placed on a wagon for the trip to the undertaker, there was an awkward silence. *Wondering if they'll be next*, Reno thought.

After the wagon lumbered off bearing the bodies, Reno left the crowd and went back inside the room. He began to go over it carefully, looking for some sort of clue to the identity of the killers.

The room was a wreck—cooking utensils scattered over the floor, clothes strewn wildly, boxes upended. A cabinet had been ripped from the wall, revealing an empty cavity. "Probably kept their dust in there," Reno murmured.

He still had found nothing when Jack Gallagher came in with half a dozen miners. He said nothing to

Reno, but looked around the room. "Anybody see who done it?"

"Reno got here first," Ringo Jukes said.

"You get a good look at 'em, Reno?" Gallagher demanded.

"No. It was too dark." As he spoke, a glitter on the floor next to the wall caught his eyes. He went to it, bent over, and picked up a sharp, pointed fragment of silver with engraving on the flat sides.

"What's that?" Gallagher asked. "I'll take that, Reno."

Reno turned to face him, then slipped the piece of silver in his pocket. He said, "No," then stood waiting to see what the deputy would do.

Gallagher straightened his back and gave Reno a hard look. "If it's evidence, I want it."

"I'll take care of it, Gallagher," Reno said steadily.

Gallagher paused, and Reno thought he meant to push it, but something in his face changed, and he shrugged his beefy shoulders, saying, "I don't care." He gave Reno a smoldering look, then wheeled and left the cabin.

"What is it, Jim?" Ringo Jukes said as soon as they were alone.

Reno reached into his pocket and held out the piece of metal. "Piece of a spur, Ringo. You ever see any this might fit?"

Jukes took it, held it to the light, then shook his head. "Not that I remember. Fancy, ain't it? You think it could have come off the spur of one of the killers?"

"Maybe. Not the sort of thing that either McKeever or Melton would wear—but it could have been a visitor."

"I doubt it, Jim. They didn't have any visitors

that'd wear fancy spurs like that." Jukes gave the piece back, saying, "I'll ask around."

"Don't do that, Ringo. If it did come from one of the killers and he heard about it, he'd get rid of the spur first thing. We'll just keep it quiet."

"What'll you do if you find them, Reno?"

Reno said evenly, "We'll take care of them, Ringo."

Something in the hard lines of Reno's mouth and the steadiness in his wedge-shaped face made Jukes nod, and he said, "No use going to the law, is there, Jim?"

"Not yet," Reno murmured. He looked around the room, and his voice was soft as he said, "Link would have made a good man if he'd had a chance—and Beans deserved a rocking chair instead of what he got." He expelled his breath and struck the wall suddenly with his left fist, the anger boiling out of him, but he said no more and the two men left the cabin.

Over five hundred people were at the funeral, mostly miners, but many townspeople as well. William Merritt stood beside the two graves, and the warm spring breeze blew his white hair over his forehead. Opening a worn black Bible, he read a few verses, made a few remarks, then said, "May we pray?"

Reno took his hat off, and as the prayer went on, he thought how alive the world was—birds singing, spring wind bearing the fresh odors of earth, buds beginning to make little knots on the tree branches. It struck him, as it always did, how the earth always comes alive again after the death of winter, and he looked at the two plain coffins bearing the bodies of McKeever and Melton.

"We thank thee, O Lord God of all things, that these two men are not as other things. That they will outlast the rocks and the hills, that though these bodies turn to dust, they will rise again in the last day." As Merritt spoke, Reno looked up and found Rachael Warren looking at him. Their eyes met, and there was a deep sorrow in the woman's eyes as her father prayed. She seemed to be searching Reno for some sign of grief, and then, apparently, she found it, for her lips softened, and she nodded to him almost imperceptibly as the prayer ended.

After the funeral, Reno went back to town with Dooley. He spent the morning with Easy and Lee at her room, then they went out to eat that afternoon at a cafe.

Easy still had a bruise on his forehead left by the blacksmith, but his natural high spirits rose as they ate, and Lee gave Reno a slight wink. "Hey, Easy, how come you let Jack Weese take Rosie away from you?"

Reno and Dooley grinned as the small puncher's face turned turkey red, but Easy quickly recovered. He said, "Why, boy, you got to understand how females operate." He shoved another enormous slice of beef in his mouth and talked around it, waving his fork wildly. "Now looky here, there was this scudder, Jack Weese, and he's bigger'n me, and some would say better lookin'—"

"Those with *eyes*!" Dooley interrupted with a grin.

"—but poor ole Jack is dumber than a barrel of hair! Now my mama didn't raise no dummies, boy, so I figures out what I can do to get that gal's mind on me, and off that big jasper—and it come to me!"

"What was it, Easy?" Lee asked.

"Why, all gals like to feel sorry for somethin'," Easy explained. He had a roguish light in his blue eyes as he went on. "You know how they take care of sick kittens and such—so I let Jack tag me and pretended to be hurt—and that's all she wrote, old son!"

Dooley laughed, saying, "Well, you gave a real good imitation of somebody being hurt. You pretended for an hour!"

"Yeah," the bandy-legged rider said, "but who was holdin' my head in her lap when I *pretended* to come to, I ask you? An who was mad as hops at ole Jack for hittin' a feller smaller than him?"

"Gosh!" Lee marveled, his thin face a study in admiration. "How'd you learn how to handle women, Easy?"

Easy let one eyelid droop in Reno's direction, and then grinned at an indignant Dooley, "Breakin' bronks, Lee. Sometimes you give 'em a carrot—and sometimes you give 'em spurs!"

Dooley said in exasperation, "You're awful, Easy! That silly girl did fall over herself, but—"

"Hello." Jay Dillingham had come through the door and approached their table unnoticed. "You leave any grub in this place for a worn-out lawman?"

"Sit down, Jay," Dooley laughed. "Easy is just giving Lee lessons in how to handle women."

Dillingham put his hat on the floor, took a seat, and joined them as they ate.

Reno noticed that the deputy didn't say anything about the murders, but he knew Dillingham well enough to know that he was aware of everything that went on. Finally, Dooley rose and the others with her. "You're all too stuffed to think about supper, but if you get hungry about six, you can come and eat at my place. Son-of-a-gun stew and apple pie."

"I'll be there," Dillingham said at once. Lee and Dooley left the cafe, and Dillingham said as soon as they were gone, "Just got back from Pine Bluff. Tell me about McKeever and Melton."

Reno told the story, and when he had finished, he fished out the fragment of the spur and handed it to Dillingham. "Might not mean anything, Jay," he said. "Anybody could have lost that."

"I don't think so, Jim. In the first place, it couldn't have been there long or it would have been picked up or swept out. Everybody teased Link about being such a neat housekeeper." He leaned back in his chair and there was a puzzled look on his face. "This reminds me of something—can't quite get a handle on it."

"Well, it shore wasn't no miner," Easy said. "They don't wear spurs. That eliminates about ninety per-cent of the gents in camp."

"That's it!" Dillingham said at once. He tapped the fragment of spur with his finger and leaned forward. "Easy's right. Soon as he said that, I started to think of how many gents I know who wear spurs, and there aren't that many. This isn't cattle country, and even when men get here wearing spurs, they pretty soon give it up."

"You got somebody in mind, Jay?" Reno asked.

"I remember about two months ago some of the fellows were riding Charley Forbes about the way he dressed—like a cowpoke right off the range." Dillingham looked at the piece of silver, then said softly, "One of the things they said was: 'Look at them fancy silver spurs ol' Charley wears.'"

Reno looked across the table and asked, "This is pretty hot, Jay. You want some help?"

"Maybe later, Jim." Dillingham's lean face broke into a smile as he said, "This could break the whole thing wide open! Forbes is a weak sister. Tries to be tough, but can't cut it. I'll lay an arm on him, and if I work it right, he'll squeal. May have to let him go for turning in evidence, but he's small fry."

"You're not Indian enough to beat a confession out of a man, Jay." Reno smiled and said, "When you were our officer we always knew you weren't as tough as you acted. Why, we soldiered on you more than once!"

"Yeah, you think I didn't know that?" Jay laughed. "But Forbes doesn't know that. I'm a pretty fair actor, and that lad will be convinced I'll pull his fingernails out with red-hot pliers! He'll talk, Jim!"

"Say when you need help," Reno said.

They got up, and the last thing Dillingham said as they parted in front of the cafe was: "Glad you're here, Jim. Always felt good with you beside me in a fight."

As he walked away, Easy said, "Reckon that there is somewhat of a man, James. He'll do to ride the river with!"

Two days later Reno and Lee looked up to see Easy riding hard along the trail. He pulled the steaming horse up, and there was a violent anger on his homely face. He slid off his horse, and gave Reno a wild glaring look.

"Dillingham's dead!" he said. He pulled his

high-crowned hat off and slapped his leg with it.

Reno slowly put his shovel on the ground, stared across the gulch and then said quietly, "Who did it, Easy?"

"Well, they arrested Haze Lyons and Buck Stinson and Charley Forbes. Way it happened, Dillingham was in the recorder's tent. Doc Steele said he'd just come in and said he had something to tell him. But Doc asked him to wait, and the next thing was that them three rode up and Lyons yelled for Dillingham to come out. Soon as he stepped outside they all three opened up on him—Jay didn't have a chance."

"How'd they get caught?"

"Why, Jack Gallagher stepped out, like he was waitin', and took 'em into custody."

"You talk to Beidler?"

"Yeah, he says for you to get to town—says we're goin' to hang those three for sure. Trial starts today. Doc Steele, Tom Bissel, and Sam Rutar gonna be the judges."

They made the ride back to Virginia City at a run and found a thousand men from towns all along the Gulch—Summit and Nevada and Central. They filled Front Street, moving like a restless tide. The judges were seated on chairs placed on the bed of a wagon.

X. Beidler waved them to where he was perched on the steps of Creighton's store. "Glad you got here, Jim. We're trying Stinson and Lyons together. That's their lawyer up there now."

As soon as the lawyer finished his speech, Sam Bible got up. He had been appointed special prosecutor, and he spoke briefly. The evidence was clear, the murderers were caught red-handed, and justice would only be served if they were hanged.

At once Steele rose and said, "You've heard the evidence. You're the jury. Guilty or not guilty?"

A yell of "Guilty!" went up, the miners waving their hands in the air. But there were other yells, as the supporters of the three began to curse and guns flourished here and there.

"Hang 'em!" The full-throated cry of the mob drowned out the partisans, but Reno noticed that Lyons and Stinson did not seem worried. He mentioned this to Beidler, who said, "They don't think we'll do it, Jim. None of that crowd ever got convicted before."

As they took Lyons and Stinson away, Steele dismounted from the wagon and came to stand beside Beidler. "Hello, Reno," he nodded. "Glad to see you here. Beidler, get three ropes ready and see that three graves get dug."

"All right." He left at once, and Reno said, "Doc, you seem pretty sure they'll hang."

"They'd better!" Steele swore. "If they get by with this, we might as well take down our sign! But you stay close and have your gun handy. The Innocents may try to take 'em if everything else fails."

All day long the town seethed, and by the time the court convened to try Forbes, most of the crowd had visited a saloon, so they were more mellow and the affair took on the form of entertainment.

Forbes was a good witness. He didn't look the part of a killer, his youthful face and neat dress giving him a genteel air. He was a bright, handsome young fellow and a capital talker. He claimed his pistol did not go off, and worked on the sympathy of the crowd by reading a letter to his mother back east.

The toughs in the crowd began to set up a cry for pity and fair play, and when Steele asked, "What's your verdict?" the cry of "Turn him loose" gave evidence that the justice Steele and the others hoped for was not going to happen.

"You can go, Forbes," Steele grunted with displeasure written on his broad face. Forbes slipped down, and there was a sly smile on his face as he was greeted by his friends.

Beidler had returned with his work party, having erected a scaffold and dug the graves. Doc Steele said, "I sentence you, Haze Lyons and Buck Stinson, to be hanged."

He got down and the crowd became unsettled. Men began to call out, "Fair play!" and Reno heard it said loudly from several points, "I'll kill the man that touches Lyons and Stinson!"

A wagon was driven forward to take the men to the gallows, and Haze Lyons, who had been laughing until now, gave a great choking cry. One of the dance hall girls began crying, and her cry was taken up by others of her kind.

It changed the mood of the crowd, and as the supporters of Lyons and Stinson kept up their loud threats, there was a sudden shift of mood.

"Let 'em go!" one of the miners called out loudly, and the cry was taken up in a chant by many of the crowd. "Let 'em go! Let 'em go!"

"Let's have another vote!" somebody hollered.

"You already voted!" Beidler shouted.

"Take another vote!"

The cry prevailed, and Beidler was shouted down

by the crowd. Lyons's lawyer got up on the wagon and shouted, "Everybody in favor of hanging, go up the hill!"

"Who wants to walk up a hill?" somebody shouted, and the roughs led a movement, shoving and pushing men down the hill.

The mob, unstable as water, was tired, and as a majority of the men moved that way, Jack Gallagher pulled his gun, got up on the wagon and shouted, "As deputy, I declare these men acquitted!"

A wild yell shook the side of the mountain, and the roughs ran to Lyons and Stinson, grabbing them from the hands of their captors. The place turned into a pandemonium, and the two men led a triumphant procession to the saloons.

George Ives passed close enough to say to Beidler, "That's the way we do it, Beidler!" Then he caught sight of Reno, and his scarred lips went pale. He stopped and said tonelessly, "I'll be seeing you, Reno."

Reno felt a tug at his arm and found Steele beside him. "Come with me, Reno." They made their way to Steele's office, where Beidler, Jim Williams, Ringo Jukes, John Creighton, Sam Bible, and a few other men were waiting.

Steele said at once, "They cried for a pair of scoundrels! None of them cried for Dillingham!"

"A shame! A shame!" Sam Bible shook his head. "Life won't be worth a dime from now on."

"We'll have to make our own law," Steele said. "Vigilantes—we have no other choice." He paused and looked around the room, then he said, "Reno, you've stood against them alone. Will you be with us?"

Reno shifted, then looked around and said, "Until

this camp forgets to cry for sinners, forming a vigilante committee won't work."

They stayed there talking about possible means, but Reno left with Easy, and as soon as they were outside, Easy said, "I take it Mr. Forbes is gonna get a visit from us?"

"He's guilty as sin, Easy." Reno frowned, then added, "I don't know how they got Jay off guard, but I know one thing."

"What's that, James?"

Reno stared at the ground, then his dark eyes fixed on the scaffold Beidler had built, the three ropes swaying gracefully in the breeze.

"Beidler didn't get his hangings, Easy—but Jay Dillingham was a square man. Somebody's going down for him, and I'm not waiting for a vote on it this time!"

SEVEN
Charley Rixie Runs Second

The day after Dillingham's funeral, Reno prowled the streets of Virginia City looking for Charley Forbes. Ringo Jukes had informed him of the regular habits of Forbes, but he caught no glimpse of him that day, nor the following. He picked up the trail by accident when three men came out of a saloon talking about the trial.

"Wasn't no way they wuz gonna hang them fellers, I tell you!" said a rangy miner with a toothpick in his mouth.

"Aw, Sid, I ain't so sure 'bout that," answered his companion, a stocky half-breed with muddy eyes. "It scared Forbes some, didn't it? He scooted out of town soon as they turned him loose."

The rangy puncher shook his head vigorously. "Devil a bit!" he spat out a gob of tobacco juice, and added, "Lessing told me that him and Forbes was goin' to Portland to pick up some fancy supplies fer

Saul Logan. Said they was gonna hurrah the hull town and they'd be back in two-three weeks."

It was already about five on Saturday when Reno got back to Dooley's place where he'd left Lee. He found Easy and Lee listening to Ivo Morgan telling about Wales, his home until he came to America. They were lounging around the grassy plot behind the stable, Easy resting on the top of the corral, and Lee beside him.

Ivo stopped and said, "Just the man I'm looking for! Here I am on the hunt for a prodigal son, and up he comes!"

Reno grinned at the small Welshman. "I'd say you'd have no trouble finding plenty of those in Virginia City, Ivo."

"You in particular, Jim. Reverend Merritt says I'm to get you in church tomorrow. 'Compel him to come in' was the way he put it."

"Ha!" Lee laughed. "I'd like to see anybody do that!"

Easy pushed his hat back and said with a wicked grin, "Never was a hoss couldn't be rode. Never was a rider couldn't be throwed!"

Lee shook his head stubbornly. "Ain't nobody could make Jim do nothin' he didn't want to do!"

"Well, now that's sure not so," Reno protested, but Easy cut him off.

"See that there corral, Lee? It's a mess, ain't it? And I got to clean it up. But I'll tell you what, I got a twenty-dollar gold piece here that I'll bet you against a good corral cleanin' that Ivo can make James Reno holler uncle in no time flat."

Lee stared at him, then he looked at Ivo, who was at least three inches shorter than Reno. He had a deep chest and his arms looked strong, but Lee shook his head. "Shoot, you might as well gimme the money now! It's a bet!"

Ivo shook his head and stripped off his coat. "Not often I get to give two men a lesson at the same time. You game for a bout, Reno?"

"Why, Ivo, I outweigh you and got the reach on you." Reno smiled.

Tossing his coat over the rail, Morgan smiled and said, "You've been dabbling around with amateurs, me boy, now come and let me instruct you in the manly art of self-defense!"

Reno had often sparred with the men in his company while he was in the army, and few of them had been able to stand up to him. He hated a real fight, but a boxing match for fun was a joy to him.

"Any rules?" he asked, stripping off his coat.

"Let's just say one knockdown ends the fight, if that's all right with you, Jim?"

"Good enough."

The two men lifted their hands, and Morgan advanced with his left far extended and his right drawn back to his chin. He came in light as a feather, his feet moving sibilantly over the grass. Reno saw at once that he was an old hand, and he moved in a circle, then whipped back, but he did not fool Morgan, who stepped back like a flash, his chin covered.

Reno feinted with his left, then flicked a right. They moved in a circle, two active, fast men in excellent condition. Reno thought he saw an opening and shot a right hand in, but Morgan simply moved his head, and Reno went off-balance, falling forward with the force of the swing. He knew he looked foolish, and as he recovered, there was a slight tinge of red on his cheeks.

"Aw, Jim, quit foolin' around!" Lee shouted.

Reno saw that he would never be able to lay a hand on the smaller man. Morgan's hands were too fast, and he moved like a dancer across the ground. Changing tactics, he raised both hands and threw himself directly at Morgan.

It was a mistake, for he let his guard down. He never even saw the blow that cracked him across the jaw. It dimmed the sun and turned his legs to rubber. He could hear Lee calling his name, but he seemed far off, his voice tinny and shrill.

His vision cleared slightly, and he shook his head. Morgan could have hit him then, but the Welshman was standing back waiting for him to recover, a smile on his face.

"With a little training you'd be a good 'un, Jim," he said. "You ready to give up?"

Reno shook his head, and then moved in, but no matter how he tried, he could not land a solid blow on Morgan's face, and few on the hard body. Time began to drag on, and he heard Easy say to Lee, "Well, boy, the shovel's right there—you can start anytime."

Reno stopped, dropped his hands slightly, and said, "Ivo, I'm going to buffalo you!"

"You just fly right at it, Mr. Reno!" Ivo said, lights dancing in his eyes.

Reno moved forward, throwing punches wildly, and a few of them got through the smaller man's guard, then a hard right caught Morgan on the temple, and Reno yelled as the man's eyes glazed. He drew back his right to finish Morgan off, then a blow came out of nowhere crashing against his jaw, and a veil of red fell over the world.

He woke up to find Dooley holding his head and Lee staring down at him with disappointment in his face. "Are you all right, Jim?"

Ivo pulled Dooley away and gave Reno a hand up, and there was a light of admiration in his eyes. "You're the best I've met in this land, Jim," he said quietly and shook his head ruefully. "I've fought some of the big ones across the water that didn't have what you got!"

"You win that one, Ivo," Reno grinned. "I'd say the church ought to be full if the preacher sends you out to get a bunch!" Then he looked at Lee and laughed at his face. "There's the shovel, Lee. I hope it teaches you not to make a sucker bet again."

Lee, disgusted, picked up the shovel and turned to the corral, muttering, "Can't even beat a little ol' foreigner!"

Lee and Reno put up in Easy's room, which was off the rear of the stable. After they were all in bed, Lee said, "Jim?"

"What?"

There was a silence, then the boy asked, "How did Ivo beat you? I've seen you whip men lots bigger than him!"

"He knows how, Lee. Ivo put in years of practice learning that game, and the average good scrapper hasn't got a chance against him. Only another professional."

Easy spoke up in the darkness, "You may be right, James, but in a *real* fight, all that don't mean much. Whut good does all that fancy dancin' mean if somebody parts your hair with a bottle? Only way that kind of fightin' works is when fellers agree to keep the rules—and that ain't the way it goes in this ol' world, is it, James?"

They were all thinking about the wild bunch that dominated the camp, and there was a weariness in Reno's voice as he said, "No, the rules don't seem to work very well, Easy." He lay there for a long time looking up at the ceiling and his next-to-last thought was of Jay Dillingham lying dead in the street. His last thought was of Charley Forbes at the end of a rope.

A stir went over the congregation as Reno entered the church with Dooley and Lee. The church was small, no larger than twenty-by-thirty, and the back seats were taken, so they had to make their way to the front. Reno took a seat next to Ivo, who grinned and touched a raw spot on his chin where Reno had clipped him.

Several of the miners Reno knew—Jim Williams and, next to him, Charley Rixie, who looked at Reno with fresh interest. Most of the congregation was composed of townspeople. John Creighton and his wife were in the front row.

Reverend Merritt brightened as they came in, and he leaned over to say something to a tall, bearded man who sat on a straight chair beside him. The bearded man nodded, then got up and said, "We will begin the service by singing 'Old Hundred.'"

Brother French, the song leader, had a clear, tenor voice, and Reno along with the others joined him in the song. French "lined out" the hymns, a practice Reno was familiar with. Since there were no songbooks, and since many of the people could not read, French said the first line aloud, then they all sang it. Then he read the second line, and so on through the hymn.

Reno looked down at Dooley once and smiled at her. She had a throaty voice, very deep for a woman, and she loved to sing. Lee, he saw, was in his latest mode—attempting to be tough. He stood there refusing to sing, and Reno bit his lip, wondering not for the first time if he were doing the wrong thing letting the boy stay with him in a rough life.

After the song service and several lengthy prayers, Merritt preached, and Reno found himself listening to the man intently.

William Merritt was certainly not an imposing figure with his thinning white hair and frail frame, nor was he of the shouting, windmilling type that Reno had encountered so often in the raw frontier. Merritt did not preach so much as *talk* to his listeners. His subject was the manhood of Jesus Christ. Jesus rubbed shoulders, Merritt insisted, with sinners of all kinds—thieves, prostitutes, murderers—and he knew not only their acts but also their hearts. For half an hour he held Reno still with his quiet flow of talk, filled with Scripture, but also filled with references to the world of Virginia City.

"You are never going to disappoint God!" Merritt said firmly. His eyes met Reno's at that moment, and he saw the surprise in his eyes. "No, to disappoint someone, you must fall below their expectations. But God knows your future as well as he knows your past!" Then he closed his Bible and said softly, "You may *grieve* God—I expect you have, as I have—but you must come to him as you are—bring him what you have, not what you'd *like* to have. He h.s gone on record as to what He will do if you simply come to him, just as you are, for the Son of God said once, 'Him that cometh to me, I will never cast out.'"

There was more to the sermon, but Reno sat thinking about that statement. He came to himself with a start when Dooley punched him and said, "Get up, Jim—the sermon's over!"

They filed out, most of the men coming to shake Reno's hand, and finally he stopped to say to Merritt, "I'll remember what you said."

Merritt gave him a warm smile, then said, "I want you to take dinner with us. We ask one family every Sunday."

He would not take no for an answer, and after the congregation broke up, they walked down the street toward the parsonage. Charley Rixie fell into step beside Reno, and they talked about a new method of mining on their way. Dooley walked with Rachel, and Lee was walking beside the preacher.

The men pitched horseshoes while Rachel cooked the dinner—fried chicken, boiled potatoes, and peach pie.

"Would you set the table, Dooley?" Rachel asked. "All the dishes are there in that cabinet."

"Oh, yes." Dooley enjoyed handling the fine china and silverware. She finished that, then came to help with the cooking. She saw the men out pitching horseshoes, and said, "Is Charley Rixie calling on you, Rachel?"

"Oh, I guess so."

"Do you like him?"

"Oh, Dooley, I like him well enough, but . . ."

"But not to marry him?"

"No. Not enough for that."

Dooley sighed and looked enviously at Rachel. "You're so pretty, Rachel! You could have any man in Virginia City!"

"Oh, Dooley, don't be silly!"

Dooley grunted, and there was a discontented look on her face. "You're so small! And I'm a big cow!"

Rachel dropped another piece of chicken into the skillet, laughed, and put her arm around the tall girl. "You're *stately*, Dooley, and a beautiful woman."

Dooley was hungry to hear such things, especially from Rachel. "Oh, I'm not! I'm too tall!"

Rachel smiled and asked gently, "Too tall for whom?"

A crimson flush leaped into Dooley's cheeks, and she covered them with her hands. "*You* know! Everybody knows—but *him*!" she wailed, and suddenly tears filled her eyes, and the unhappiness in her youthful face went to Rachel's heart.

She put her arms around her, and though she was not as tall as Dooley, there was a broad maternal expression on her face as she held the girl close. Dooley's shoulders shook and she sobbed, "He'll never love me, Rachel, never! He thinks I'm a little girl. And I love him so!"

Rachel was too wise to force counsel at such a time. She simply held her, making small comforting noises, then finally when Dooley straightened up, she handed her a lace handkerchief and said only, "Things are never as bad as you think, Dooley. God won't let you down."

Dooley wiped her eyes, then forced a smile. "Guess you think I'm an awful crybaby, Rachel."

"No—just growing up," the older woman said, smiling sadly. "We all have to cry our tears, I think."

Dooley felt better somehow, and she watched Rixie carefully, not missing how his eyes followed Rachel's every move. They finished the meal, and Merritt was talking about how hard life was in mining camps. He finally said, "There was no school at all here for the children until Rachel started a small one last year."

Reno lifted his head. "A school?"

"Oh, not much of one, I'm afraid," Rachel said. "I'm not a trained teacher."

"She's better than any of that breed I ever saw," Charley Rixie said at once. "I *was* a teacher, and Rachel is a fine one, I say."

Reno asked, "Can you stand another pupil?" He looked at Lee and said, "I've been worried about the way Lee's getting shortchanged on his education."

"Why, I'd be glad to have him!" Rachel said, smiling at Lee. "I'm not too good on composition, but I do pretty well with mathematics."

"Is that right?" Reno said, and he surprised them all by saying, "Could you handle *two* new students— one of them an old man?" He laughed at their expressions, and added, "I've always wanted to learn math. In fact, I've always wanted to learn how to survey—but my education was cut short by the war. Sure would like to learn geometry!"

Rachel laughed. "Well, if you can behave yourself, I think we have an empty desk, Jim!"

Lee protested, claiming they were going to get rich. "Rich people don't have to know any old arithmetic!"

Reno laughed at him and gave his head a rub, which Lee had grown to dislike. "Guess you're not too rich if I'm not too old, Lee."

Before they left, they had agreed to spend Saturday and Sunday afternoons and Monday mornings.

"We'll be there at eight," Reno said as they left, and all the way home he talked the thing up, hoping to get Lee excited.

Finally Lee said, "Jim, I guess it's all right, but I just hate arithmetic! I'll do it, but I think you ought to teach me somethin' I really *want* to learn to make up for it."

Reno knew what he meant. They'd had several arguments in recent days over the matter.

"Guess you mean about my teaching you to use a gun."

"Yes."

"You're too young, Lee."

"You said there were fellows in the army no older than me!"

"Yes . . ." Reno tried to find a way out. He knew what it was like, and he remembered suddenly how when he was Lee's age he'd had the same longing to join the world of men. Finally he said, "Well, all right, Lee. I'll do it."

Lee was happy, then, and he ran ahead to tell Easy. Dooley and Reno walked slowly along in the afternoon sun.

"You don't like it, do you, Jim?" she asked quietly.

"No. I wish he'd never put a gun on." Then after a brief silence he burst out with the most revealing thing she'd ever heard him say.

"I wish to heaven *I'd* never picked up a gun." Then in a voice so soft she barely heard it, he said, "Once you pick up a gun, it's awful hard to put it down!"

For the next three weeks, Reno and Lee fell into a pattern. They worked at the claim, putting in long hours, and the sacks that held their dust grew plump. It was hard, backbreaking work, but Lee never complained. He kept up with Reno, and his thin frame began to fill out with a padding of muscle as he worked.

They quit on Saturday, going into Virginia City at noon. Rachel met with them in the small log cabin she used as a classroom for the children of the townspeople, and they worked all afternoon, Reno on geometry, and Lee on arithmetic, spelling, and history.

They went to church on Sunday morning, then had another lesson with Rachel, usually a short one, in the afternoon. They stayed overnight in Easy's quarters and met with Rachel again on Monday morning.

It was a welcome break for Reno. He cared little for money, and the hard, grinding labor at the claim was something he could bear, but he found himself more and more looking for the end of the week.

Lee griped about having to work on his studies, but Reno knew that secretly he enjoyed it. Besides, the lessons on the use of a gun filled his time, and those hours not spent working on his studies or at the claim, were spent practicing with the .44 Colt he had bought out of his earnings. Reno quickly discovered that Lee had a steady hand and a sure eye, and after giving a few pointers, he mostly let Lee practice on his own.

Two people were not so happy with the situation—Dooley and Charley Rixie.

Dooley felt cheated, as Reno and Lee spent most of their free time at the schoolhouse working with Rachel. On the second week she went by late on

Saturday to invite them to a late supper and found Lee already finished and gone. Rachel was sitting next to Reno at a scarred desk, and they were so engrossed in the paper before them that they didn't hear her come in. As Dooley watched, Rachel looked up at Reno, the beauty of her fair, round face enhanced by the glow of sunset flooding through the window, and Reno smiled down at her—a smile that Dooley coveted for herself. She left the room without saying a word, sick at heart and with a fear nagging at her.

Charley Rixie had been hopelessly in love with Rachel for months. Sometimes his hopes rose, for she did not seem interested in another man. But then he saw nothing in her eyes to encourage him as a lover.

He was not a colorful man. There was nothing flamboyant in him, either in thought or appearance. Perhaps that was why, when he saw Reno looking darkly handsome as Rachel smiled at him, he decided to give up his hope.

He came to Rachel as she was locking the door to the schoolhouse one Wednesday evening. He walked home with her, and when they stood beside her door, he said abruptly, "What about me, Rachel?"

She paused and turned to face him, and there was a silence in her face that warned him of the words to follow.

"You've been a long time coming to that, haven't you, Charley?"

"Yes. I ask without much hope. I'm not a dashing figure, Rachel. I'm just a schoolteacher."

She shook her head. "You're a fine man, Charley. I admire you so much!"

He searched those words, then said, "I hear you saying what I've been afraid I'd hear, Rachel."

"I don't love you, Charley," she said quietly. "It wouldn't be fair to you."

He said only, "I thought it would be like that." Then he turned and walked away. There was something in the firm set of his narrow back that gave her sorrow, and she brushed away the tears that filled her eyes.

Rixie said nothing for several days, then on Friday he came to Sam Bible and said, "Sam, I'm pulling out."

Bible was visibly surprised. He scratched his chin with the tip of his steel hook, and said, "Sorry to hear that, Charley. You goin' back east?"

"Yes." He hesitated, then shrugged fatalistically. "I've made some money, Sam, but it's no good for me anymore."

Bible said nothing. He had been aware of Rixie's feeling for Rachel, and he guessed that was what was behind the man's decision.

"I need a little help, Sam," Rixie said finally. "The toughs know I've got money. I think they watch every stage as it leaves here."

"In that, you'd be right."

"There's no way to keep them from hitting the stage, but I've been thinking of it, Sam, and there's one thing that might work. If I could get somebody to wait outside of town with a fast horse, I could get on the stage. The Innocents would know that, but I could get off a little way out of town, get on the horse, and make it to Fort Payne. I'd be all right there."

Bible's eyes glinted. He nodded and said, "That

ought to work, Charley. I'll see what I can do. When you want to leave?"

"I'd like to leave right now," Rixie said, and there was a sadness in his gray eyes. "But I guess Wednesday will do it."

He left, and Sam talked to John Creighton. The two of them put their heads together and came up with the same answer.

Reno was surprised to see Bible ride up to the claim. Bible stayed in town pretty much, not being much of an active man.

"Got a job for you, Jim," Bible said. He explained the job, and when he was finished, said, "It ought to be all right, but I don't like one part of Rixie's plan. I want whoever takes the horse to go all the way to Fort Payne with him. Them yahoos are pretty tough, Jim. They'd butcher him if they caught him alone."

"Sure, Sam. I'll do it," Reno said at once. He liked Rixie and asked, "Wonder why Charley's leaving. He's got a good claim."

Bible stared at him, opened his mouth, then changed his mind. "Don't know. You know where Dempsey's place is?"

"Sure."

"There's an old shack about five miles this side of it. You be there on Wednesday. I've got a good horse you can take. He'll be all saddled and waiting for you. Pick him up early and don't hang around town. When the stage gets there, you and Rixie hightail it to Fort Payne."

"Sure."

"Maybe you could take Easy with you. You might

run into a bunch." He got on his horse and rode back toward Virginia City at a slow trot.

"What'd he want, Jim?" Lee asked.

Reno told him the story, and Lee said, "Let me go, Jim."

"Too dangerous, Lee," Reno answered.

"Jim, you got to let me grow up," Lee said, and there was an intensity in his thin face.

"Sure, Lee, but there may be trouble."

"I'll do just what you say, Jim. Just let me go. I'm asking you."

Reno stared at the boy, almost as tall as he was now. He had grown like a weed and was beginning to fill out. His blue eyes were clear, and there were the beginnings of manhood in his face and body.

"Aching to grow up, aren't you, Lee?" Then he nodded, saying, "All right. I don't think we'll have any trouble, but it's always a chance."

They got up before dawn on Wednesday, Lee strapping the .44 on for the first time. It was still dark when they pulled up in front of the livery stable and found Easy waiting for them, two horses saddled. They left town in the early light of dawn, with not a soul stirring on the street.

There was no rush, so they made a leisurely trip to the rendezvous point and pulled off into a grove of alders to wait for the stage. It was nearly noon when Reno said, "Something's wrong. Stage should have been here two hours ago." He went to his horse, saying, "Let's get back to town."

They rode hard, keeping their eyes peeled for a glimpse of the stage, but saw nothing.

As they rode into town, Easy said, "There's the stage—over there at the depot."

As they dismounted, Bible and X. Beidler came out of the depot, and by the look on their faces Reno guessed what they would say.

"They hit the stage?"

Beidler nodded grimly. "I think they smelled something, Jim. They've never held up a stage so close to town."

"What about Charley?"

"Dead!" Bible cried out, anger in his eyes. "He tried to tough it out and they shot him down!"

Reno's face showed nothing, but there was an anger raging inside him. He had not known Rixie long, but the man was good, and he had died a bloody death at the hands of vicious dogs.

He turned and left the depot, not saying a word.

"Hit him pretty hard," Bible said. "Didn't think he was that close to Charley."

"I think it's the whole thing that's eating on him," Beidler said. "He's going to boil over soon, Sam."

Reno walked quickly through the town, then along the bluff that arose to guard its eastern border. He was blind to the beauty of the day, his mind struggling with the death of Rixie.

He walked for a long time, then came back. He wanted to talk to Merritt. He stepped up on the porch and started to knock on the door, but paused when he heard a small sound to his right.

It was almost dark, but there was enough light to see Rachel sitting in the swing. He hesitated, then stepped to her. She was sitting bolt upright, her fists tightly clenched, and she was staring blindly across the yard.

Reno knew that there had been something

between the two, and he turned to leave, then changed his mind.

"Rachel," he said quietly, "are you all right?"

"Yes."

Her voice was somehow thick and wooden. There was no life or expression in it.

Reno sat down beside her, and for a long moment he said nothing. Her hands were trembling, and her breast was rising and falling in an agitated fashion.

"I'm sorry, Rachel."

She turned to face him, and her fine eyes were dry and her face seemed frozen as she tried to answer. "He loved me, Jim. Did you know that?"

"No, I didn't."

"Oh, yes." She put her fist suddenly against her mouth to choke the cry that tried to arise, then said, "But I didn't love him."

She sat there without moving for a long time, and he was afraid to speak, not knowing what to say.

She turned to face him again and whispered, "Something always happens to people who love me—something terrible."

"No. You can't blame yourself."

"Oh, you don't know. Nobody knows, Jim!" In a strangely empty voice she said, "My husband loved me—and he died. We only had a week, then he went away. I never saw him again. There was just a letter from the War Department telling me he was dead."

He shook his head, then put his hand on hers. It was cold as ice, and he took it in both of his. "Rachel, listen to me, men died by the thousands in the war. Some loved their wives, some didn't. But that had nothing to do with their deaths, don't you see?"

She looked up at him, and her soft lips trembled

as she said, "Charley came here last week. If I'd married him, he'd still be alive."

Reno said gently, "Rachel, you've got to listen to me." He stood up and pulled her up with him. Holding her by the shoulders, he looked down into her face and said, "I've lost friends, and I know the emptiness that comes. Never had a wife, so your loss of a husband was probably worse. But we have to let go. You have to, Rachel! You can't think that your husband would want you to blame yourself. Or that Charley would."

She looked up at him, and there was a hope in her eyes. She whispered, "Oh, Jim, I've been so miserable!"

Then the tears filled her eyes, and she began to tremble like a leaf in the wind.

"Maybe," he said softly, "I can help."

He put his arms around her, and she fell against him with a cry, her body shaking wildly. She sobbed against his chest, and the fear and uncertainty that had built up in her were released as she clung to him. He stood there until the sobs stopped, and then she lifted her head.

It was a strange moment. Her emotions had boiled over for the first time in years, and there was an innocence in her face and a hunger that suddenly touched him. She lay against him, warm and yielding, and without thinking, he lowered his head and kissed her.

Her lips were soft, and she responded to his kiss by lifting her arms and putting her hands on his neck. She was fragile, but there was a firm womanliness to her that revived old hungers. He lifted his head, and there was a light of wonder in her eyes as she looked up at him.

"That's the first time I've cried since I got the letter saying Mark was dead," she whispered. Then she stepped back and stared at him. "And you're the first man I've kissed."

He stood there, waiting, and then he said, "You've been too hard on yourself, Rachel. And life is hard enough without adding one ounce of unearned grief to the load."

She came to him again and touched his cheek lightly. There was sorrow in her eyes, but there was hope in her voice as she said, "I feel all cleaned out, Jim." Then she shook her head. "Poor Charley!"

Reno stood there, a solid figure in the falling darkness, and he took a deep breath, then expelled it.

"Everybody dies, Rachel; all of us." Then he shrugged and in a soft voice added, "We have to make the living worthwhile before it happens!"

EIGHT
Trouble at the El Dorado

Virginia City grew, swelling out of the small fold in the Montana hills. The noise of its sluice boxes and the stamp and shuffle of its many thousand feet carried to the East, so that the impatient ones, the dispossessed ones, the misfits, and the daring ones came up the Missouri to Benton and across the wild Rocky passes, or from Lewiston through the Bitterroots, or over the Oregon Trail to Fort Hall in a headlong rush.

By March there were five thousand people in Alder Gulch alone, and by the next month that number had swelled to seven thousand of all kinds and classes—veterans from the Civil War and frontiersmen from the Platte and the Purgatoire, trappers out of Ogden's Hole, Maine men and Ohio men and Arkansas men, doctors who turned miners. Lawyers who had gone bad stood in the El Dorado quoting Shakespeare and begging the price of another drink. Black sheep fleeing from their families sought their fortune that they might return home. Desperadoes guided by an unerring scent, dance-hall girls, and ladies no longer ladies crowded into Virginia City.

The Gulch was staked out solidly, and the steady stream of newly arrived gold-seekers was pushed farther into other gulches and deeper into the Rockies. A. J. Oliver and Peabody and Caldwell had their stage lines established from Virginia City through Bannack and on to Salt Lake City. The Virginia Hotel went up, wood began to replace canvas, and an air of permanence began to form over the town.

The toughs were in the saddle. Two men were killed on Front Street in broad daylight for the contents of their pockets. A miner named Lenton left Virginia City for Salt Lake City and vanished completely. A merchant was shot down under view of twenty people outside the blacksmith shop, and the murderers rode away without fear. The roughs became more predatory daily, so that X. Beidler said sourly to Reno one morning as they met at Creighton's Store, "This place is rotten, Jim. It's got to have its man for breakfast every day."

Reno had resisted all efforts to join the movement to organize a protective force. He worked his claim, he and Lee kept working on their books with Rachel, and now he picked up the sack of supplies he'd come for, saying briefly, "It'll get worse, X. You don't expect the Innocents to reform, do you?"

Beidler stared at him, a curious light in his eyes. "You're a hard one, Jim. But you'll find out one day that you can't be a lone wolf forever—not unless you want to be an old hermit living in a shack and hating the world."

Reno started to answer, then his eye caught something outside. He said, "See you later, X." He left the store abruptly, and, walking along the street, kept his eye on Ron Lessing and Charley Forbes. The pair sat on the seat of a heavily loaded Conestoga wagon, and Forbes was smiling and shouting to men as Lessing guided the team through the crowds of men and animals that milled thickly on Front Street. They pulled up in front of the El Dorado, and as Forbes jumped down, Saul Logan came out, leaning on his cane. "You're late," Reno heard him say.

"Got held up by the rivers, Saul," Forbes said as the two went inside.

Reno went quickly to Easy's place, dumped the sack of groceries, and pulled his gun from the bunk where he'd left it.

He was strapping it on when Lee came in. He wore his .44 on his side, and he asked, "Jim, do we have to go study today? Easy said him and me could go out to the river and fish if I could play hooky."

He had little hope of Reno agreeing with that plan, and surprise swept his face as Reno nodded. "All right, but you go by and tell Rachel we'll make it up tomorrow."

Lee stared at him, and there was a tightness in Reno's lips that made him ask, "Somethin' wrong, Jim?"

"Got a little chore, Lee."

He left at once and made his way back to the El Dorado. He'd made it a point to go in every week, not to drink but to let the toughs know he wasn't afraid. He spotted Charley Forbes drinking with Logan and Ives at the saloon owner's private table. He did not look directly at them, but stood at the bar for ten minutes talking with Ed Rachaner. Then he left without looking back.

Logan had observed him the moment he came in, and a ruffle of emotion swept his pale handsome features. He did not miss the venomous look Ives gave the man, and he said, "Reno's been pretty quiet lately, George. Maybe he decided to mind his own business."

Ives said at once, "He's too late for that, Saul. He won't live to see another month." The scar on Ives's mouth had healed, but it pulled the upper corner of his lip up in a lopsided fashion, spoiling his good looks.

"He must have dug a fortune out of Tatum's claim," Saul said. "He hasn't been out of town, so it's probably in his cabin."

"I'll be drinking it up when Reno's a piece of meat in the ground," Ives muttered.

Forbes got up. "I need some money, Saul."

Logan reached into his pocket, took out a sheaf of bills, and counted out several to him. Forbes left and went to the blackjack tables. Saul laughed and put the money back into his pocket. "The fool. He knows the game is crooked, and he goes to it like an ox to the slaughter. The table and the women will have every dime of that money."

After leaving the El Dorado, Reno crossed the street and sat down in one of the worn cane-bottomed chairs in front of the hotel. He tilted his chair back and pulled his hat over his eyes, feigning sleep, but he never took his eyes off the front door of the saloon. The day wore on, but he kept his station until finally Forbes came out with Haze Lyons and the pair went down the street. Reno got to his feet and kept well behind on his side of the street.

They went into a cafe and spent an hour there, then went back to the El Dorado.

As the crowd thinned out, Reno felt exposed, and he moved away from the hotel front and took a station in the opening of a narrow alley. It was after two when Forbes came out, and Reno's mouth tightened when he saw Lyons still with him. The two separated, Lyons heading north, while Forbes crossed the street and headed south.

Reno kept his distance, but he was close enough to hear Forbes singing drunkenly, and he saw that the man's steps were unsteady. Forbes jovially greeted a man he passed, then turned off and headed down a side street that led to a cluster of cabins thrown up with little idea of order. It was darker away from the lanterns of Front Street, and Reno moved closer as Forbes followed a twisting path between the cabins, finally stopping at one.

Reno watched as Forbes fumbled in his pocket for a key, singing to himself softly. He let Forbes unlock the padlock and open the door, then he stepped forward and gave him a shove, driving him headlong into the cabin.

"Hey!" Forbes yelled as he scrambled around, getting to his feet. It was dark in the cabin, but Reno could see him plainly outlined by the light of the single lantern that hung on a pine tree outside. Forbes was pulling at his gun, and when it was free, Reno drew his own and smashed down at Forbes's wrist. He cried out, and the gun fell to the dirt floor of the cabin.

"Look, you can have my money," Forbes said, holding his wrist, "but I just dropped most of it at the El Dorado."

Reno spotted a lamp on a table. He pulled a match from his vest pocket, struck it, and, holstering his gun, lifted the glass and lit the wick.

Forbes saw his face and a wave of fear ran through him. He began to say in a high-pitched voice, "Reno, now look—let's talk about this. . . ."

Reno reached into his pocket, pulled out the fragment of silver, then said in a hard voice, "Yeah, that's what we'll do, Charley. We're going to have a nice talk." He pushed Forbes backward into a chair with a quick motion, then pulled Forbes's boot up and held the piece of metal into place. "A perfect fit," he said, then dropped the foot. He pulled his gun, and the hammer being drawn back sounded loud to Forbes in the silence of the room.

"What—what you gonna do?" he whispered. His face was pale and sweat stood on his forehead, gleaming in the golden light of the lantern. Then he cried out loudly in a voice that cracked with sudden fear, "I didn't do it, Reno! I didn't even pull my gun that night!"

Reno laid the muzzle of his gun between Forbes's eyes, and there was death in his face as he said, "You convince me of that, Charley, and you may live to see the sun come up."

Forbes began to tremble in every limb, and he began to talk at once, the words sometimes crowded as if he couldn't get them out fast enough. But if he was afraid of Reno's gun, he was equally terrified of what would happen to him if he gave evidence against the Innocents.

Reno made him go over and over the details of that night, but when he pressed him for the names of the others, Forbes would only gasp, "They'd kill me, you know they would!"

Light came through the single pane of the cabin, and Reno knew that he had to get away with Forbes. "Get up," he said, and he shoved the man out the door.

"Where you taking me—to jail?"

Reno laughed, and gave Forbes another push. "To Jack Gallagher? You'd like that, wouldn't you, Charley? No, I'm going to put you on ice for awhile. Get going."

As Forbes stumbled along, Reno threw out a thought. "You know Ed Rachaner?"

"What about him?"

Reno said, "I guess I'm too tender to torture a man, Charley, but Ed, now, he lived with the Sioux for a spell. And he was a good friend of McKeever and Melton. He told me last week if he ever got the man that did them in, he'd pull the flesh from his bones and fill the gaps with salt."

"You wouldn't let him do that, Reno!"

"No, not if I was there. So guess what I'll do is leave you alone with Ed for a couple of hours. And you know what I think, Forbes? I think you'll be wishing you had *more* to spill by the time I get back!"

Reno ignored Forbes's pleas, and he hurried along so fast, he missed seeing a very tall man who came out of a cabin. Seeing Forbes being pushed along by the gun in Reno's hand, the man ducked back inside. He waited until the two were out of sight, then emerged and made for the center of town at an awkward run.

Saul Logan was awakened by a thunderous knocking at his door. Pulling the .38 from the table beside his bed, he got up, grasped his cane, and hobbled to the door. "Who is it?"

"Ives—let me in, Saul!"

Logan unlocked the door and Ives stepped in at once, accompanied by Long John Frank. "We've got trouble, Saul!" Ives said. He was unshaved and his clothes were rumpled. "Frank saw Reno taking Forbes somewhere at the point of a gun an hour ago."

"Forbes? Why would he be taking Charley anywhere?"

Long John Frank said, "There was a lot of talk after McKeever and Melton was killed. Some said that Reno had some kind of evidence on who done it."

Logan's eyes narrowed and he said, "If Charley talks, we all may go down."

Ives said, "He's yellow, but he won't talk. He knows what would happen to him if he did."

"Yeah," Long John said, "but he knows what'll happen to him if he *don't*, George. And that's *now*! He'll spill his guts."

"I think you're right." Saul conceded, then said, "We got to get him away from Reno, George."

"Be hard to do," Ives answered at once. "He sure won't take him to jail. Likely hide him out in some miner's shack. We'll find him, though."

Saul Logan grew still, and his mind raced, considering every possibility. He had built an empire of sorts in Virginia City, and he was not going to see it tumble now. An idea came to him, and he went to his chair, sat down, and let it take form in his head. Ives and Frank had seen this happen before, and they stood silently waiting until Logan finally nodded.

"All right, this is what we do. . . ."

They listened carefully, and then Ives grinned.

"That'll settle Reno's hash, Saul."

Logan picked up a cigar, and when he got it going, he said, "You've missed Reno twice, George. You'd better make this good."

"I'm not afraid of him," Ives snapped, "but we'll do like you say, Saul."

"Do it, then!"

Reno tried to think of the last place the Innocents would look for Forbes. *They'll hit my place first, I reckon,* he thought as he herded Forbes along. Already people were stirring, and he didn't want word to get out that he had Forbes.

He made it to the livery stable, and Easy came out of his room as Reno entered.

"What's up?" he asked, taking in the harried face of Charley Forbes and the gun in Reno's hand.

Reno told him about the piece of spur, then said, "Charley's not saying who was there with him, but he will. We have to get him in a safe place."

"That's gonna be kinda tough, James." He scratched his head and said, "They'll be looking in every rat hole soon as they find out."

They considered half a dozen places, rejecting them all, then Easy said, "Well, what about that old harness room here? Full of junk, but it's tight, and there's a stout lock on the door."

"What if he makes a racket?"

"Why, I'll jest step in and put the quietus on him, won't I now, Charley?"

Reno said slowly, "I don't like it much, but it's the best we can do. Lock him up, and if he tries anything, shoot him in the leg. I don't want him dead before Ed Rachaner has a little talk with him." Reno fluttered one eyelid, and Easy picked up on the game at once.

"That Indian!" he exclaimed. "Why, Jim, you wouldn't turn a white man over to *him!*"

Reno nodded, saying, "I got some calls to make. I'll be back with Ed sometime today."

As Easy shoved the protesting Forbes into the harness room, Reno left, heading straight for X. Beidler's house. Beidler was eating breakfast, but his eyes gleamed when he heard Reno's story.

"If that jasper will talk, we'll have another trial."

"But it's going to be touchy, X. If they find out we've got Forbes, they'll pull Virginia City apart to get him.

"Sure they will. I'll get Creighton. You think he'll talk, Jim?

Reno rubbed his chin and said finally, "I'm going to let him simmer in his juices for a few hours. I'd like to get him away from here, but that's too dangerous in daylight. I think we better get him away after dark. Then we can work on him."

"What are you going to do now?"

"I better get back and help Easy watch him. He has to run that stable, and all Forbes needs is one break and he's gone."

Reno returned to the stable, and all morning he dozed on a pile of hay as Easy ran the business. It was a busy place, and Easy was in and out often. At noon Easy said, "I'll spell you, Jim. Go greasy up yore mouth."

Reno ate a quick meal at the cafe, then hurried back. There were few customers that afternoon, and it was about five o'clock when Ivo Morgan came scurrying in, alarm on his face.

"Jim! Glad I found you!"

"What's up, Ivo?"

"It's the boy—Lee. He's at the El Dorado, and he's in bad trouble."

Reno came off of his chair like a cat, his eyes blazing. "Tell me!"

"The boy came in like he was looking for somebody, and then some of the roughs began making fun of him—about his being too young to wear a gun. Said they were gonna give him a paddling and send him home to his mother, that kind of thing."

Reno started for the door, his face fixed. Ivo grabbed him, saying, "Wait a minute! Slow down, Jim!"

Reno paid no heed. He left the stable at a fast walk, and Easy had to stretch his legs to keep up with him. The short wrangler had a wild streak, but now he had a saving coolness. "Jim, wait, this don't smell good. Let's get some help on this thing."

Reno didn't even answer, but plowed across the street, shoving men aside with his broad shoulders. The fighting impulses that lay not deep beneath the indolence of his manner revealed themselves in the loss of caution.

He wheeled into the El Dorado, Easy close on his heels. Easy murmured softly, "We ain't got too many friends here, Jim." He saw Ives and Haze Lyons standing at the bar, and there was something revealing in the way they kept their faces turned away from the two men who thrust suddenly into the bar. Boone Helm, Sam Brunton, and Long John Frank were sitting at a table to their left, and Steve Marshland and Red Yeager lounged at the bar toward the front of the room.

"Heads up, James," Easy said. He moved away

from Reno, taking a place directly across from where Ives and Lyons were sitting. He hoped Reno would notice how thick Ives's men were in the room.

Reno saw it all, but he ignored Ives and did not waste a glance at Saul Logan, who did not look up from his drink. Reno saw Lee backed up against the wall, facing two men. One of them was Dan Brown, a tough man by reputation, and the other was a thin Mexican wearing tight pants and a jacket with silver buttons.

Lee's face was pale, and he looked even younger than his age as he stood there. Then he tore his eyes away from the two men in front of him. A light of relief touched his blue eyes at the sight of Reno and Easy, and he licked his lips, saying, "Jim . . ."

"Lee, what's the trouble?"

Reno moved smoothly to stand just to the left of Brown and the Mexican. He could see Ives out of the corner of his eye, but he didn't turn his head.

Brown turned to face Reno, and his eyes swept the room slyly. Then he said, "This kid is too brash, Reno." He let his hand brush against his gun, then said louder, "He's wearin' a gun and he's gotta stand to his remarks—ain't that right, Miguel?"

Reno had heard nothing good about Miguel, who had killed a man with a knife the month before. There was a cruel glitter in his almond-shaped eyes as he nodded. "*Sí*, that is so." He slowly turned so that now both men were facing Reno squarely.

The room was filled with silence, and Reno let it run slow and thick, ignoring the threat of the men behind him, his eyes putting pressure on Brown and Miguel. His mouth was a long streak across the weathered bronze of his skin, narrowed to a tough half-smile.

He turned and walked five steps, and with his back to the two men, he came to stand before Ives and Lyons. "You too yellow to take a crack at me yourself, George?"

Ives jerked his arm at the question. His hand darted toward his gun, but he hesitated. His eyes swept quickly right and left. Easy had moved over to face Helm, Brunton, and Long John Frank, but Ives saw Red Yeager give him a nod, and answered loudly, "You drunk, Reno? I'm not in this."

"Don't lie, George. You've let other men do your fighting so long, you're gutless!"

Easy saw how it would be. They had pulled Reno into the saloon by using Lee. Now they would gun him down, and no one in town would dare make a protest. He kept his eyes locked on the three men at the table, but Yeager and Marshland were too far to his left. Reno faced Ives and could not see Miguel or Brown.

Ives's face was flushed, and he said, "All right, Reno, you've made a splash, but it ends here!" He stepped to his right, and Lyons stepped to his left. Men began diving for cover, and then there was the sound of a door closing. Ives darted a look to see Ringo Jukes step in behind Brown and Miguel. The two pulled around instantly, facing Jukes instead of Reno. At the same time Ivo Morgan walked through the front door. He was wearing a gun, and he moved to the left of the building, keeping his dark eyes fixed on Yeager and Marshland.

Ives hesitated. There were still at least ten of his men to their four, but Reno's gaze was locked into his.

"What's the matter, George?" Reno said. "You got to have an army?"

Ives stood there, knowing that if he backed down he was through in Virginia City. He had gone against men before, but the chill in Reno's eyes and the steadiness of his gaze shook him.

Then he pulled himself up and glanced around. All of his men were facing opponents of their own— except for Alec Carter, who stood back against the wall directly behind Reno. He had drawn his gun, and points of light came to Ives's face as he saw his chance. As he saw Carter's gun pull down on the center of Reno's back, he yelled, "Reno, you're dead!" and his hand stabbed for the gun at his side.

Reno did the one thing that saved his life. As Ives went for his gun, Reno turned his body to one side in the classic duelist position, and his gun leapt into his hand. He heard the sound of a gun behind him and felt the slug tug at his shirt, but he never stopped his movement. He did not shoot from the hip, but as Ives's weapon cleared the holster, his arm straightened and Ives's mouth dropped open in an agonizing shape as he saw that Reno's gun had locked on his heart.

"No!" he screamed, but the cry was drowned out as Reno's gun exploded. The slug caught Ives high in the chest and drove him back against the bar, then he sprawled on the floor clutching at his chest, the blood spurting through his fingers.

The room was rocked with gunfire as Miguel drew and got off one shot that creased Jukes's thigh. He dropped dead as Ringo put two bullets in his heart.

Yeager dropped to the floor, fired twice at Ringo, missed, and rolled away as Ivo Morgan drew and began firing at Yeager and at Marshland, who was pulling down on Easy.

The three men at the table took a dive, Long John firing once, then grabbing his throat, which was ripped open by a slug from Easy's gun. He gurgled and tried to call for help, but everyone was ducking for cover.

"Help me! Get Steele!" he kept calling, trying to staunch the blood that boiled through his fingers.

Yeager scrambled behind the bar, and Marshland followed, and they kept up a running fire.

The instant Reno saw his slug strike Ives, he whirled and took a shot at Alec Carter, but it missed. It came close to Carter's head, and he flinched, then dropped down behind a table, firing wildly at Reno.

Brown started to shoot at Reno's back, but Jukes said, "Drop it!" Brown saw Jukes holding a gun right at his head, and he dropped his own, saying loudly, "Don't shoot!"

That seemed to turn the tide, for Yeager and Marshland both had run out of shells. Carter began hollering, "I'm out! I'm out!"

A quiet came over the place, and Reno, with his ears ringing from the gunfire, swept the room with a swift glance.

Ivo, Easy, and Jukes were all up, and Lee came from where he'd dropped. Reno ignored Long John's wailing and came to stand over Ives.

He was alive, and as Reno stood over him, he struggled to his feet. The slug had caught him as he had turned, gouging a track through the flesh of his upper chest but not penetrating the lungs. He looked at his gun lying on the floor, and his eyes were dull with shock as he muttered, "I wish I'd gut-shot you." Then he walked unsteadily to the door, saying, "Come on, Long John, let's find that doctor."

The two men left, and Reno whirled and stepped to the table where Saul Logan sat.

The dapper owner had not moved even when bullets were flying.

Reno stopped, looked down at him, then pulled a chair off the floor and sat down. He shook the loads and spent shells from his gun, put one live load in, then put the gun on the table.

"Logan, you're a cripple, but there's nothing wrong with your hands. You hired your murders done. Now you're going to have to stand up to one fight yourself."

The silence spread out over the room as Reno folded his arms, his eyes daring Logan to go for the gun. They all saw that Reno had given him an edge. The gun was close to his hand, and Reno sat there with his arms folded.

The pressure built up, then suddenly Logan shook his head. "I'm no gunman!"

"You're nothing, Logan," Reno said quietly. He picked up the gun and then walked to the bar, stopping at the free lunch counter. He picked up a bowl, filled it with thick, greasy chili, then walked back to Logan. Without a word he poured it over the saloon owner's head, then slapped him twice in the face.

"Let's get out of here," Reno said. He moved out of the saloon, and the others followed.

Logan sat there, the chili running down his cheeks and staining his immaculate white shirt. He did not raise his hand to wipe it away, and every man in the room stared at him, waiting.

Finally he stood up and picked up his cane. He wiped his eyes with a handkerchief, hobbled across the room to the stairs, then turned and said, "Red," and went up slowly, grasping the rail with his free hand. He moved like an old man, and when Yeager followed him to his room, he said nothing until he went to a pitcher and washed his face.

Then he said in a thin voice, "Get Zane."

Yeager's mouth dropped open, and he said, "Saul, he's in that Mex prison for another five years!"

Logan went to a desk and opened a steel box. Taking out a wad of bills, he said, "Bribe him out. Hire an army and take the prison. Whatever it takes, get him!"

Yeager took the money but still hesitated. "Saul, think about it. He wouldn't be in that jail if it wasn't for—"

"For me," Logan said with a thin smile. Then he nodded, and there was dead certainty in his voice as he said, "For me, he'll come. And he's the only one who can take Reno out. Get Zane—and get the Simmons brothers from El Paso."

"You sure you want them two? They're poison."

"Get them!" Logan allowed a smile to touch his thin lips, and he touched his mustache in a feline gesture. "I want to be there when Reno tries to pull on Zane!"

NINE
The Pit

After having been a general of sorts in the Mexican army, Juan Mateo Rivera took little pleasure in his position as superintendent of Magdegara Prison. His only diversions were drinking huge quantities of cheap red wine, which dulled his memories of better days, and his "experiments" with prisoners. The latter ranged all the way from withholding all mail and privileges to having a man beaten and thrown into the Pit—a hole the size of a grave but only twelve inches deep and covered with a sheet of steel. Under the blazing sun of southern Mexico, the temperature of the Pit mounted to well over 150 degrees, and more than one prisoner had been removed directly to a deeper grave. Others had lost their reason, and the very threat of the Pit was enough to turn a hardened desperado into a fawning, cringing thing.

In his eleven years at Magdegara, the superintendent had only failed to tame five prisoners. Four of those were dead, and a frown creased his brow as he thought of the fifth. The resistance of the gringo had added a spice to his life that he needed. He leaned back in his chair, recalling the means he had taken to break the tall man who was now going through his seventh day in the Pit—a record.

He recalled the beginning, over two years ago when the man had come. The man had been thin, and the doctor who took a desultory look at prisoners from time to time had said with a shrug, "This one will not last."

Rivera had agreed with him, but not only had the man lived but had grown strong on the terrible working conditions and miserable food. And his spirit! He had refused to degenerate into the cowed state of a prisoner. Rivera had quickly found out that no matter how much work he was forced to do, the man with the greenish hazel eyes would not be quenched.

Rivera smiled at the memory of how he had tested the man. Beatings, starvation, the Pit—nothing could dim the fire of those eyes!

"If I had time!" the superintendent whispered. He opened the desk drawer in front of him, pulled out a heavy steel box, and unlocked it with the key that dangled from a heavy chain at his waist. Taking out one of the five thick sheaves of bills, he rippled the notes, and then frowned. "If I had time I would make the gringo crawl to my boot!" he whispered, and an angry expression crossed his face as he started to throw the money back into the box. But Rivera was a practical man, and he knew that the pleasure of breaking the man was too expensive. He fingered the notes, took the others out, and made a stack on his scarred desk.

There would be another stack exactly that size when he followed the instructions that had accompanied the first payment—enough money to leave Magdegara and retire to a resort on the coast.

"One cannot have everything," he murmured sadly. Putting the cash back in the box, he remembered with a frown how he had received that first stack of notes.

A red-haired American had walked into his office the previous day, and said without preamble, "Señor Rivera, I am here to bribe you."

"Ah! What a refreshing experience!" he had said with a grin. "You know such a thing could result in a long prison term for both of us."

The red-haired man had returned his grin. "Life is a gamble. What's your price?"

Rivera had stared at him, then asked softly, "What is it you want?"

"The gringo, Zane Logan."

Rivera knew how to bargain. "Ah, Señor, that is impossible!" And he had begun to go over the reasons why Logan absolutely could not be allowed to escape.

Ignoring Rivera's eloquent speech, the visitor had reached into his pocket and pulled out a large sheaf of bills, freshly printed U.S. notes. "That's plenty for the job," he had said carelessly. Then he caught the unbelieving look on the other's face and pulled out four more stacks. "That will retire you for life, Superintendent."

Rivera had been stunned by the amount, more than he had made in his entire life—or was apt to. But he said, "Señor, I cannot."

The red-haired man had stopped smiling. Sweeping up the packets of money he stood up. "I don't bargain, Rivera. This is *half* the bribe. The other half will be in your hand when Logan is in mine. And you've got until I get out that door to say yes or no."

Rivera had managed to call out "Stop!" as the other got to the door, and there was a grin on the wide lips of the redhead as he swung back. "The arrangements are simple. You bring Logan to the crossroads over by Corozza tomorrow at dusk. Have him on a good horse and come alone."

"But I cannot personally—"

"Yes or no?"

He had said yes.

Now Rivera, sitting alone in his office, frowned at the thought of how he'd been forced to nod. He lifted the stack of bills and said again, "One cannot have everything."

He replaced the money, took out a small derringer, concealed it in his sleeve, strapped a .45 on his thigh, and walked out the door.

The sun-baked earth surrounding the barracks sent up heat waves that blurred the far-off hills, and a hot breath of air met him as he made his way toward the lone sentry who stood guard at a barbed wire enclosure. The guard, a short, stocky Indian with obsidian eyes, saluted Rivera and stood at attention, awaiting a command.

"Is he still alive?"

The guard shrugged, nothing showing through his stolid expression. "I cannot say, my Comandante."

"How long has he been inside this time?"

"Seven days, sir." The dark, expressionless eyes of

the Indian flashed for one second with a brief admiration. "He never begs, this one."

"Saddle my horse—and also saddle the bay with three white stockings."

"Yes, my general." With a nod, the Indian went at a trot to the corral at the far end of the camp. He did not question the command, though behind the stolid face anything might have been going on.

Rivera lit a cigar, threw the match away, then leaned down and grasped the iron handle welded to a steel plate. It burned his hand, and he took out his handkerchief, wrapped it around the hot steel, and, with a grunt, lifted the heavy cover.

Stepping back, the superintendent drew his .44 and said, "Come out of that hole, dog!"

Seven days with only a single canteen of warm water every third morning under that steel plate. No room to turn over. The burning heat of the sun transforming the steel cover into a radiant heater that did not cool down for hours after the sun went down. Three days of thirst, not knowing how long the water had to last. Three days of breathing the fetid scent of the miniature prison, the only air coming through a tiny gap at the foot of the Pit.

Rivera shivered as he thought of the horror of spending one hour in the Pit, much less seven days. He took a firmer grip on his weapon and said with a trace of nervousness in his voice, "That's close enough. Stand there, dog of a gringo."

Rivera had no lack of personal courage, having been a soldier and a good one. And his reason told him that the emaciated figure that had slowly risen Lazarus-like from the shallow trench could offer no threat to him. But he had to force himself not to take another step backward.

Indeed, there seemed nothing dreadful about Zane Logan as he stood there, weaving in the fading sunlight. He was tall, well over six feet, but there was not an ounce of excess flesh on his body. He wore only a pair of thin shorts, and every muscle in his body was evident—thin and stretched over the bones. Yet despite the emaciated condition, there was still the impression of strength, and even as he lifted his hand slowly to wipe the sweat out of his eyes, the muscles in his arm and chest moved like steel cables.

His hair was long, and the chestnut color had just a tinge of reddish gold. A rugged chin proclaimed stubbornly the iron will that lay somewhere behind the high forehead. The features were craggy—a roman nose and broad cheekbones, deep-set eyes under heavy bone, a broad mouth, and small, close-set ears.

He did not speak at all, but his hearing was good, for though his eyes were shut tight against the blinding light of the sun, he turned his face directly toward Rivera.

"Did you enjoy your vacation, pig?" Rivera asked. He did not expect a reply, for experience had taught him that nothing could make the gringo speak until he chose. He moved three steps to his left, keeping Logan carefully in his gaze. He picked up the guard's canteen and shook it so that the sound of the sloshing water was evident. "Perhaps you'd like a drink of water?"

The tightly shut eyes of Logan opened a fraction of an inch, and the greenish eyes that Rivera had learned to hate peered out. Then the cracked lips opened and he said in a raspy voice, "No, I've got plenty."

He stooped, picked up the canteen, and tossed it at Rivera. It caught the superintendent in the chest. He cursed, and his face grew livid as he saw the mockery in the green eyes of the prisoner. Even as he swore he was thinking, *This man is not human! Anyone else would have drunk all that water the first day!*

A streak of fear shot through him, and he forced himself to laugh. "Not thirsty, eh? Well, maybe you'd better think again. Where you're going today, gringo, you'll be dry forever. Better have one last drink—and put on those rags!"

As Logan pulled on the prison rags, his eyes were opening wider, and they stared at the Mexican steadily. Rivera grew furious at this man who could not be frightened, who would take the worst and stare back out of those green eyes.

They stood there locked in silence until the sound of hoofbeats drew Rivera's head around. The Indian rode up, mounted on the bay and leading the superintendent's rangy chestnut. He slid to the ground and stood there watching with his expressionless eyes.

"Put iron on his hands!" Rivera snapped, and while the Indian put a pair of heavy manacles on the thin wrists of the prisoner, he mounted his horse and waited. When the Indian was finished, he said, "Put him on that horse!"

The bay was a large horse, and full of life. It took an active man to mount him, and after seven days in the Pit, Rivera expected that Logan would have to be lifted into the saddle like a sack of grain.

But Logan moved suddenly. Taking two short steps, he moved to the bay, then, lifting his heavily ironed hands, he grabbed the horn and pulled himself into the saddle with a smooth motion. The bay whickered once, gave a sudden sidestep, then steadied under the pressure of the rein.

Rivera stared at Logan, then pulled his horse around. "Get moving," he said, then nodding to the guard, said, "Open the gate."

The Indian trotted in front of the two men, crossing to the steel-barred gate that gave entrance to the narrow road that led across the desert. He slid a massive key into a padlock and drew a heavy iron bolt. It took all his strength to swing the gate open.

"Move ahead. If you try to run, you'll get the back of your head blown off!"

Zane Logan put his animal through the gate at a walk, and Rivera followed behind, his gun drawn and his eyes glued on the thin form of the man ahead of him. He did not turn to see the guard standing there staring at him, curiosity rising to break the dull surface of his black eyes. And he did not hear the faint whisper as the guard watched them grow smaller in the distance. "The gringo has beaten my superintendent—and now he will die for it." He shrugged and turned back to bar the gate, knowing that the official would come back with the report—*Prisoner shot while trying to escape.* It had happened before.

Rivera said nothing to the prisoner for three hours, nor did Logan speak. The sun was a huge orange ball casting brilliant fingers of light over the peaks of the far-off mountains, and the blistering

154

heat rising from the rocky ground began to be tinged with the first faint trace of coolness coming from those same peaks.

They were only half a mile from the rendezvous point when Rivera said, "All right. This is as far as you go. Get off your horse."

Logan slid off the bay and turned to face the other, his eyes reflecting the dying rays of the sun. He stood there loosely, holding the reins of the mount with no trace of tension in his body.

Rivera said, "You've become boring, Logan. I could break you, given the time, but it's not worth the bother." He lifted his gun and aimed right at Logan's face. "You can say a prayer if you wish. Make it a short one."

Logan did not move. His eyes took in the muzzle of the gun trained on his face, and he said, "No prayer, Rivera."

Rivera shouted, "All right—take it then!" He drew the hammer of the .45 back, the loud click striking through the stillness of the desert air. He steadied his hand, and with the gun aimed right between those greenish eyes he'd learned to hate, he said, "May you rot in hell!"

But if he expected Zane Logan to show fear, he was disappointed. He held the gun rigidly and saw that except for swaying forward slightly as if in anticipation of the bullet, the tall man did not react. He didn't even blink. He stared at the man before him, then shouted, "Get on your horse!"

Zane watched Rivera for a long moment, then mounted the horse and again they made their way along the narrow road.

When they reached the crossroads, Rivera looked

around nervously. There was nothing there except a tall outcropping of basalt two hundred yards down the east road and a small grove of spindly trees to the west.

Suddenly a man rode out from behind the rock formation, and Rivera recognized the American. He rode right up to them, his hand close to the gun at his side.

"Here's your money, Mex," he said, taking a package out of his pocket and tossing it to Rivera.

Rivera had to lean forward to catch it, and when he recovered his balance, he saw that the red-haired man had drawn his gun in that instant. Fear ran through him, and he sat there, dry-mouthed, with his heart pumping wildly.

"Give me the key to them irons, Mex, then get movin'!" the red-haired man said. "And don't even think about tryin' anything cute!"

Rivera swallowed, handed over the key, pulled his horse around, and rode away in a wild plunging gait. When he finally stopped the horse and looked around, the other two men were mere dots on the darkening horizon. He pulled the wrapper off the package, half-expecting to find only newspaper, but real cash was there.

He was already thinking of ways to intercept the two, to bring them into his grasp for revenge, when he saw a small slip of white paper inside the first packet of notes.

He saw the words printed in a strong, bold handwriting: IF YOU TRY ANYTHING FUNNY, MEX, YOU WON'T LIVE TO SPEND THIS MONEY.

Rivera wiped the sweat off his face and drove his horse back toward the prison. In a few days he'd be away from the cursed place, beside the sea, living like a king.

But he knew as he made his way back that his sleep would be forever haunted by a pair of mocking eyes, eyes that didn't blink at a cocked pistol.

Yeager had said nothing to the man beside him, thinking it wise to move away from Rivera, but finally he pulled his horse to a halt and turned to say, "Let me get that iron off you, Zane."

Zane extended his hands, and Yeager unlocked the manacles and threw them into the brush. "We better make time, I reckon. Never did trust a greaser."

He spurred his horse into a fast walk, and for a time the two men rode silently. Then as the ground began to rise, Yeager said, "We'll make camp in those mountains tonight. Tomorrow we'll cut east and catch the train to the border."

"All right, Red."

Yeager cut his eyes around, a little nervousness in his manner, but there was nothing in the face or manner of Zane to give alarm. For the next six hours they made their way up into the foothills.

Yeager found the spot he'd selected, high on a plateau, with good cover and a small stream, cold with mountain snows.

They made a fire, and Yeager cooked up a meal of bacon and gravy. They poured the gravy over biscuits he'd brought and washed it down with steaming coffee.

Finally, Yeager could stand it no longer. "Zane, you ain't changed a bit. Any other man would at least *ask* why I got you outta that Mex jail!"

"You must want something, Red."

The remark caught Yeager off guard, and he cursed. "Well, that's a fine—"

"What is it?" Zane asked, his deep-set eyes fixed on Yeager.

Yeager shut his mouth with a click, then, after staring at the tall figure across the fire, laughed nervously, saying, "Well, Zane, it ain't so much that *I* want something—it's Saul who sent me." He stared at Logan to see the effect of that, but there was only a watchfulness in his eyes, and that unnerved him. "Well, that's the way it is. And lemme tell you, it cost Saul a *bundle* to get you outta that hole!"

"What's he want, Red?"

"Why, to tell the truth, Zane," Red said with a shrug, "Saul's done real well. Maybe he wrote you about what's he's done up in Virginia City?"

"No," Zane said quietly. "Saul didn't write."

Something in that remark stopped Yeager, and he had to swallow before he could go on. "Well, anyway, he's doin' good, but there're some pretty hard characters there who want to cut him down. One in particular is a hairpin named Reno. He's a hard one, and Saul says you're the only one who can take him."

Zane stared at Yeager, saying nothing. He finally lay back, his head pillowed on the saddle, and said, "Good night, Red."

"What!" Yeager exclaimed. "Is that all you gotta say to me?" He started to go over and pull Logan out of his blankets, but a thought crossed his mind and he sat back hurriedly. "Well, you gonna go help Saul or not?"

An owl drifted overhead, falling to the ground somewhere off to their left. There was a shrill squeal, a rustle, then silence.

Finally, after a long time, Zane Logan said, "Good night, Red."

Yeager spent a sleepless night. The next day they made it to a small town where the train stopped, and Yeager said, "I've got to hightail it to El Paso, but you better start for Virginia City, Zane."

He had outfitted the tall man and given him money for his fare, but Zane had not said a word about his intentions. Yeager said finally, "Well, you got a pretty raw deal last time, Zane. Guess I can't blame you if you don't run to pull Saul's apples outta the fire."

Zane lifted his head, and there was a sadness in his face as he regarded Yeager. With his thin hand he touched the butt of the new .44 at his side. Then he said quietly, "I'll be there, Red."

TEN

"He's Faster Than Anybody!"

Spring swept across the Montana highlands, its warm breath freeing the streams and bringing life to the seeds that had lain cold and dormant under the weight of winter ice. The hills around Virginia City exploded with wildflowers, spotting the land with brilliant red, violet, and yellow.

Dooley had thrown herself into the laundry, but after hiring two Chinese to help Jackson and Leah with the hard work, she found herself idle. She began to invest herself in the work of the church. Back in Arkansas she had been a regular church-goer, but it had been more out of habit than anything else.

The raw life of the Gulch, with its ever-present violence, the painted women hailing customers from upper-story windows, and the steady stream of humanity with all its foibles had something to do with her new interest. With new graves, raw and ugly, gaping almost daily, she was more and more aware of the narrow gap that spanned life and death.

William Merritt and Rachel observed this. The minister remarked, "Dooley's a good one to have in a congregation. It's easy to preach when you can look down into a face that's taking everything in." Then he added with a smile, "And have you noticed how many young fellows have gotten interested in church since she's started attending? I suppose she's the best evangelist we have!"

Rachel looked up from her sewing and frowned. "It won't do them any good. She's so smitten with Jim Reno she doesn't even *see* other men."

Merritt gave Rachel an odd look, then remarked quietly, "She's jealous of you, Rachel."

A flush rose on Rachel's smooth cheeks, and she looked up with a startled expression. "Why— that's ridiculous!"

"No, it's not. Reno spends more time with you at the school than he spends with Dooley. And you're a beautiful woman his own age. Perfectly natural thing, I'd say."

"Why, I hardly *know* the man, and even if I were interested in him, he's not the sort of person I'd look at. He's not at all like . . ."

When he saw her confusion, he said quietly, "He's not at all like Mark? Is that what you almost said?" He shook his head, thinking about Rachel and her obsession with the death of her husband and her hatred for the South. He examined her keenly as he added, "Mark is dead, Rachel. I've been waiting for you to admit that—to accept it. You're a young woman, and it's the right thing for you to find another man and make a life for yourself."

She fingered the scarf she was embroidering, then looked up into his eyes, her face more open than usual. She was a calm woman, not easily stirred, but now her bosom rose quickly and her fingers trembled slightly as she said, "I don't know, Dad, why it's been so hard for me. Ever since Mark died I've felt *guilty* somehow, like I didn't do my best for him. It's been like–like I've been in a trance . . . and just starting to wake up."

Merritt wanted to say that it had been Jim Reno's presence that had shaken her, but he was too wise to press the issue.

"Well, maybe you can convince Dooley you've got no designs on her man while we're over at Bannack." He laughed then, and rubbed his chin. "Better yet, maybe she'll fall in love with that skinny preacher. That'd take care of the whole thing!"

Rachel smiled and shook her head. "He's more likely to fall in love with her, Dad."

Her words proved to be prophetic. Brett Stevens, a rawboned, inexperienced young man, was so smitten by Dooley's charms he was practically paralyzed. Stevens was beginning a new church in Bannack, and Merritt went over twice a month to help him. Rachel usually accompanied him, and she asked Dooley to make the trip.

It was a break in the monotony for Dooley, and after her first smile at Stevens it was obvious to all three of the visitors that the preacher was captivated.

They attended two services, at which young Stevens had preached to a congregation of thirty people as if they were a host, but he lost his eloquence when he tried to carry on a simple conversation with Dooley.

After their last breakfast at the cafe, Stevens managed to ask Dooley to accompany him to the general store to help pick out some goods for mission work. After the two left, Rachel said, "He's eloquent in the pulpit, but when he looks at Dooley he can't even make a sentence!"

Merritt nodded. "He's pretty well fragmented, all right. But I guess most men look pretty colorless to a girl who's been looking at Jim Reno."

Rachel knew that his words had a double meaning, partly directed at her. She merely nodded, saying, "Jim's colorful enough. And I suppose most women are drawn to a man with a wild streak." She smiled at her own words, then said, "We plan to reform them, or housebreak them, I suppose."

Merritt shook his head. "I'm worried about Jim. Sam Bible told me that the roughs have his number. He says they'll get him sooner or later."

"He knows that." Rachel sipped her coffee, lost in thought, and Merritt, though he knew her well, could not read what lay behind her smooth expression.

Half an hour later the stage rolled in and unloaded. There was an hour layover, and Stevens spent most of that time trying to unearth some excuse for seeing Dooley again. Finally Rachel took pity on him.

"We're having a special service next Saturday night, Brett. Why don't you try to join us?" She added with a wink at her father, "Miss Wade will be favoring us with special music."

They all nearly laughed at the frantic manner of his acceptance, and he kept promising to attend, clinging to Dooley's hand so tightly that she had to pull it away.

Merritt helped them into the coach, which had only two other passengers. Merritt put Rachel next to a window, then sat down between her and a rancher named Greeson that he knew. A fat man with a checkered vest sat at a window on the opposite side, and Dooley sat down by the other window.

She watched as the bandy-legged driver came out of the station carrying a leather pouch. He walked to the double doors of a saloon, called, "Leavin' now!" then came to the coach and tossed the pouch up to the guard.

As the coach swayed, two men walked out of the saloon and pulled themselves into the coach. One of them was a tall, heavy man in his middle twenties. He had muddy brown eyes and tow-colored hair, and he wore two ivory-handled guns. The other man was obviously his brother, but was older. He had the same hair and eyes, but was thinner, and an old scar began at the right corner of his mouth, ran backward to his neck and disappeared under his collar like a snake. Both men had obviously been drinking and smelled of rank tobacco smoke and raw whiskey.

The younger man's eyes swept the other passengers, and he deliberately sat down next to Dooley. He motioned to the other man, who sat down beside him. "Well, ain't this nice, Ben? We got some ladies for the rest of the trip." He had a bold look, and he turned his eyes on Dooley, allowing his leg to press against hers as he said, "Well, now, guess we might as well get acquainted. I'm Curt Simmons and this here is my brother, Ben."

Merritt saw Dooley's discomfort and said, "I'm

William Merritt, this is my daughter, Mrs. Warren, and this is Miss Wade."

Curt Simmons grinned and would have said more, but the door opened and another man entered. Dooley, staring straight ahead to avoid looking at Curt, got a good look at the newcomer as he sat down across the aisle between Merritt and the rancher.

He was very tall, the crown of his soft, gray hat almost brushing the top of the coach. His skin was burned to a dark mahogany texture, except for where a fresh shave and haircut exposed a whiter surface. The short-cropped hair was dark auburn with a slight curl, and his heavy eyebrows formed a cover for the oddly colored eyes that peered out from deep sockets. His features were not handsome, she decided, being rough and craggy, much like the pictures she had seen of Abraham Lincoln. High cheekbones and a chin that looked durable added to the impression. He wore a soft cream-colored shirt, a plain black vest and dark trousers tucked into brown boots. His clothing, like the .44 he wore on his right side, looked new.

"Hup! Hup! Go, Babe!" the driver called, and the coach threw the passengers around as it left the stage office.

The trip from Bannack to Virginia City took at least eight hours, and the Simmons brothers put their heads back and snored away. Only once before noon did Curt Simmons wake up. His bulk was spilling over, pressing Dooley against the side of the coach, and Merritt spotted her ineffectual efforts to pull away. "Change seats with me," he murmured, and in the process, Curt opened his eyes and took it in.

Dooley sat beside the tall man but did not look at him directly. He was not asleep, but watched the scenery roll by, finding in the far-off snowcaps and the flat plains something that pleased him. He said nothing, and he kept himself pulled up so that they did not touch.

The stage rolled and pitched considerably, so that by the time they pulled into a dilapidated stage station halfway to Virginia City, Dooley and Rachel were ready for a rest.

A slovenly man who had given up any attempts at personal grooming met them as they dismounted. "Grub's ready."

He left to change the horses, and the driver said, "Half an hour to eat and do the necessary."

Dooley and Rachel used the station keeper's bedroom to wash up, drying off with their handkerchiefs instead of the filthy towels left for the purpose.

The meal was cold and poorly cooked, so when Dooley had picked at it and noted that Rachel did the same, she said, "Let's walk a little before we leave."

Curt Simmons's eyes followed the women as they left, and he nudged his brother, who lifted his head from the half-cooked steak to see them leave. The younger man whispered, "Goin' to have a little fun with that filly, Ben."

Rachel and Dooley took a brief walk, and when they returned, the driver emerged, picking his teeth. "Better git, I reckon," he said.

Curt Simmons stepped outside the shack, and he came at once to stand beside Dooley. "Say, I been thinkin', a fine-lookin' woman like you and a good-lookin' hairpin like me, why, we'd make a right big splash." When Dooley didn't respond, he took her arm with a suddenness that caught her off guard. "What say you and me do a little high-steppin' when we get in, honey?"

Dooley attempted to pull away, but he held her fast, a wide smile on his face.

"Let go of my arm!" she cried angrily, but her efforts to free herself seemed to please him.

"Why, this gal's got a temper, Ben! But I like that— makes it fun to tame 'em down a mite."

Merritt turned pale as he came out of the door. He quickly came to stand beside Dooley, saying in a tight voice, "Turn the young woman loose, Simmons. She's not one of your dance hall women!"

"Oh, she ain't *good* enough for me, Preacher?" Curt had picked up Merritt's occupation during the meal, and he pulled Dooley a little closer, saying, "Now, me and Ben, we might want to attend your church, ain't that right, Ben? Might even put a big offerin' in your collection plate—and I never seen a preacher turn nothin' down." He winked at his brother, and added, "I swan, Ben, this pretty little gal, why's she's liable to *convert* me!"

Merritt reached out and took Curt Simmons's arm, attempting to pull Dooley away, and the big man's reaction was vicious and catlike. He swung his left arm back, then lashed out, catching Merritt on the side of the head. The blow drove him violently to the side, and he fell heavily to the ground.

"Dad!" Rachel ran to his side and helped him up. Her violet eyes flashed as she said to Curt Simmons, "You're disgusting!"

The scene pleased Curt. It was the sort of thing he liked, and he looked around at the men who were watching. "Ain't none of you fellers goin' to jump in and rescue this gal? That's what always happens in the story books!" There was brief silence, and the driver said, "Better not mess with the passengers," but it was a token resistance that Simmons laughed at. A thought struck him, and he pulled Dooley closer in an embrace, ignoring her frantic struggles. "Tell you what, let's have one little kiss, and that'll satisfy me for a spell."

"Let her go, Simmons."

The tall man had come out last, and he had been observing the scene from the door. He moved now to stand ten feet from where Simmons was holding Dooley, and his face was as calm as the voice in which he spoke.

Dooley felt the swift reaction of Curt Simmons, for he at first gripped her harder. Then she saw his eyes grow wider, and he let her go. She moved over to where Rachel and Merritt were standing, and the three of them moved away toward the shack. In the sudden silence, the other men all jumped nervously out of the way, leaving the tall man to face the Simmons brothers, who stood near the coach.

"You tellin' me what to do?" Curt Simmons grated out. "Nobody tells me what to do—nobody!"

Dooley noted at once that Ben Simmons was edging away from his brother. He moved stealthily to his left, stopping when he stood ten feet away. Curt took that in with one swift glance. Dooley could tell it was a maneuver they had used before, but the tall man did not appear to notice that the two men had him hipped.

He stood there, making a high shape in the brilliance of the noon sun. He let the silence run on, and it was as if Simmons had not spoken.

Suddenly a red flush crossed the countenance of Curt Simmons, and he touched the handles of his twin Colts. "I been hearin' lots of talk from Red about what a tough hombre you are—but I don't see nothin' to worry about." He waited for the other to speak, and when nothing came, he said loudly, "I'm gonna get me that kiss, you hear me?"

Curt made the threat, but did not move toward Dooley. Instead his hands suddenly gripped his weapons, and there was a fierce tension in his arms. Ben's hand slapped his .44, making a loud noise in the silence. Both men were powder kegs that one spark would set off.

The tall man slowly lifted his right hand, the one he would use to draw his gun, and he fingered the leather lanyard that dangled from his hat beneath his chin. Dooley could not see his face, but there was no tension at all in his slender body. He was as relaxed as if he were alone admiring a sunset, and his voice was summer-soft as he said:

"You boys won't be ridin' the stage into Virginia City with the rest of us. You need to learn how to behave."

Curt Simmons's face turned pale, and his eye took in the tall man, observing that his right hand was chin high, while both he and his brother gripped the handles of their weapons.

A cruel smile was on his heavy lips, and he whispered, "You think you can put me off the stage? Ain't *nobody* can put me off!"

It was a ruse, the talk, and suddenly his hands jerked at the twin revolvers at his side, and at the same instant, as if they had practiced it, his brother made a pull at his gun.

Dooley had moved around to the far right. Standing slightly behind the tall man, she could not believe what she saw.

The arm of the tall man did not move until both brothers began their draw. Curt was much faster than his brother, but when his guns were almost clear of leather, the arm of the man in front of them dropped.

It was too fast to be seen—a blur of action like the flickering sweep of a rattler's lightning stroke. One moment the gun was in the holster, then, suddenly Curt Simmons with his draw half-completed stared into the muzzle of a Colt!

"No! Wait!" Curt cried out, throwing his hands up into the air. "I ain't drawin'!"

Ben Simmons stared stupidly at the gun that was trained on his brother's chest, unable to take it in. He was a dull, stupid man, accustomed to easy victories. But he was not too stupid to see that neither of them would live if they tried to pull on the tall man.

"Just toss your guns in the coach, both of you," he murmured, and when they had done so and moved away from the coach, keeping their arms stiffly in the air, he slipped the Colt into his holster with the same flash of movement as when he'd drawn it.

He nodded at the driver, then reached out his hand to Dooley. He gave her a hand up, then did the same for Rachel, and nodded to Merritt and the others. "Guess we're ready."

They all got in, but he paused for one second, turning to give a sober look at the Simmons brothers.

He cocked one eyebrow, and murmured, "Well, Curt, what do you know? This all turned out just like it does in the stories, didn't it?"

Then he entered with effortless motion and sat down.

Merritt said huskily, "We are in your debt. But I'm afraid you've made trouble for yourself. Those men won't forget this."

The tall man removed his hat, gave the preacher a straight glance, then shrugged. "Give no thought for the morrow," he said, humor a thin edge in his voice. "Sufficient unto the day is the evil thereof."

Merritt straightened at once, his face lit with a smile. "You know the Bible?"

The question sobered the man, and he shrugged again, saying so quietly that they almost missed it as the horses' hooves beat against the ground. "Know it—but don't do it."

As the stage rolled along, the guard looked back at the two men who stood staring at the departing stage.

"Them Simmons brothers is tough," he said. "Wonder why they didn't tough it out?"

" 'Cause they wasn't ready to die, you dummy!" The driver spat an amber stream over the side. "I seen Wild Bill draw once in Tombstone. He was fast, but he wouldn't have no show against that skinny hairpin down there."

The guard stared at him. "You mean he's faster than Hickok?"

The driver said slowly, "He's faster than *anybody!*"

ELEVEN
New Deputy

"There he is, Saul."

Red Yeager's comment pulled Saul Logan's attention away from the poker game. He looked up and saw Zane coming through the front door. Throwing his cards down, he said, "I'm out."

He picked up his cane and made his way through the crowd, coming to stand directly before Zane. Saul Logan was rarely at a loss for words, but he hesitated before putting his hand out and saying with a trace of embarrassment, "Hello, Zane."

"Hello, Saul."

"Well, come on over and have a drink. We've got lots to talk about."

Saul crossed the floor with his hitching gait and waved his hand, saying heartily, "You know Red. Take a chair." He waited until Zane was seated and asked, "You want a drink? Something to eat?"

"No, thanks."

"Well, maybe later." There was a brief silence,

and Saul said, "You lost weight, kid."

"Guess the food in that Mex jail wasn't nothin' to write home about, was it?" Yeager said.

Zane shrugged, and Saul's cheeks were touched by a slight redness. He leaned forward, spread his hands out, then said quietly, "Sorry about the way it turned out, kid. Never thought the job would turn out like that. Guess you know I tried everything I knew to get you out of that jail."

"Sure, Saul," Zane said. He gave Saul a direct look but said no more.

Saul twisted in his chair, and there was a trace of anger in his face. He tapped his leg with the cane, and snapped, "Well, if I had two legs, I could have done something, kid, but a cripple doesn't have much of a chance. I have to depend on other people."

At the reference to the crippled leg, Zane's lips tightened and he could not meet Saul's eyes. He wet his lips and said hurriedly, "Sure, I understand, Saul."

Yeager understood none of this, but he gave a look toward the saloon door and asked, "Where's Curt and Ben? Thought they'd be with you."

Zane shrugged, saying, "They'll probably be in tomorrow." He caught the inquiring look of both men and added, "They wasn't acting right, so I put them off at the stage station."

"You put them off!" Saul stared at him wide-eyed for an instant, then he leaned back in his chair and laughed. "Did the fools draw on you, Zane?"

"They had second thoughts."

"They won't forget it, Zane," Red Yeager said. "Those two stay mad forever."

Zane leaned back in his chair and said softly, "The wrath of man worketh not the righteousness of God."

Yeager's jaw dropped, and he stared first at Zane, then looked at Saul, who shrugged and said, "Kid, you're still reading too many books."

"Guess so, Saul."

"Well, Red filled you in on the problem I've got here. We've got a nice operation—making lots of money, but there's a group of soreheads who don't like us." Saul kept his sharp eyes fixed on Zane while he talked, and there was a trace of anxiety in his face as he said, "You want in? I mean money's no object, kid."

"I don't need a lot of money, Saul. I'll help you if I can."

Saul's face lightened, and he patted Zane on the shoulder. "Right! I knew you wouldn't let me down! Now, here's the setup. . . ." He talked rapidly for several minutes, then stopped, saying, "So we can handle the miners, and the townspeople won't do anything to hurt business. But there's the fancy gunman named Reno who's got quite a following. He's crooked, Zane, and treacherous as a snake. But he's got the camp fooled. They make him out some kind of a hero."

"Long as he's around," Yeager put in, "our whole operation is dead. He's got to go!"

Zane shook his head. "I'm not goin' gunnin' for him, Saul."

"You won't have to." Saul reached into his pocket and pulled something out. He grinned and handed it to Zane.

"A deputy? Me?"

"Gallagher will swear you in," Saul said. "Then you just do your job and sooner or later Reno will come after you."

Zane looked at the star, then glanced across the table. "Saul, if I help you out, are we even? I mean . . ." He glanced at Yeager, then searched for words. Finally he said, "I mean, we're square for everything?"

Saul Logan's eyes narrowed, but he said at once, "You do this job, kid, and everything between us is all square—*everything!*"

Zane nodded, got to his feet, and said, "Where do I stay?"

"Take the third room on the right up those stairs." He added as Zane turned to go, "Be ready to move tomorrow. I've got a chore that might smoke Reno out for you."

"All right."

Yeager watched him go, and there was a light of curiosity in his eyes. "He's kind of simple, ain't he, Saul?"

"Dumb." Saul bit the end off a cigar, got it going, then watched as the tall form of Zane mounted the stairs. "I let him rot in that jail for two years, and he's too dumb to get mad."

"Saul, what is it he wants square between you two?"

A flush touched Logan's cheeks and he said, "Mind your own business, Red!" Then he forced himself to calm down, and said, "Tomorrow Gallagher will take Zane and put the squeeze on the darkie over at the Gulch."

"Washington's claim?" Red said, his voice shaded with doubt. "That's pretty raw, Saul. He's in with Mike Ryan, and Ryan will put up a fight."

Saul leaned forward, satisfaction making his cheeks smooth as he remarked, "Sure. And it'll be the last fight he ever puts up, Red."

"He's a hard man. Gallagher won't stand up against him."

"No. But Zane will. And once Ryan and that darkie are out, sooner or later Reno will have to face him. The town expects it." He threw his cigar on the floor, and there was a savage look in his eyes as he ground out, "I want to be there when Zane gives it to Reno!"

Lee wrote the last sentences on the paper in front of him, jumped to his feet, and dashed over to Rachel's desk. Throwing it down, he said, "All done. Can I go over to Lyle's now?"

Lyle Muller was the stocky son of Dutch Muller. He and Lee were the same age and had become close friends over the months.

Rachel said, "If you've done it well, Lee, I think you might." She read the composition slowly, pointing out a few minor errors while Lee twisted anxiously, then smiled. "This is very good, Lee."

The boy wheeled and ran out the door saying, "See you later, Jim!"

As the door slammed, Rachel looked up at Reno, the smile still on her face. "I'm afraid he's a better scholar than you are, Jim."

Getting to his feet, Reno grinned and walked over to the stove, poured two cups of coffee, then said, "You didn't know what a thick head I have, Rachel, or you would never have agreed to take me on."

She got up, and there was a natural grace in her walk as she moved to take the cup. Standing beside him she touched his arm and laughed. "Oh, yes, I would!"

He took a deep drink of his coffee, then stood

there, looking down into her eyes. He liked the gift of silence that was part of her nature, the ability to let time run on without talk. But he liked as well the sudden gusts of anger that from time to time swept over her. She was a calm woman on the surface, but he sensed the depths of emotion that she kept closely guarded.

She looked up at him suddenly and a strange smile touched her full lips as she remembered something. "Do you remember when I cut your hair, Jim?"

"Sure."

She put the coffee cup down on the window sill and crossed her arms over her breasts. After a silence broken only by the loud ticking of the clock on the wall, she looked up into his face and said, "That was a hard time for me. When you asked me if I was going to hate all Southerners always, it was like getting hit right in the pit of the stomach."

"Reckon I was too harsh."

"No!" She smiled tremulously, reached out one hand, and gripped his arm. "No, it was the *right* thing to say, Jim! I'd been feeding on hate. Not just the South, but everything—myself, and even God!"

His voice was gentle, and there was a smile on his face as he said, "Guess we all get tangled up in our own harness at times, Rachel."

She nodded, but her eyes were moist as she whispered, "Jim, I've been wanting to thank you for that— for helping me see what I was doing."

She blinked, and a smile trembled on her lips. There was an intimacy in the way she watched him, and the warm light in her eyes grew. He had thought of her as a woman far off, distant and hard to know, but as he looked into her face, suddenly she was a shape and a melody and a fragrance. The only sound was her quick, soft breathing, and he saw only her fair, smooth skin and her violet eyes opened wide in the silence. The walls they had built around themselves fell away, and the loneliness that they both knew became unbearable. He never remembered putting his arms around her, nor was she aware of placing her hands on his neck. It was a natural response, and the softness of her lips stirred him.

Then she pulled her head back, and there was wonder in her eyes as she whispered, "Is this pity, Jim?"

He said at once, "No, not pity. I think—"

What he might have said she would never know, for the schoolroom door swung open abruptly, and Dooley rushed in, saying, "Rachel, Doctor Steele wants—!"

She came to a full stop, her words cut off as if with a knife. The sight of Reno and Rachel embracing drove the color from her face.

Rachel pulled away from Reno, her face flushed. "Dooley, what is it?" she asked as she stepped toward the girl.

Dooley's lips were white as she clamped them together, and a mixture of hurt and anger flashed from her eyes as she looked into Reno's eyes. Then she said harshly, "A man's been hurt. The doctor asked me to get you." She straightened up and said weakly, "I'm sorry to interrupt you."

"Dooley!" Rachel said and started toward her, but Dooley whirled and dashed blindly from the room. The woman turned and bit her lip in vexation. "She's hurt, Jim."

He was angry and did not know why. "Oh, she's

just embarrassed, Rachel. It's nothing personal."

She stared at him, gave a pitying smile, then said, "You think that? Jim, it's nice to be humble, but that's *dumb!*"

He walked with her to Steele's house, and neither of them said much. The kiss had opened a door that they had gone through, but the appearance of Dooley had somehow closed it.

Easy pulled away from the crowd that milled around in front of the doctor's front porch, coming over to meet them. "Dooley found you, huh?" he asked. "Better git on in, Miz Warren."

"Who is it, Easy?" Reno asked.

"Feller named Mike Ryan. Him and that darkie there talkin' to Beidler and Creighton, they got a good claim over on Nevada Gulch. Come on, let's give a listen, James!"

A tall, thin Negro man in mud-stained overalls and a shapeless hat was surrounded by a group of miners and townspeople. His speech was not slurred, but crisp and clear, unlike the Negroes Reno had been accustomed to in the South.

". . . and they just rode in and said we had to leave, Mr. Creighton." He shook his head, and there was anger in his voice as he added, "I tried to get Mike to let it go, but you know him!"

"Who was it, Wash?" Creighton asked.

"Deputy Gallagher and another deputy. I'd never seen him before. Gallagher said his name was Logan—Zane Logan."

"How'd the shooting start?" Beidler demanded.

"Why, Deputy Gallagher had a piece of paper he said proved our claim belonged to the Syndicate. He told us to get off. Then Mike, why, he laughed and told them to leave. Gallagher backed off when Mike said that, and he kinda motioned the Logan fellow in."

"Did he draw on Mike, Wash?"

The black face of Ned Washington grew perplexed. "No, I can't honestly say that." His brow wrinkled and he shook his head. "You know how Mike is, all hotheaded. Soon as this feller stepped forward, Mike made a grab for his gun. But he didn't have no chance at all! I seen it all clear, but I still can't believe it, Mr. Beidler!"

"What happened, Wash?"

"Why, this Zane Logan didn't even move his hand until Mike's gun was out and pointed right at him. Then all of a sudden there was a shot and Mike was down."

"He have a hideout gun, Wash?" Ringo Jukes demanded.

"No, he just pulled that gun and got a shot off before I could blink."

"Self-defense they'll call it," Beidler said heavily. "Stage driver told me about a ruckus on his last run. Said this tall, thin man had a run-in with a couple of toughs. Andy told it about like Wash here. Said Zane Logan could draw a gun quicker than any man he ever saw."

"And his name is Logan," Creighton said slowly. "Must be some of Saul Logan's kin. And a bad one at that."

"What are we gonna do, Mr. Creighton?" Washington asked quietly. He had large intelligent eyes that were filled with smoldering anger, and his hands twitched as if he yearned to use them on someone. "They can't just steal our claim, can they?"

Creighton shook his head. "First let's see how

Mike is, then we'll see about what to do."

They milled around for an hour, the heat of their anger growing as time passed. Everybody liked Mike and Washington, and angry talk went around the yard. Finally Doc Steele came out. Wiping his hands on a towel, he said, "He'll live. Took a slug high in the chest."

"Let's go see Gallagher!" someone yelled. His cry was taken up by a dozen men, and when Ringo Jukes whirled and headed toward the center of town, he was joined by every man in the yard.

Easy joined Reno, gave him a sour grin, and asked, "You goin' to attend the services, James?"

Reno nodded, and they followed the yelling crowd down the crooked streets, coming at last to stand in front of the jail.

"Gallagher! Come outta there!" Jukes yelled.

The door opened at once, and Gallagher stepped out, followed by a tall man who looked at the crowd once, then calmly leaned back against the wall of the jail.

"You're not gonna get away with it, Jack!" Jukes said. He looked around at the men behind him, and then added, "You can't hide behind that tin star this time."

Gallagher shook his head, saying at once, "Listen to me, you men. We went over to serve a legal paper on Ryan, and he tried to kill us. The darkie will tell you that Ryan drew first. Zane could have put a bullet right through his head, but he didn't."

"Let him talk for himself, Jack," Jukes said. He set himself and let his hand hang beside his gun. "You, Logan, come over here!"

A hush fell over the crowd, and several men

moved to one side as Zane Logan came to stand before the crowd. His face was relaxed, and he said softly, "You'd best break up this group and go home."

Ringo Jukes was a tough one. His face bore the scars of many battles, and he did not back up one inch from the tall deputy.

"Logan, Jack's a liar! You claimin' you placed that shot on purpose to keep from killin' Mike?"

"Would you believe me if I said yes?"

"Not likely!"

Zane Logan's greenish eyes swept over the street. It was almost dark, but he pointed at a sign across the street. There were three balls on top of it, each about six inches in diameter. "You see that middle ball?" The men all turned to look and he said, "You call the shot, mister."

Jukes yelled, "Shoot!" but before the word was out of his mouth, there was an explosion that set the horses tied to the rail to plunging.

Every man looked first at the sign. The middle ball was gone. Then they looked back, every man thinking of the fragment of a second that had elapsed between the time Jukes yelled and the gun exploded.

Zane's gun slid back into his holster and he stood there, his face unstirred by the scene.

Then John Creighton said, "We'll take this thing to the state court, Gallagher!"

Gallagher grinned and nodded. "Sure, you do that, Mr. Creighton!" The crowd broke up, fading away into the darkening streets.

Easy and Reno fell into step with Creighton and Jim Williams and it was Williams who said, "We won't get anywhere going to law, John."

"No. I was just making talk," Creighton said sadly. "We've been feeling pretty good, Jim, thinking that things were getting better. But the lid will be off now."

"I'm afraid so," Williams agreed. He looked at Reno and asked, "Did you ever see anyone who could handle a gun like that, Jim?"

"Maybe two or three almost that good," Reno said slowly. "I've seen some about as fast, and one or two have been dead shots. And I've run across some who could pull fast and shoot straight, but they couldn't face up to a real fight—just good for target practice and exhibition." He let the silence run on, then said, "This one, though, puts it all together—fast, accurate, and not afraid of anybody."

"Could you beat him, Jim?" Williams asked hesitantly.

"No." The answer came back instantly. "I'm no gunman. Oh, I've carried a gun, smelled powder a few times, but this one is a professional. Good to begin with, probably, and spent lots of time practicing. No man has a chance against a man like that."

Easy nodded, his homely face screwed into a frown. "Reckon Brother James is right on that. It's gonna take somebody special to hang Zane Logan's hide on a fence."

The crowd broke up. Reno rounded up Lee, and they went back to the stable. As they were going inside, Dooley came down the stairs. She would have passed without speaking, but Reno said, "Dooley, let's go down to the cafe and get a steak."

She turned to face him, and her face was stiff as she said, "No, thanks."

He stood there feeling helpless, angry at himself and at her. Finally he said, "Dooley, don't make too much of things."

"Oh, no, I won't do that!" she said instantly. Her lips trembled but she pressed them together firmly and said quietly, "I've been a fool, Jim, but you won't have to worry about me any more. Good-bye!"

As she whirled and raced off down the street, Lee stared at her, then looked at Reno with puzzlement on his thin face. "What in the world was that all about, Jim?"

Reno slapped his hands together and said in a grating voice, "It was about me being ten different kinds of a fool, Lee! Or else it's about how a kid of a girl turns into a woman. Take your choice!"

He left the yard abruptly and Easy, who had been taking it all in, came to stand beside Lee. A smile creased his wide mouth, but he shook his head sadly. "Feller starts in tryin' to understand women, he's liable to get his comeuppance, boy. Me, I'd rather get hit in the face with a wet squirrel!"

TWELVE
Second Meeting

Dempsey's ranch, halfway between Virginia City and Bannack, served as a meeting place for the Innocents. The main room was crowded with men as Henry Plummer walked through the front door, and he gave them a careful glance as the talk died down. Jack Gallagher, Buck Stinson, and Haze Lyons stood together close to him, and Long John Frank, Alec Carter and Boone Helm formed a cluster in one corner. The Brunton brothers, Sam and Bill, stood alongside Thad Hilderman and Red Yeager. Bill Hunter, Clubfoot George, Steve Marshland, Jen Romaine, Bob Zachary, and Joe Pizanthia were seated around the room. The Simmons brothers stood close to George Ives, who was moving carefully, the wound in his chest being still painful.

Plummer gave the room a short and thorough glance, his eyes stopping on the Simmons brothers. Ives said, "They're all right, Henry—Curt and Ben Simmons."

Plummer nodded and said, "Things have got to pick up. The dust has been getting out of the Gulch in big chunks. From now on, I want you to keep up with things. Listen to the talk; find out who's got money and when they're leaving. Get some confederates to spy. You can afford to pay them big for information."

Ives said, "There's been talk of a vigilante committee, Henry."

"Put the fear to them, George," Plummer snapped, and there was a coldness in his small eyes as he smiled. "There's more of them than of us, but they'll never get together if every man's afraid for his own skin." He frowned, and looked at Ives. "What about Reno? Has he got you buffaloed?"

A flush rose in Ives's face, and the scar on his lip stood out like a signal. He glared around the room, then said, "Don't worry about him, Henry. He'll get his ticket punched soon."

Gallagher spoke up instantly. "That's right. Saul got his brother here from Mexico. I put a star on him. He don't do much, but he pulled off a stunt that's got every man in camp scared to blink when he's around. But his one job is to bury Reno."

Plummer stared at Gallagher, then said slowly, "All right, see to it. Now listen, this place is rich and we're in the saddle. None of us will ever have a chance like this again! Men will be coming out with dust all summer. Any man that stands against us, we'll wipe him out. I'll stay in Bannack, and you fellows here take your orders from George.

Plummer outlined a few more details, then left abruptly. As the others were milling around getting ready to leave, Curt Simmons came over to stand beside Ives. "George, what's the game now? Me and Ben need to make some big money."

"Take what you want from these people, Curt," Ives said at once. "Do what you please with the little fish, but when we move together, every one of us moves."

"What if I double-cross you?" Curt asked curiously.

"You won't, Curt. We'd find out about it. Nothing happens in the Gulch that we don't find out. Anyhow, you don't need to think about that. By the time summer is over you'll be fat. We all will."

Curt nodded, then said, "About Zane Logan . . ." A scowl contoured his lips, and his muddy eyes flared with hatred. "I don't let no man put me off a stage, George. He's goin' to get real dead."

"Let him and Reno meet, Curt," George said. "Reno's not as fast, but he'll take a lot of killin', so maybe they'll shoot each other's lights out. If either one of them's left, we'll take care of him."

"He's Saul's brother. Maybe he'll—"

Ives shook his head. "Don't worry about that. Nobody knows what goes on between those two, but I'll tell you this—Saul hates Zane. Shows up in his eyes. And the poor sap doesn't even *know* it! Did time in a Mex jail for Saul, and would be rotting there yet if Saul hadn't needed him." Ives shook his head and the two men parted.

The Innocents threw an iron ring around the camps, and lawlessness swept the country. Two miners were shot to death, their bodies left sprawling beside their claim, their pockets stripped. The stage line doubled its caution and increased the guard, but it did not help. Anyone getting on as a passenger ran the chance of losing his money or worse if the guards resisted.

In two months the Syndicate took four claims by simply putting pressure on the owners and buying them out for a pittance. Zane Logan played a role in this, for the story of his shooting of Ryan and his use of a Colt in front of the mob swept the camp.

Dooley had seen Zane at a distance several times since his arrival, and she heard the stories about him like everyone else in Virginia City. She thought of him often, going over the scene when he had faced down the Simmons brothers, but there was something in him she couldn't fathom. She had tried to mention the matter to Bible, but he had shaken his head stubbornly. "You're trying to make a hero out of the man, Dooley, because he got you out of a bad spot. But he's a low-down killer, and he'd let you go down without a thought!"

Easy had said pretty much the same. "Aw, Dooley, he's a bad one. And he's gonna be worse before he gets through." His homely face screwed up in thought, and he added, "Right now he's kinda in the middle—mebbe on the fence, don't you see? But he's got somethin' eatin' on his liver. Dunno what, but he's gettin' sour, and when a hombre who can use a shootin' iron like he can finally goes bad, it's bad news!"

Dooley thought she knew what he meant, for despite what she had heard about Zane Logan's wickedness, she could not put him in the same category as the other toughs such as Ives and the Simmons brothers. She got some confirmation from Mike Ryan.

Ryan's progress had been slow, and Dooley went

almost every day to take food and help with the nursing. Washington was often there, and one day Dooley entered to find Rachel and Reno visiting the partners. "Oh, Dooley, I'm glad I caught you," Rachel smiled. "Dad says you're to sing next Sunday morning."

"Been hearing about your singing, Miss Dooley," Washington said. "Sure would admire to hear you."

"Oh, I'm not all that good," Dooley said. There was a restraint in her manner that both Rachel and Reno noticed as she went to pick up the dirty bed-clothes, and she did not look at either of them as she said, "I'll get these back tomorrow, Mr. Ryan."

"Aw, thank you, Miss Wade," Ryan said with a smile. He turned carefully to face her, and a thought caught at him, turning his expression sober. "Miss Rachel's been tellin' us about how that Logan bird helped you out on the stage." He lay back and shook his head, saying, "Guess he's a ladies' man."

"I don't think it was that, Mr. Ryan," Rachel answered. "He really didn't pay any attention to us after he put those two off the stage."

"Well, he's not goin' to get by with throwin' us off our claim!" Ryan pronounced. "Soon as I can get up, I'm headed right back there. Maybe I can't beat that draw of his, but Washington and me went through some tough times, and we worked hard for that claim."

"You're not the only ones hurt," Reno said. "Ringo told me that Logan and Gallagher made a visit to Ivo Morgan on Monday."

"Ivo won't budge!" Ryan said.

"His claim is next to yours, isn't it, Jim?" Rachel asked.

"Yes."

She was waiting for him to say he'd help Morgan, but he said nothing at all. They were all looking at Reno, and he felt the pressure they were putting on him. Slowly he shook his head, stubbornness in his wide mouth as he said, "If Zane Logan or Gallagher comes at me, I'll take care of it. And I won't ask for help from anybody." He turned and left the room, leaving a silence behind him.

With a gusty sigh Ryan let his head fall back, the lines in his face deepening. "Can't blame him much. But it shore don't look like a man's got a chance."

Dooley turned to leave, saying, "I'll bring you some pie tonight."

Rachel said quickly, "I'll walk with you part of the way, Dooley." The two women left the shack and fell into step as they made their way toward town. They said nothing, and Rachel felt her face flushing. She was nervous, but finally she said in a halting voice, "Dooley, about what you saw . . ." She felt guilty as she turned to meet Dooley's steady gaze, and finally she said, "I know how you feel, and I'm sorry."

"You don't know how I feel!"

"Well, maybe not. It's hard for one person to know another's heart, but it would be very strange if you didn't have feelings for Jim. He's a very attractive man, and from what you've told me, he's filled a place in your life." She smiled gently and added, "You're not very good at hiding your feelings, Dooley."

The tall girl flushed, and her back was rigid as she said angrily, "Well, neither are you! You've done everything but put a halter on him, haven't you? All these *lessons*—I've got a pretty good idea what they've been!" She broke away from the hand that

Rachel laid on her arm and turned to run blindly away from her. "Go on and get him. Who cares!"

Ignoring Rachel's call, she raced away down the street, stopping only when she arrived at the stable. She threw a saddle on her mare and headed out of town at a fast gallop, heading for the foothills east of town.

She crossed the low pine-sloped hills that formed the walls of the valley and headed for the buttes that seemed to shut the valley off. Two hours later she rode out of a heavy growth of scrub pine into a piece of open ground where a small mountain stream curled around a huge outcropping of basalt. Hitching her horse to a limb, she made her way to an opening worn by the wind, little more than two feet deep and four high. She sat down, let the sibilant breeze run over her. Her agitation had been all out of proportion, and in the solitude she regretted her behavior toward Rachel.

Her lips grew firm, and she nodded as if she had made a decision. She walked purposely to her mount, vaulted into the saddle, and started back toward Virginia City. She was almost through the timber when a shot rang out that made her horse shy, and she almost fell to the ground.

Getting control of the animal, she rode on around a gully to find Zane Logan bending over a freshly-killed deer. He straightened up at once, his eyes alert. He made a quick move toward the rifle on the ground, then recognition came to him, and he stood there giving her a close attention that seemed characteristic.

Ordinarily she would have been cautious, even afraid, of meeting a man alone in the wilderness. But a curiosity had been building in her, and she rode up to look down at the deer, then turned her attention toward him. "I didn't thank you for what you did on the stage."

"Not necessary."

His brief answer was not discourtesy. He was relaxed, and there was a sober quality in his face. She had seen many hard men in Virginia City, but there were none of the marks of hard living on Zane Logan's face. A desire to shake his calm made her say, "You helped me, and I thank you." She paused, then looked directly into his eyes, saying, "They say you're a hired killer doing your brother's dirty work."

If she expected anger, she was disappointed, for he only shrugged, saying quietly, "Guess that's natural for people to think."

A streak of anger ran through her, and she thought of Ryan lying in his bed, his face marked with pain. "Are you going to shoot Ivo Morgan down like you did Ryan?"

She was pleased to see that her words did stir him. His mouth tightened, and he gave an involuntary shake of his head as he answered. "Those fellows didn't have title to their claims."

"Says Saul Logan!" Her eyes sent off a flare of anger and she said, "Logan, if you're going to be a crook, then be one, but don't try to cover up your killing and robbing by pinning on a badge!"

He stepped forward, and fear shot through her for one instant, but she saw that he was not angry. Regret scored his face, and there was a profound sadness in his eyes as he said, "People don't understand Saul. He's had a hard time."

"You mean because he's got a bad leg he's got a

right to steal what he wants and get his killer of a brother to back it up?" She saw the words cut him, and for one instant she wondered why it gave her such pleasure to hurt him. It never occurred to her that she was venting the anger she felt for Reno and Rachel on him.

"I haven't killed anyone."

"But you will, won't you? Sooner or later you'll pull that fast gun of yours and be just a little off. Then you'll be sorry, and your brother will have another claim."

He stood there, looking up at her, and there was a strange vulnerability in him. Despite his fighting skills and his reputation, there was no danger in him as he stood here, searching for words. Finally he said, "Sorry you think like that, Miss Wade."

She stared at him, not understanding how he could be so humble before her when an hour later he might be putting a bullet into a man's body.

She lifted her reins, gave him one pitying look as she said, "One day you'll wake up, Zane Logan, and you'll look back on your life. Maybe it'll be while you're lying in your own blood after you've been dry-gulched. And what'll you see?" There was a merciless quality in her husky voice as she ended: "You'll see you've spent your whole life being a bloody killer for a man who's nothing but a cheap crook!"

She left Zane Logan standing there watching as she raised a cloud of dust.

He stared at her for a long time, then said gently, "Guess she's got my number pretty well." Then he turned slowly and began to dress the carcass of the deer.

THIRTEEN
Grizzly

Lee Morgan divided his history into two parts—
before and after Jim Reno had come into his life.
Sometimes he had nightmares of his early life,
dreaming that he was a ragged, half-starved kid of
twelve, barely surviving by running errands for men
in saloons. He would lie there thrashing and moaning, feeling the kicks and blows of callous fists and
hearing no kind word to soften his hard life. Then he
would come awake with a wild jolt, his heart beating
wildly, and the knowledge that he was no longer in
that terrible time brought a flood of relief. He would
lie there and think of how Reno had ridden into his
life and taken him away from it all. He would think
how the man had not only taught him how to be a
man, but had instilled in him a sense of self-worth he
had never known.

It was no wonder that Lee's admiration for Reno
came close to idolatry. During the three years that
they had been together, Lee had seen no man that

was Reno's equal, and he had formed a rigid conviction concerning Reno—he believed that the man was invincible.

A fragment of conversation between Ringo Jukes and Easy had disturbed Lee. He had been loafing outside the livery stable, half-dozing in the sun, listening indolently to the two men. He had come awake when Jukes said, ". . . and you know how much I think of Jim, Easy, but he wouldn't have a chance against Zane Logan!"

Lee waited for Easy to defend Reno, but he said instead, "In that, I'd reckon you'd be right, Ringo. That jasper ain't *human!*"

Lee said nothing until Jukes left, then he got up and came to where Easy was leaning on the corral fence. "I didn't think you'd put Jim down like that, Easy," he said defiantly. "You've seen him draw before."

Easy turned to look at the boy, and he saw at once how deeply felt the boy's idolatry was. Biting off a piece of straw, he paused to consider how to answer. Finally he said soberly, "Lee, I don't reckon as how I ever met a man I admire like I do Jim Reno. Far as I'm concerned, he'll stand in the hedge and take up the gap."

"But you said—"

"Yeah, I said Zane Logan was a faster man on the draw. And he is, Lee. And I guess somewhere on this earth there's a faster man than Logan." He took in the disappointment on the boy's face, and put his hand on Lee's shoulder. "That's the way this ol' world is, I guess."

"But what if him and Jim face each other?"

Easy shook his head, a grim look replacing the

customary smile. "Jim's got a lot of fool notions about honor—like lettin' the other feller go for his gun first and all that crock of oatmeal. But *I* ain't been infected! If it comes to a showdown between Logan and Jim, I'll pot that lean drink of water with a Sharps buffalo gun right in the back of the head!"

Lee said nothing to anyone, but as the days passed he became aware that despite Reno's reputation as a tough fighter, the eyes of the camp were on Zane Logan. The tall gunman kept to himself, and except for walking the streets of Virginia City and making a call with Jack Gallagher to pressure some miner into selling out to the Syndicate, he kept out of sight.

The mystery of the man drew Lee's curiosity, and he began stalking Zane Logan. He took every occasion when in town to loiter on Front Street, and several times he followed Logan's progress as he made his cursory rounds. Lee saw at once that Zane was both admired and feared, for men went out of the way to catch his attention. "Top gun is always looked up to, boy," X. Beidler grunted as he saw Lee watching Zane make his way down the street. "But he'll stretch a rope like the rest of the trash one day."

Lee could see that Zane Logan was like Reno in one respect—he was quiet and had no need to call attention to himself. Although he took no notice of brawls, Lee once saw him shove his way through a crowd and take a gun away from Tom Lowry, one of the toughest men in the camp. Lowry was drunk, but he sobered up instantly when he found himself looking into the eyes of Zane Logan who said, "I'll take your gun, Tom."

Lowry, a huge man with a bloody record in Texas,

had stared at him, then his face had dropped, and he had simply handed his gun to Logan and turned to walk away abruptly. Zane's face had not changed during the encounter. He had stood in front of the tough, letting him make the decision, and every man in the crowd had known that Tom Lowry would not have given his gun to any other man in Virginia City.

The only time Lee had spoken to Zane Logan was when he had come in from swimming under the bridge on Roaring Creek. Lee had come to sit on the boardwalk, waiting for his lesson with Rachel, and he had almost dozed off when a voice said, "Be a good day for a swim, wouldn't it now?"

Startled, Lee looked around to see Zane standing behind him, leaning against the wall, a slight smile on his lips.

Lee got up at once, and, staring cautiously at the man, said, "I been." He stood a little straighter and said, "I took a dive off the trestle. Touched bottom."

Zane nodded and said, "Why, that's good divin'! Bottom must be twelve foot deep in the middle."

Lee felt a thrill of pride at the sound of Zane's praise, but he had learned to say little of his deeds. "Not hard when you know how."

Zane's smile had broadened, and he said, "Well, you learned how. What's your name?"

"Lee Morgan."

"I'm Zane Logan." He put out his hand, and his grip was firm as Lee took it. Lee thought it was odd that he should give his name since he was one man that everyone in town knew.

"Glad to know you," Lee said, and felt guilty saying it. He had listened to the miners and the towns-people enough to know that this was the man who made his brother's word law in Virginia City. He was a killer, and there was always the possibility that he might face Jim Reno in a death struggle.

But Lee could not find a trace of evil in Logan's countenance. His eyes were clear and the rough features of his face were not marked by hard living as most of the toughs. He stood there, and Lee found himself thinking, *He's bad, I guess, but it wouldn't be hard to like him.*

Then Zane said, "See you later, Morgan." He had known how to please a young fellow, calling him by his last name as he would another man, and Lee watched him walk away with his feelings agitated, and feeling not a little guilty for almost liking the enemy.

After that chance encounter, Lee's thoughts went more and more to Zane Logan. He wanted to ask Reno what he thought, but something kept him back, and despite telling himself that the man was a crook, he could not hate Logan.

As the summer wore on, Lee became more and more aware that Dooley was having a hard time. The two of them had become fast friends on the trail to Oregon, and the boy would have been subject to a violent crush on Dooley except for one reason—he had seen that Jim Reno occupied all her thoughts. He had finally accepted the idea that sooner or later Reno would see Dooley not as a child to be taken care of but as a woman to be desired. The thought satisfied him, since they were the two people in the world he most loved.

But something had gone wrong, and he realized that the relationship between Rachel and Reno had rocked Dooley's world. With all the reluctance of youth to speak about deeply felt things, he had kept his own thoughts, hoping that either Dooley would give up her dream or that Reno would see her in a different light.

Out of his earnings he had bought a new Spencer rifle, and he formed the habit of going hunting at every possible opportunity. He had little spare time and was not a skilled hunter, but the delight in the weapon was keen, so it was a welcome relief when he got Friday off. Reno had seen the need for a relief from the hard labor for the boy, and had said, "You go kill us a deer, Lee. I'll clean all you shoot."

Lee rode into town to buy ammunition. At Creighton's Store he encountered Dooley. "I'm going to kill a deer."

"Going hunting?" Dooley brightened up, and said, "Take me with you, Lee. I'm bored to death!"

"You don't even have a rifle."

"I don't want to shoot anything." There was a look of dissatisfaction on her smooth face, and she added, "I won't be any trouble."

"Sure, Dooley." Lee brightened up and said, "Say, let's go now and camp out. It'll be more fun that way."

Dooley eagerly agreed, and two hours later the two of them rode out of Virginia City, headed south toward the foothills. They rode steadily, and by the time they had reached the thick woods that Lee had picked out, the sun was dropping over the peaks in a flashing sheet of flame, and violet began to flow across the valley. Lee took a short ax and cut some dry wood while Dooley made their beds out of boughs and blankets. Then the two of them pitched in to cook their supper. They ate bacon, canned corn, and cold biscuits dipped in hot-water gravy, all washed down with steaming black coffee and topped off with a whole apple pie that Dooley had stolen from Leah.

After cleaning up, they sat around the fire, sometimes talking, but more often just looking up at the millions of stars that dotted the heavens. Finally Dooley said, "It's so peaceful out here, Lee!" Then she sighed and added wistfully, "Too bad we can't stay out here always."

Lee gave her a quick look, then said cautiously, "Well, I guess it would get pretty rough, Dooley." He gave a short laugh, then said, "I mean, it's *fun*, but the reason it's fun is because it's *different*, you know?"

The cry of a hunting bird split the silence of the woods, and they listened, then Dooley got up. She went to her blankets and lay down before she answered him.

"Sure, I know. It's just that . . ." She paused, and he could see by the flickering light of the fire that she looked tired. There was none of the liveliness in her face that he had grown to expect.

He rose and went to his own bed, and for a time he struggled to find something to say that might encourage her, but nothing came. Finally, just as the fire was dying out, he said sleepily, "Well, Dooley, I guess the Lord knows about how we feel, don't you reckon?"

She turned her head toward him, smiling at his awkward attempts at comfort. It pleased her that he had put it the way he did, for he had shown no interest in attending church, and she had been afraid that he would grow up into a man not fearing God. She said in a warmer voice than he had heard, "That's good, Lee!"

Lee dropped off at once, but she lay there for a long time listening to the night sounds and looking up at the stars. They were more brilliant than she could remember, strewn across the velvet skies like winking fragments of fire. She had been unhappy since she had seen Reno kissing Rachel, but now as she stared up at the panorama in the skies, her problems seemed less terrible. She felt the magnificence of the heavens and a sense of worship washed through her, causing her problems to fade away. Before she dropped off to sleep, she prayed a very simple prayer, much like the ones she had prayed when she was a little girl: *God, help me to be good! Don't let me be angry with Jim and Rachel—just let me be what you want me to be.*

She drifted off, feeling better than she had in weeks, and when she awoke the next morning, Lee noticed that there was a sprightliness in her that had been lacking.

They ate a big breakfast, then Lee led her through the woods looking for game. It was not surprising that they saw none, for they made enough noise to frighten away any deer that might have been there. Lee said once, "We'll *still* hunt, Dooley. Let them suckers come to us!" So they had tried that, but Dooley soon spotted a squirrel and Lee blasted him out of the tree, blowing the small animal into fragments with the heavy slug and signaling any big game in five square miles that this was a place to avoid.

None came and they decided to go back to camp to eat. Lee insisted on taking the mutilated body of the squirrel. "Going to have to tell Easy and Jim that we killed our own food," he explained to Dooley with a grin.

Dooley teased him about starving to death on his hunting, and they were almost back to the spot where their horses were tethered when she cried out, "Look!" Lee followed the direction of her gesture and saw a small animal disappearing into the timber.

"Hey, it's a bear cub!" he shouted. Running to the animal, he grabbed it and brought it back to Dooley. "Look, it's just a baby!"

"It's so cute!" Dooley said. She stroked his fur and it playfully tried to bite her hand. Looking around, she asked, "Is it big enough to take care of itself?"

Lee shrugged. "Guess so. Maybe they get put out of the nest like eagles when they're big enough to take care of themselves."

"Better put it down, Lee. It might scratch you."

"Aw, I'll just play with it until we get packed up," Lee said. They continued back toward the camp, which was less than a hundred yards away, and Lee said, "Look, Dooley, there's somebody there. See his horse? Here, hold the cub while I load the gun."

Dooley took the cub, and Lee chambered a shell into the rifle. He went first, and Dooley followed with the cub, which was making feeble attempts to escape and making mewling growls.

"It's Zane Logan!" Lee said in surprise. He lowered the gun, and as the tall rider standing beside his horse saw them, he called out, "Hello, Zane."

Surprise crossed Zane's face, but he smiled and answered, "Why, hello, Morgan. Didn't know this was your camp. I came out for a deer."

"Yeah, we been hunting deer, too. Didn't get one, though."

"You're in the wrong spot," Zane said. "If you want a shot, I'll take you to a crossing about two miles from here just stiff with deer."

"Hey, will you? Gee, let's get this stuff packed, Dooley!"

Dooley stood there holding the cub, feeling the flush mount to her cheeks. She remembered her last words to Zane: *You've spent your whole life being a bloody killer!*

"Where'd you pick that one up, Miss Wade?"

"Oh, back there a way."

"That's a grizzly cub," he remarked. "Hope its mama doesn't come lookin' for it."

"Lee, I'm not going to hold this thing any more," she said. Putting the cub down, she began to pull their blankets together, hoping that Logan would leave, but Lee was chattering away about the possibility of getting a deer.

The cub waddled over to the tree line, then sat down. Raising its nose into the air, it began to keen a plaintive cry. It sat there until they had packed their horses and were ready to go.

Lee and Dooley were standing together, and Zane was twenty feet away, close to the trail, when a muffled grunt drew the attention of all three. There was a rustle of bushes and a low-pitched grunting sound. At first Dooley thought it was a hog snorting. She'd heard them often in the woods in Arkansas, but when she looked up she saw the bushes part about fifty feet away, and then her heart nearly stopped. Suddenly, out of the timber, an enormous bear broke cover and ran toward them with the speed of a racehorse!

She and Lee turned to run, but in their fright they bumped into each other and fell sprawling. Frantically they scrambled on the ground, and it seemed to Dooley that she was moving through water, so slowly did she get to her feet. The bear's massive jaws gaped and the little red eyes glowed like coals. Dooley heard Zane calling loudly, telling them to do something, but fear had numbed her and Lee as well.

The grizzly was so close that she could see the drops of froth on the jaws. The bear gave a savage cry and launched her bulk at the two, who were still unable to get their balance.

Time seemed to freeze for Dooley, and as the bear suddenly reared up, she received a tremendous shove in her back that drove her into Lee. The two of them were driven forcibly out of the path of the raging animal, and they rolled through the fallen needles of the pines. Scrambling to her feet, she whirled to see a terrible sight. Zane had shoved the two of them out of the way, and turned in time to catch the full force of the charge!

He was still half-turned from the animal when she struck, rearing up and slashing downward with a mighty sweep of one thick forearm. Dooley saw the claw rip through Zane's shirt, tearing it like paper and leaving bloody furrows across his chest. The other paw struck, catching him on the right shoulder and driving him away as if he'd been shot from a gun. He went cartwheeling away. As the bear whirled to charge, he came to his feet, and Dooley saw the bear rise up on her hind legs and loom over him.

Dooley screamed, for Zane was dwarfed by the

mighty bulk of the grizzly. Then she saw the lightning draw she'd heard about.

Even as the bear reached out to envelope Zane, he drew. Raising his gun, he got off four shots so quickly that they sounded like one rolling explosion right in the grizzly's open jaws.

The force of the animal's charge carried her into Zane, and one final blow from her massive paw smashed against his head, then she fell dead on top of his sprawling body.

"Zane!" Dooley cried. She and Lee ran to where the two lay locked together, and together they managed to roll the bulk of the grizzly over. Both of them were sick when they saw the body of Zane Logan.

"He's dead!" Dooley moaned, staring down at the bloody chest. Zane's eyes were closed and there were bloody furrows on his left temple where the last blow had taken him.

"No, he's alive!" Lee cried. "See, he's breathin'!"

Dooley's heart leapt as she saw Zane's chest rise, and she said, "We've got to get him to a doctor!"

Lee jumped to his feet. "There's a farm down the road about three miles. I'll go borrow a wagon!"

Dooley nodded, and after Lee went pounding down the road she tried to make the wounded man more comfortable. The ragged claw marks were deep, and she took some cloths from her provisions and attempted to stanch the flow of blood by forming pads, but they were soaked almost at once. His breathing grew ragged, and he moved his head from side to side without opening his eyes. He was saying something, but she could not understand his words.

As she knelt there in the silence of the woods

with his head pillowed on her lap, she looked up into the skies and said in a whisper, "Let him live, God!"

An eternity seemed to pass before Lee got back in a wagon driven by an elderly man named Bill Clark. He took one look at Zane and said, "We better get him to Doc Steele."

Dooley made a bed in the wagon, and together they managed to get Zane into it. "I'll ride with him to keep his head from bumping," she said. "I think he's got some kind of head injury."

Clark drove slowly to avoid jostling the injured man, and Lee followed closely, leading Dooley's horse. When they were five miles from town, Lee said, "I'll ride on in and find Doc and have a place ready."

He galloped off at a fast pace, and when they were half a mile from town, he met them, pulling up his horse from a dead run to say, "Drive to the preacher's house. Doc says he'll be easier to take care of there."

Clark pulled the wagon up in front of Merritt's house, and they carried the limp body of Zane Logan into a bedroom. Dooley and Rachel stayed while Steele made an examination. Finally he said, "We'll get these chest cuts stitched up. What a mess!"

"Is he going to live?" Dooley asked faintly.

"Don't know. Chest wounds won't kill him. But that head wound may be more serious. Got a concussion."

Steele worked quickly, cleaning the gashes and stitching them up where necessary. Then he cleaned the face, saying, "These aren't too deep, but gettin' hit by a paw of a grizzly's a little like getting hit by a freight train." He got up and turned to leave, saying,

"He ought to have somebody with him all the time. You two work that out."

As he left, Dooley said, "Rachel, he can't die!" Then with a face pale as paper she told the older woman the terrible things she'd said to Logan.

Rachel looked at the girl's trembling form with compassion, and there was a broad maternal smile on her lips as she slipped her arm around Dooley, saying, "We'll believe God, won't we?"

And through her tears, Dooley nodded, and as the two sat there through the long hours, sometimes speaking quietly, sometimes seeing to the needs of Zane, Dooley felt that the wall she had built between herself and Rachel had been broken down.

FOURTEEN
Left-Handed Gun

Always there was the darkness, black as velvet, cold and empty. It lay over him like an ocean, and when he came to the surface from time to time, the pain came as the light grew stronger. When that happened, he tried to go back into the depths of oblivion, but there would be a voice urging him to stay, to awaken.

Not just one voice. Sometimes the voice was rough, and along with it came pain. The other voice was soft and was accompanied by a soothing feeling as the pain ebbed and he could relax.

Sometimes he came out of the depths of darkness almost to the surface so that the light burned his eyes, and then he would dream and call out to somebody. But he never knew who it was he was calling, and once he knew he was weeping bitterly as he had not wept since he had been a small child. Then there was a softness that enveloped him, and he surrendered to it, falling into a natural sleep instead of the black depths.

When he awoke he heard the sound of a bird chattering and a creaking sound. Opening his eyes slowly, blinking against the light, he saw a ceiling papered with tiny red roses and green leaves. Letting his eyes fall, he saw an oak chest with a vase of yellow wild flowers on top, and over it a large framed picture of a man sitting stiffly in a chair, with a woman beside him. Both were stern-faced and rigid as they stared back at him.

Again the bird chattered, and turning his head to the right, he gazed out a window at the bright sunlight illuminating a small gray bird perched on a limb.

Nothing was familiar, and a sudden start of fear ran through him. He made a sudden motion, and the sharp pain that cut through his chest and right shoulder drew a grunt of pain from him. Glancing down, he saw that he was covered with a quilt. His chest was swathed in layers of white bandages and his right arm was bound tightly to his body.

"You're awake!"

He turned his head quickly to the right, and a woman who had been rocking in a chair placed close to his bed got up with a quick motion and came to stand over him. She had olive skin, smooth and clear, set off by a wide mouth. Her eyes were almond-shaped, and there was a light of pleasure in their gray-green depths. She leaned over, put her hand on his forehead, and smiled.

"Your fever's gone."

He licked his lips and tried to remember, but he was confused. She reached over, poured a glass of water from a pitcher on the bedside table, and placed it to his lips. As she said, "Drink this," memory came flooding back.

He drained the glass, and as she put it back on the table, he stared at her and asked in a voice rusty with disuse, "How long have I been here?"

She leaned over him, and he saw that there was fatigue in the lines of her face. "Tomorrow, it will be five days." She took a towel and dipped it into a pan on the table. Wringing it out, she began to clean his face. He recognized the soothing act as one of the sensations he'd had while unconscious.

He felt strange, helpless, but he lay there calmly as she bathed his upper body and said, "I need to change your bandages. It would be easier if you could sit up."

He pulled himself up, and the room suddenly went around. Only when she put her arm around him, holding him upright, did it stop. She asked, "All right?" and when he nodded, she began to remove the bandages. As she worked, he had an opportunity to study her. She moved quickly and there was no embarrassment in her face. She had long lashes, and from time to time, as she eased a stubborn bandage loose, she bit her full lower lip in steady concentration. A faint odor of some perfume came to him, and again he felt more vulnerable than he could remember.

When the bandages were off, she picked up a brown bottle and poured a clear liquid onto a piece of cotton. Then she began going over the wounds on his chest and arms. "This will hurt," she said.

He looked down as she began wiping the huge scars that ran from a point high on his chest in a diagonal direction almost to his belt line—four angry-looking welts pulled together by black thread at intervals. He smiled and asked, "Your needlework, Miss Wade?"

"No, Doctor Steele's. The one high on your shoulder got infected. That's what gave you such a bad fever." She began wrapping his chest with a roll of fresh bandages, saying, "The wound on your shoulder was the worst. You were thrashing around so much the stitches kept coming out. That's why we had to keep your arm tied up in a sling."

He looked down at his shoulder and slowly flexed his right arm. It was stiff and painful, but he said, "Guess I don't need a sling now."

"All right. It'll be better if you begin to exercise it a little. Not too much at first, though."

She gathered the old bandages, but as she turned to go he said, "Miss Wade . . ."

"Yes?"

"I'm not used to anybody taking care of me. Guess I've pretty well done that for myself." He struggled to put his feelings into words, his deep-set eyes searching her face. Then he added, "Guess I'd have been finished if you hadn't taken care of me."

She looked at him soberly, shook her head, and then smiled. "That's backward, Zane. Lee and I would have been killed if you hadn't stepped in. It was the most courageous thing I've ever seen in my life."

She saw that this embarrassed him. He dropped his eyes and picked at the quilt. Finally he looked up and smiled. "Guess we saved each other, Miss Wade."

She nodded, and said, "Dooley—that's what they call me."

"Dooley—funny name for a pretty girl."

She flushed and gave a short laugh. "Well, it's Julie, really. But nobody calls me that."

"Think I will, if it's all right with you."

"Why . . . I guess so."

He looked at her and asked with a puzzled light in his eyes, "I remember some bad dreams, Julie, and it seems like someone was always there when it got bad. Was that you?"

"Well, usually."

"Did I say anything?"

She stared at him, and shook her head. "Not really. Things I couldn't understand. Mostly you kept calling for your brother, trying to get him to do something, but I couldn't understand what."

He was silent, then he looked up and pain scored his gaunt face. "I was dreamin' about the time he got crippled. I always dream about that."

She came closer, put the bandages down, then sat down on the chair. "What was it, Zane? It's something bad, isn't it?"

"Bad? It's the worst thing in the world!" he said bitterly. Then he gave her a look so filled with black despair that it hurt her to meet his gaze.

"You want to tell me about it?"

He stared at her, then dropped his eyes to look at his hands. Finally in a voice that was not steady he said, "We were just kids. Saul was older, but I was always bigger and stronger. And that bothered him. He was always trying to outdo me, and he never could. 'Course he was smarter than me, but that didn't seem to help. I could whip him when he was twelve and I was only nine."

He gave her a bleak look and then added, "We

were playing out in the barn one day, jumping into the hay, and I climbed up pretty high and shouted, 'Bet you're afraid to jump from *here!*' And then I jumped." Sweat broke out on his face and he dashed it away with his left hand, then went on. "He climbed up to the very top of one of the beams—way too high. And he was afraid—he was always afraid of heights."

He broke off suddenly and stared at the opposite wall so long that she finally whispered, "What happened, Zane?"

He bent his head, not looking at her, then said huskily, "I shouted at him, 'You're scared to jump!' And then he jumped! He missed the hay, and there was this awful sound as he hit a beam!"

The room was quiet, so quiet that she could hear his irregular breathing, and then he looked up. There were tears in his eyes, and he blinked them away quickly. "I know Saul's not the best man in the world, and he's done some things I wish he hadn't. But it's my fault, Julie—my fault!"

The words covered a wound so ancient and so painful that she could read in his eyes the hurt. He was like a small boy who'd hurt himself, and without giving her action a thought, she rose and bent over him. Putting her arms around him and drawing him close, she whispered fiercely, "No, it's *not* your fault! You shouldn't say that!"

She felt his muscular shoulders heave, and time ran on endlessly as they sat there. She held him tightly. Slowly the spasms in his body stopped, and she drew back. With her arms still around him, his face only inches away, she said, "Your brother is like all the rest of us, Zane. He makes his own life. Look at Sam Bible. He lost an arm, but he didn't let it spoil him! Ask yourself this, if it had been *you* that was hurt, would you have become a crook?"

Then suddenly she realized the intimacy of the position, and color came to her cheeks. Rising swiftly, she picked up the bandages, saying just before she left the room, "I'm glad you're better."

He sat there, his face pale. He had never told anyone about his past, and now that it was said, a sense of wonder filled his mind. He felt more free, somehow, and for a long time he sat there, thinking of his life with Saul. Finally he sighed gustily, threw the covers back, and carefully stood up. When the room stopped swaying, he began walking carefully, holding on to the bed and the wall. When he came to the chair, he saw his gun belt draped over it, and paused. A thought came to him, and he stood upright, and moved his right hand to his hip, then brought it up with his elbow bent. The effort and pain of the movement tightened his lips, and he stared at the gun. Finally he gave a short laugh and said quietly, "Going to be interesting." Then be began walking, lifting his right arm painfully as he went.

Dooley found Rachel and her father in the kitchen, and said at once, "He's awake!"

Rachel noted the heightened color in Dooley's cheeks, but said only, "Is he? How does he feel?"

"Fine. I changed his bandages. It's lots easier when he's awake."

"Well, that's good," Merritt said, then he gave her a searching look. "You'd better go get some sleep, child. You've worn yourself thin sitting up with him."

"I didn't mind. After all, he saved our lives."

She left, and Rachel said, "We'd better have a look at him, Dad."

Going to the sick man's room, they entered and were amazed to find him standing up, clinging to the bed.

"You shouldn't be out of bed!" Rachel said at once.

He stood there, thin and gaunt, but the eyes were bright and he smiled gently. "Want to thank you folks for takin' care of me."

"Why, we owe you a favor, Mr. Logan," Merritt said at once. "Besides, as Christians, it was our duty."

He considered that, then nodded. "I'll be out of your way as soon as I can manage. You must be tired of waitin' on me."

"Not at all," Rachel said at once. "You're welcome to stay until you're well. Besides," she added with a smile, "Miss Wade did most of the work."

He thought that over, then said, "I'm in your debt, all of you. But I'll be movin' as soon as I can."

"Your brother sent word for you to come as soon as you were well."

"Did he?" Zane's voice was toneless, and he did not seem surprised at the news.

"Well, Doc Steele will decide what's best, Logan," Merritt said. "I'll send word for him to stop by this evening."

Steele pronounced the patient over the crisis, but was adamant about his not moving. "You'll stay right here until I take those stitches out!" he said loudly, drowning out Zane's protests that he was able to be gone. "You can wait a week. You're weak as a kitten, and those wounds need to heal up. I can count on Dooley and Mrs. Warren keeping you still."

The next week was the strangest, and in some

ways the happiest, in Zane Logan's life. He was up and about almost at once, but Merritt and the two women would not permit him to do a thing. He ate his meals with them, spent long hours reading, and found Merritt to be good company. The minister had been a chaplain in the Union army and could paint a picture of the many actions he had seen that made the war come alive for Zane.

The evenings were quiet, mostly talk around the kitchen, and he was surprised to find Dooley in and out of the house night and day. She told him the story of how she had been forced to run away from her home in Arkansas to escape the advances of her stepfather. She could not keep Reno out of the story, and as she told how he had been the means of getting her free, he saw her eyes light up.

He said only, "That Reno, he's quite a man."

"Yes, the best I've ever known," she replied quietly.

Merritt and Rachel had not missed the way Dooley kept returning to the house, nor were they unsure of the reason.

Finally Rachel said, "Dad, I was worried about Dooley's feelings about Jim, but this is worse!"

"I know. He's an attractive man, isn't he, Rachel? And the circumstances are romantic enough to catch any young girl's fancy."

"We've got to do something."

"What would you suggest?" he said, almost harshly. "Throw him out? Tell her he's no better than a criminal? She knows what he is, but she's seeing the best side of him." He sighed heavily, then said, "No, we can't say anything. That would just make her more determined, I think."

"Well, he'll be gone tomorrow. That'll help."

"No, it won't," Merritt said slowly. Shaking his head he added, "He'll still be in her head, and this is a small town."

The next morning they stood at the door to receive Zane Logan's thanks. He had his gun belt draped over his left shoulder and was wearing a new shirt. "Guess I'll never be able to thank you folks enough for all the trouble you've gone to. Maybe I'll find some way of makin' it up to you."

"Come to church, Zane," Merritt said, shaking his hand. "We'll call it an even swap."

Zane stared at him, then gave a crooked smile. "Might get your folks down on you, havin' a maverick like me in the congregation."

"We're all mavericks from God, Zane," Merritt said simply.

The tall man narrowed his eyes at that, then said, "I'll be there." Then he turned and left.

He made his way down the side street, turned left, and walked slowly along Front Street until he came to Creighton's Store. He was aware of the looks he got from those he passed, but paid no heed. Creighton was standing behind the counter, his arms crossed. He straightened up, came to where Logan stood, and said evenly, "Can I help you, Deputy?"

"You have a left-hand holster to fit this?" Zane plucked the gun belt from his shoulder, removed the .44, and handed it to Creighton.

"I think so." The merchant went to a shelf, pulled down a brown leather holster and inserted the weapon. "Good enough fit?"

Zane tried it. "That's fine. How much?"

Creighton named the price, took the money, and watched silently as Logan threaded the holster on the belt, buckled it around his waist, and left the store. A thought ran through his mind, and he smiled grimly. "Don't think he can make it stick," he muttered.

The El Dorado was almost empty, but one of the bartenders saw Logan enter. He straightened up, nodded, and said, "Good to see you on your feet. You lookin' for Saul?"

"Yes."

"Go on up. He's out of bed."

Zane made his way up the stairs, and knocked on Saul's door. "Come in," a voice said, and he pushed the door open and went inside. Saul was fully dressed, and he got up quickly from his desk and stared at his brother.

"You look bad," he said finally.

"Better than bein' dead."

Saul's lips tightened at that, but he forced himself to smile. "Would have come to see you, Zane, but it wouldn't have done that preacher any good having me there."

"It's all right."

Saul pulled on his coat. "Let's go get—" A knock on the door sounded, and he said, "Come in."

George Ives stepped in, his eyes lighting on Zane at once. "Up again, eh?" His eyes lit on the gun on Zane's left hip. He looked at Saul, then asked, "Left-hand gun? Can you do any good with that?"

"We'll have to let somebody find out," Zane said with a shrug.

Saul took the cigar out of his mouth, and there was a frown on his face. "How long before your right arm is well enough to pull iron?"

"Don't know," Zane said. "Probably never will be

as good as it was. Guess I won't be much help to you, will I?"

"You running out?" Saul snapped.

"No. Just tellin' you how it is."

Saul thought about it, then said, "I remember you were always pretty good with your left. Not like the right, but it'll do for Reno—if you get some help."

Ives said at once, "We better make it quick, Saul. There's a lot of talk about vigilantes, and it'll be Reno they'll center around."

Saul thought about it, then shrugged. "Can't be too soon for me—but we'll have to work it so he makes the first move."

"I think it'll be when we move in on Ivo Morgan," Ives said quickly. "I been picking up a few things, and Reno makes a lot of talk about how he won't help anybody else, but he's gotten pretty close to Morgan. I think if we push a little, it'll be all we'll need."

"Do it, then." Saul gave Ives a curious look, then shifted his gaze to Zane. "You ready to go to work, Zane?"

A silence ran across the room, and there was something in his brother's face that bothered Saul Logan. He shifted uncomfortably, then said angrily, "If I didn't have this bad leg, I'd never ask you; you know that!"

Zane did not change expression, and he said, "I said I'd play this hand out, then we're square."

"Do it, then!"

Logan and Ives waited until Zane left, then Ives said, "He's gone sour, Saul. What happened, that preacher convert him while he was getting well?"

"I don't know. But he'll do what I tell him,

George. Now, what's new?"

"Everything's OK, but I'm going to get on Morgan and Tbolt. They're both pretty popular, but once we put them down, we have a free hand in camp."

"Do it! I want to milk these people, George, then get away from here. Go to Europe maybe, where people are civilized!"

The remark amused Ives, but he said only, "Give me a week, Saul, and this camp will be as easy to pluck as summer blackberries!"

For the next week the town watched Zane Logan. He moved more slowly and obviously favored his right side. Endless arguments went on about the gun on his left side.

"He can't be as fast with his left hand," Ringo Jukes said to Ivo Morgan. "No man could be as good with his off hand."

Nick Tbolt shook his head stubbornly. "Some are just as good with either hand. I knew a feller once could write with either hand."

"Not the same thing at all!" Ed Rachaner protested. "Gettin' a gun unlimbered and gettin' off a shot ain't nothin' like writin'!"

But nobody cared to test it out, or did not until late Saturday night in the Nugget, a sleazy joint run by Don Futrell. Zane and Gallagher went in to find a rough named Zach Pounders getting set to tear the house apart.

"Get him outta here, Jack!" Futrell pleaded.

Gallagher gave a sly look at Zane and said, "Take him out, will you, Zane?"

It was clearly a test, but a smile was on Zane's lips as he said, "Sure, Jack."

He walked up to stand in front of Pounders, a

thick-bodied miner with a bad reputation for brawling, and said, "Time to go home, Zach."

Pounders stared at him, and his gaze wavered. Then he glanced down at the gun on Logan's left side, and when he looked up there was a grin on his face. "Got your right wing broke, didn't you, Deputy?"

"That's right, Zach."

"Well, now, that makes things a little different, don't it now?"

"Difference is I put a bullet in your liver with my left hand instead of my right one," Zane remarked. "You want to try it now, Zach?"

The room went quiet, and suddenly the sweat broke out on Pounder's broad face. He gave another glance around the room, then looked back at the tall man in front of him. Then he blustered, saying, "You ain't got the gall to pull against me with your off hand, Logan!"

Zane Logan shrugged and said nothing, then when the silence ran on, somebody said, "What you waitin' for, Zach?" He laughed and said, "Zach's tryin' to figure out if it's a good day to die."

The big miner kept his hands stiffly at his sides, and he searched the face of the tall deputy for a flicker of weakness. He didn't find it. A reluctant grin broke across his thick lips. "Well, maybe you ain't as good with that left hand, Logan, but I'll let somebody else do the findin' out!"

"Better get home, Zach," Zane said.

The week ran out, and on Sunday Merritt looked up to see Zane Logan enter the church and take a seat near the rear. This created a small stir, but Merritt was glad to see that several of the members went out of their way to speak to Logan after the service.

Dooley had seen him from her position in the choir, and she caught up with him as he was making his way back toward the center of town.

"I'm glad you came," she said breathlessly. "I was hoping you would."

He stood looking down at her, and then he looked back at the crowd milling around the church. "When I was a little boy, my mother used to take me to church." There was a light of regret in his eyes as he remarked, "Somethin' I've missed out on."

"Not too late, is it, Zane?" she asked.

He turned his hat slowly in his hands and then gave her a swift look. "I thought it was, but maybe I was wrong. Pretty hard for a fellow like me to change directions, Julie."

"You want to buy my dinner?" she asked suddenly, and without waiting for his answer she took his arm and walked with him toward the cafe.

"Your reputation will never survive this—havin' dinner with a notorious sinner like me," he said with a grin.

Her eyes sparkled as she said, "Well, if I can give you a bath, I can eat lunch with you!"

Her audacity caught him off guard. He stopped dead still, and people passing by stopped to stare at the tall deputy who stood there laughing at the pretty girl who stood before him.

Saul Logan was sitting at his private table with Gallagher and Ives, and Gallagher reported the incident. "Steve Marshland saw Zane come out of church, then him and that Wade girl went to eat together."

Ives scowled and said, "This business gets worse

all the time, Saul. Looks like Zane is straying out of line."

Saul picked up a drink, sipped it, then said steadily, "We'll have to smoke him out, George. You don't know him like I do."

"Yeah? Well, I'll take him over to Ivo Morgan's tomorrow, Saul," Gallagher said. "We'll find out something about him then."

"And I'll put the pressure on Nick Tbolt," Ives put in, leaning back in his chair. "Nick will hand over that claim or I'll bust him wide open!"

Saul nodded, adding, "I want Zane put in the oven. See to it!"

FIFTEEN
Dooley Finds a Man

Midsummer heat fell across the land, drying up
streams and sending dust clouds billowing high.
Reno and Lee were stripped to the waist as they
dumped ore into a box, then sluiced it with water
from the flume. Reno noticed that Lee was filling
out. *Going to be a big man when he gets through
growing,* he thought.

The two of them had worked hard all week, and
by midafternoon Reno said, "Let's give this dang
claim to the Indians, Lee!" He grinned at the boy and
added, "At least for this week. I'm bound to go into
town and sit down to a meal I didn't cook myself.
You game?"

Lee threw down his shovel, saying, "I thought
you'd never ask. Come on, last one to get cleaned up
is a skunk!"

They bathed in the creek, and later on Reno
teased Lee about shaving. "Watch out, you might cut
that poor struggling whisker off, boy!"

They battened the hut down, saddled up, and rode toward Virginia City. The creek made a sharp bend three hundred yards away from their claim, and as they turned out onto the road they spotted William Merritt in a buggy headed toward town. They waited for him, and Reno asked, "Where you been, Reverend?"

Merritt answered, "Over to Branch. Bob Engstrom's down with something. Might be cholera."

"Hope not," Reno said. "We don't need that around here."

They rode along slowly, Merritt giving the news from town, Reno and Lee idly keeping beside the buggy.

Suddenly Reno looked up, and said, "Looks like Morgan's got company."

Ivo Morgan's claim was off the main road, a slice of ground between an outcropping of rock and a thick grove of scrub pines. Reno took in the five horses tied to the trees and recognized none of them.

"What's wrong, Jim?" Lee asked. He was wise enough in the ways of the camp to know something was wrong, and the look on Reno's face was an additional sign. "You think it's trouble?"

"We'll just have a look-see," Reno murmured. "You better steer clear of this, Merritt," he added. But as Reno spurred off, closely followed by Lee, Merritt spoke to the team and they broke into a gallop.

Reno slowed enough to allow Lee to pull up, and he said quickly, "Watch yourself, Lee. Don't be too quick to pull that gun."

Lee nodded, and his heart began to beat faster as they rounded the screen of pines and rode directly at the group of men gathered in front of the shack.

Ivo Morgan was standing in front of his shack, and in a semicircle stood Gallagher, Zane Logan, Long John Frank, and the Simmons brothers.

Reno stopped his horse, dismounted in one easy motion, and moved without pause to stand beside Ivo Morgan. Morgan's face showed instant relief as Reno and Lee moved to stand beside him. "Hello, Jim."

"Hello, Ivo," Reno said. He was aware that the crowd facing him was disturbed by his action, and he fixed his eyes on Gallagher.

"What's going on, Jack?"

Gallagher gave a quick look at the others and seemed to come to a decision. "Got to move Morgan off this claim, Reno. Got a paper here that says he sold this place to somebody else."

"Which is a lie of Saul Logan!" Morgan said. His face was red with anger, and he did not let his hand get far from the gun on his hip. "You can take that paper and eat it for breakfast, Gallagher. I'm not moving!"

"You're talking to the law, Morgan," Gallagher said. He settled his feet, and once again his eyes cut around. He measured the odds, found them favorable, then said, "You're not giving us much choice, are you, Morgan?"

"You got some new deputies, Jack?" Reno asked. He nodded toward Long John Frank and the Simmons brothers. "Or are they just along for fun and games?"

"I figured some of Morgan's friends would try to buy into his troubles," Gallagher said, "so I deputized them to give me and Zane a hand."

Reno took a brass button from his shirt pocket, and the silence ran on as he began to flip it into the air with his thumb. The action seemed to paralyze Gallagher, and he stood there watching Reno, who then said quietly, "You should have brought more help, Jack. I don't see anything to brag about in that pack of dogs."

The insult hung on the air, and Curt Simmons cursed loudly. "Gallagher, don't let that clown slow us down!"

The moment was tense, and Reno was afraid for Lee. The boy was a good shot, but he was untried. Ivo Morgan was tough, but no match for these hard cases. Gallagher said suddenly, "Zane, Reno's your meat if he moves!"

Zane Logan stood there, slightly to the left, but he moved to face Reno. He said quietly, "Reno, it'd be better if you and the boy pulled out of this."

Reno studied Zane Logan carefully, noting the steady eye and the fearless stance. He knew all about this man, that his right arm was too stiff to draw, but he saw that there was no give in him. He knew from what Rachel and Merritt had said that Dooley had become interested in him, and that bothered him.

"I don't know you, Logan," he said directly, and he turned to face the man squarely. "But you're running with a pack of dogs. Don't move that hand of yours unless you mean to draw."

Tension was thick, and Lee's face was pale, but he stood there steadily facing the men across the yard. He found himself suddenly free from fear, and he could not understand that. He knew that in a matter of seconds he might be lying in the dust dying, but he concentrated on one thing—keeping his hand ready to pull the gun at his side.

Gallagher said, "Zane! Get the—!"

But even as he raised his voice, the sound of Merritt's buggy being driven at a hard clip struck them, and Gallagher whirled to see who it was.

Merritt pulled the wagon to an abrupt halt and looked at the two groups. Then he did a strange thing. He wound the reins tightly, then pulled a rifle from the floor of the buggy and got out. His face was steady as he crossed the yard, coming to stand beside Lee. He said nothing, but the rifle in his hand was enough to make his intention clear.

Gallagher was thrown off by this maneuver, and he said loudly, "Get away from here, Preacher!"

Merritt chambered a shell, then held the rifle with both hands, muzzle down but ready for action. "I'm not a man of war usually, Gallagher, but I guess this time I'll have to do what I think is right."

Gallagher stared at him, his face turning red, and he glanced at the others, uncertain.

Curt Simmons's face had a broad grin as he said, "Well, looks like the preacher has joined the outlaws, Jack!" Then his face went mean, and he said, "Frank, you take the preacher—Ben, you get the boy. I'll take Morgan. That leaves you to get Reno, Logan."

Reno knew that Curt Simmons had seen a weakness, for except for the possibility that Reno might match Logan's draw, the others were out of their class. Desperately he tried to think of a way out, but nothing came. For himself he did not care, but Lee and Merritt were vulnerable, and he didn't want to see them die like this.

Gallagher, having sized up the situation, cried, "All right, let's get 'em!"

But even as Gallagher's hand moved toward his

gun, Zane Logan cried out loudly, "Hold it!"

Gallagher, caught off balance, whirled to stare at Logan, his face rigid with anger. "What did you—?"

"Show's over, Jack," Logan said. He moved away from the others, coming to stand to the left between the two groups. He stood with his feet wide apart, and he half-turned his back on Morgan and the others to face Gallagher.

Curt Simmons turned, but felt flanked as he tried to keep his eyes on the group in front of the house and Logan at the same time. Ben started to move to one side, but Zane Logan riveted him by saying sharply, "Take on more step, Ben, and you're dead!"

They stood there, frozen into inaction by Logan's sudden move. Reno didn't understand it, didn't trust the man, but he saw the sudden uncertainty in the faces of men who stood across the yard, and he knew that they were shaken by Logan's switch.

"You gone crazy, Zane?" Gallagher asked.

Logan said, "You fellows better move out."

Gallagher longed to go for his gun. The desire was on his face, but the odds had changed. He clamped his jaws shut and said, "Let's get out of here!" He led the others away, all of them walking stiffly, and it was not until the sound of their horses running came that Reno relaxed his position.

"That was close!" Morgan said. He pulled a trembling hand across his brow, then stared at it. "Must be getting old! Use' to be it took more than that to give me the shakes!" Then he looked up, warmth in his eyes, saying, "You folks didn't do yourselves any good today. They won't forget."

Merritt wasn't listening. He said to Zane, "You kind of turned a corner, didn't you, boy?"

232

Zane shrugged and turned to go, but Morgan said, "Logan, I guess I've said some pretty rough things about you. I guess I got to take them back. If you hadn't pitched in with us, it would have ended a lot different."

Lee's eyes were shining with admiration, and he said, "Zane! Boy, you sure did make that bunch take water!"

There was a puzzled look in Zane Logan's eye, and he stood there staring toward the column of dust created by the galloping horses. He finally looked at Reno and gave a crooked smile. There seemed to be something in the two men that each recognized, and it was to Reno that he spoke.

"Guess I've been a fool most of my life. But I don't think I'll have any regrets about this."

Reno suddenly stepped forward, held out his hand, and as the other gripped it, he murmured, "You come of age, old son!"

The remark reddened Zane's cheeks, but he shook his head, saying, "Guess I'm finished here."

"You won't be too welcome in some quarters, Zane," Merritt said quickly, "but you've made some friends here today, and there could be more."

The offer caught at Zane, and he stood there looking down, then after a long silence, he shook his head. "Guess I'll have to be leavin'."

He turned and left, walking quickly around the screen of pines, and they heard his horse gallop away.

"He pulled our bacon out of the fire for sure," Morgan said. "Wonder what made him do that?"

Merritt stared toward the trees and said, "He's a very unhappy man, Ivo. All mixed up. But he seems to be struggling to do the right thing."

Morgan said, "Where does this leave us, Reno? Gallagher will be back with a bunch. All we've done is put the thing off!"

Reno shook his head. "Can't see any end to it."

"No, it just gets worse," Morgan agreed. "Think I'll go into town with you."

They waited until he got his horse, then made their way slowly along the road, and Lee said, "Jim, I thought you weren't goin' to help Morgan. That's what you said."

Reno looked at the boy, then shrugged, "So I did. That's what I meant to do—just mind my own business." He lifted his head and released a gusty sigh, then looked at Lee with a sudden angry light in his eyes. "And it's a sorry way to live, Lee! I thought I could do it, but I know I can't. Might as well go back into a cave somewhere if we can't have a friend to stand by!"

Merritt had heard the last part of this, and he asked, "Does that mean you'll join in with the vigilantes, Jim?"

Reno thought about it, then said, "I reckon so, Merritt." Then he gave Lee a quick look, saying, "I hate to see you thrown into all this Lee, but I know you wouldn't be set off on the shelf. You stood there like a rock when it looked pretty bad. I like that."

Lee flushed, the compliment being the sweetest thing he'd ever known. He swallowed and said, "Well, Jim, I had some good teachin'!"

Zane walked into the El Dorado, finding Saul sitting at his table, Gallagher by his side.

"Guess you heard the good news, Saul," he said.

Saul's face was rigid with anger. He stood up, and the rage that ran through him thinned his voice as he whispered, "Why'd you bother to come back, you Judas?"

"Wanted to say good-bye, I guess."

Saul raised his cane and brought it across Zane's face. It left a red mark that stood out against the cheek. "Get out of my sight! Get out of this town! If you're in town in one hour, I'll have you shot down!" Then he said what he had said many times before: "If I wasn't a cripple, I'd kill you myself."

Always that formula had worked, but something was different in Zane this time. He stood there, the lash mark on his cheek glowing, and he said softly, "That dog won't hunt anymore, Saul."

"What?"

Zane Logan's face contained a touch of amazement. "I can't believe I spent all these years listenin' to you sayin' that—and didn't have sense enough to see how you used me." Then he said, "That's your crutch, Saul—not the cane you walk with. Men hurt worse than you have picked up and made it. You're crippled in your head more than in your leg."

Saul Logan stood there, his face pale as paste, and he could not find a word in the silence that followed. He looked as if he had received a sudden blow in the stomach, and his eyes were wild.

Zane stared at his brother, then said, "Sorry for you, Saul. Not because of your leg. Sorry you've let it turn you into what you are. I'm leavin'—and I won't ever feel guilty again about you, Saul."

Then he whirled and walked out of the saloon so quickly that Saul was left staring at him.

Gallagher understood none of this. He waited for Saul to speak, but he seemed to be paralyzed. Finally Gallagher said, "Well, *he's* out of it—that's clear! Been better off if you'd left him to rot in that Mexican pen!"

Then Saul leaned forward and said in a thick voice, "Take him out, Jack!"

Gallagher was surprised. "Zane?"

"Yes, you big ox!"

Gallagher hesitated, then got up, "Your own brother? You want him put down?"

A fierce light of unholy joy leapt into Saul Logan's face. "Yes, my own brother! I want him dead. Don't let him get out of town alive, you hear me! It's worth five thousand!"

Greed leapt into Gallagher's face. "I'll take care of it myself, Saul!"

Word of Zane Logan's rebellion swept through the town. Dooley heard it from Merritt when he came to the stable to put his horse up. She was on her way to the laundry when she heard him call her.

"You'll be happy to hear this," he said gently, then he related the story to the girl. She listened without a word, but when he was finished, she let her breath out in a long sigh. "I *knew* he would get free from his brother!"

"Well, he's leaving town, and that's best, I suppose!"

"But I thought . . ." She hesitated, and Merritt wanted to put his arm around her.

"Dooley, he's not for you," he said gently.

She shook her head, then walked away ignoring his call. She went upstairs to her room, and for a long time she sat there, calling herself a fool for even thinking thoughts about Zane Logan. But it did no good. Finally she dashed the tears from her eyes, saying angrily, "First Reno, now Zane Logan. I really am a glutton for punishment!"

Ten minutes later a knock at her door came, and she opened it to find Zane Logan standing there, hat in his hand.

Her hand went to her throat, and she stepped back, saying, "Come in."

He hesitated, then came in. There was a hesitancy in his manner as he said, "Julie, I—"

She interrupted him. "I heard how you helped Morgan, Zane."

"Well . . ." he stammered slightly, then shrugged. "I couldn't let them hurt Reno, Julie."

"It's like you, Zane," she murmured.

He shook his head. "It's *not* like me, Julie, not at all! I've got nothin' to brag about." He let the anger that was in him show on his craggy face, and there was a touch of sadness in his eyes as he said, "I've wasted my whole life, Julie. Because I was better with my fists and with a gun, I just sort of took the easy way out."

She put her hand on his arm, and urgency ran through her husky voice as she said, "But you've changed, Zane. You know you have!"

He gave her a smile. "Guess I've got you to thank for that, Julie. After I told you about how it was with Saul and me, and after what you said, why, it seems like a load was just lifted off me." He looked at her with wonder in his eyes. "When I told Saul I was leavin' and how I'd never feel guilty again over him, why it made me feel . . ." He shrugged, and finally said, "Well, anyway, I came to say thank you—and good-bye."

She bit her lip, and her voice was unsteady as she

looked up and said, "I don't want you to go!"

He stared at her, disbelief in his face. He put his hands on her shoulders, and gently said, "Julie, you're the best girl I've ever seen, but it would be no good for us, don't you see that? Why, I'm nothin'— I've got nothin'." He shook his head and added, "I don't even have a trade."

She looked up at him and said instantly, "Zane Logan, I expect you could do just about anything you put your mind to!"

He stared at her, laughed, and then grew still. She was close to him, and the freshness of her youth and the feminine qualities of her face and form struck him like a blow. Her face was turned upward, and he lowered his head, kissing her gently at first, then as she put her arms around him, he drew her closer, savoring the freshness of her lips. She met his kiss and pulled herself against him. He had not been a womanizing man, and the shock of her firm body against his sent a shock through him. *This is what it ought to be like—a man and a woman!* he thought.

Then she pulled her head back and said, "I love you, Zane."

He put his arms on her shoulders, saying gently, "I'll remember that, Julie, always. But tyin' up with me would be the worst thing that could happen to you."

She did not argue, but said, "You won't be able to forget me, Zane. You'll try, but you won't forget how I kissed you. And I'll be waiting for you to come back."

He stepped back and said, "Don't do that, Julie! Marry some nice young fellow, and think of me once in a while."

He turned and left the room hurriedly, not giving

her a chance to respond. She stood there weeping
openly as his footsteps sounded down the steps.

He reached the ground and started toward his
horse, but a voice caught him in midstride.

"Well, Logan, let's see if it ends like it does in the
storybooks this time!"

Whirling quickly, he saw Curt Simmons standing
in the shadows of the stable door, his gun lifted and
aimed. Zane stopped dead still, then heard a muted
chuckle to the left of Curt Simmons and knew that it
was Ben.

Got me hipped! he thought, and stood there rigidly waiting for the tearing of led through his body.

But Curt had waited for this moment too long
not to savor it. He grinned and said, "Now if this
was a storybook, why, Ben and me would put up
our guns and give you a fair chance, ain't that the
way of it, Logan?"

"Goes that way," Zane murmured. He was staring
at the bore of Curt's gun, wondering if he could
throw himself to one side, but he knew the big man
was quick on the trigger, so he stood there hoping
for a break.

Curt shook his head and said in a mocking voice,
"Well, Ben, you reckon we ought to give ol' Zane
here a fair chance?" He listened to the muted
chuckle from his brother, then shook his head sadly.
"Ben says no, Logan."

"Thought he might."

Curt dropped his smile and said, "You got nerve, I'll
give you that, Logan. You know you'll be dead in less
than a minute, but you ain't crawlin'. I admire that."

"But not enough to let me off?"

"If you hadn't put me off that stage, I might do

that," Curt stated. "But you did, and I can't let no man treat me like that. You can see that, can't you, Logan?"

A flicker of movement caught Zane's eye. He did not turn his head, but behind Curt Simmons, who was framed in the stable door, a shadow moved, then disappeared.

"Sure, I can see that, Curt," Zane said. "You've got a lot of pride."

Curt swelled up, and then he laughed. "That's it. I've got pride. Why, if I let one man push me around, there'd be another one, and then I'd be finished."

The shadow moved, and Zane saw the shape of a hat.

"Guess you've had to deal with gents quite a few times, haven't you, Curt?"

The shadow moved again, and Curt began to tell of men he'd downed, then all of a sudden he stopped and said, "Think I don't know what you're doin', Logan? You're tryin' to live a few seconds longer. But it won't do you no good." He lifted his gun, pointed it right at Zane's head, then laughed. "One more thing—the last you'll ever know. Know who's payin' for this job? Your own brother! Now you can go out chewin' on that!"

Zane sensed the coming shot and flung himself violently to his left. The shot that came brushed his cheek, and another shot came right on its heels, but he was rolling in the dust, pulling his own weapon. Curt was down, and Zane threw a single shot at Ben, who got off one shot of his own. The bullet plowed up dust at Zane's feet, and his own slug struck Ben in the mouth, driving the life out of him instantly.

Zane heard a voice from the stable, "You OK?"

240

"Yes." Zane saw Easy come out of the stable, gun in his hand, his eyes glinting with the light of battle. He paused to look down at the form of Curt Simmons, then looked up at Zane. "They had you in a pocket, didn't they now?"

"I was dead, sure enough." He looked at the small rider, remembering that he'd been antagonistic before. "Why'd you step in, Easy?"

"Aw, I heard about what you did for Reno and Ivo. Thought it was pretty good."

A clattering of boots on the stairs made them both turn, and Dooley hit the ground running, throwing herself into Zane's arms.

"I thought you were dead!" she moaned, her face pressed against his chest.

Holding her, and looking into the wide eyes of Easy, Zane smiled, then pulled back. Looking down at her, he said, "You told me the truth, Julie."

"The truth?"

He laughed and said, "That I wouldn't be able to forget you—that I'd be back." He held her tightly, and said, "It was a short trip, Julie, because I'm back. And I won't leave you again!"

Easy looked at the two and muttered, "Well, ain't *that* a pretty come-off!" He shook his head at the sight, then turned to face the men who were running to investigate the sound of the shooting.

SIXTEEN
The Posse

The deaths of the Simmons brothers did not disturb the Gulch. They had no friends and were buried in unmarked graves in the raw earth, with only Reverend Merritt and the two gravediggers in attendance. A week after they died it was as if they had never existed, and the memory of their faces had faded in the minds of most of the miners.

Two weeks after the shooting, however, the people of the Gulch were stirred by another death.

X. Beidler came into Creighton's General Store with a hurried gait. He spotted Reno and Creighton at the rear and made straight for them.

"Hello, X.," Reno said, looking up from the pile of supplies. His greeting was casual, but he saw that Beidler's face was set and rigid with anger. "What's the trouble?"

Beidler planted his feet on the floor squarely and aimed his gaze at Reno. Without preamble he demanded, "You mean what you said, Jim, about doing something about the Innocents?"

Reno glanced at Creighton, then nodded. "I've been thinking a lot about Link McKeever, X. Somebody's going to go down for that."

Beidler nodded, and there was a sadness in his sharp eyes. "I'll give you another reason—Bill Clark just came into town with Nick Tbolt. Nick's got a bullet in the head."

"Nick?" asked Reno, and his face filled with sadness. "Young Nick?"

"Clark found him in the brush," Beidler said. "He went over to ask Wiley Hildebrand and Long John Frank to help him load the body, but they acted plumb spooky, Bill said."

"That's too much, Beidler!" Creighton said at once, his aristocratic face filled with anger. "We can't let this go!"

"You sure you're ready, Jim?" Beidler demanded. "Once we start, there'll be no backing down."

Reno nodded slowly. "Young Nick had a good life ahead of him," he said softly. Then his lips tightened, and he said, "We'll pay a call on Frank and Hildebrand."

By the time a posse could be rounded up, it was after midnight. At one o'clock, eight men left Virginia City. Sam Bible and Jim Williams flanked Reno in the lead, and the others kept close behind. They wound around Stinking Water Creek, took a low ford, and still under the cover of night they entered the flat, wedge-shaped plateau that fell sharply toward the lowland prairie. There was little talk. Most of them were thinking of Tbolt. He had been one of the most popular young men in camp, and his death was the catalyst that stirred them to action.

It was close to daybreak when Reno said, "Hold up." He waited until they all grouped close, then said, "We want to catch them by surprise if we can. I'll go have a look-see."

He slipped off his horse and disappeared into the timber, making no sound. "Hate to have him on my trail," Jukes said. Half an hour later they were startled when a voice right at their feet spoke up.

"We've got something." Reno slipped out of the timber, mounted his horse, and said, "There's a bunch at the cabin. Quite a few horses, and there's eight or nine men sleeping outside. Maybe four or five inside."

"You think it could be the Innocents, Jim?" Beidler asked.

"Maybe. They're not just camping out."

"Want to bust 'em now?" Easy asked.

"Guess we'll have the light." He looked up and saw the first gray in the dark sky. "Let's get moving. Ringo, you and I will take the cabin. The rest of you put a gun on those fellows outside."

They moved forward in the gray light, spreading out, and the sleepers were quickly surrounded by a ring of rifles.

Reno moved to the door, opened it, and called out, "Long John Frank!"

The sleepers began stirring, and from inside the cabin a sleepy voice said, "What's up?"

"Get out here!"

A tall shape filled the doorway, and Long John Frank stepped out, rubbing his eyes. He stopped short when he saw the armed men in the yard. The sleepers were all now risen, and Reno held his gun on Frank. "Hold the rest of them here. Beidler, you come with me."

Reno led Long John Frank away from the cabin and then pulled him around. "You're in a bind, Frank. You killed Nick Tbolt, didn't you?"

The sudden accusation caught Frank like a blow in the face. He began to tremble, seeing the stern faces of Beidler and Reno.

"No! I didn't kill him!"

"Why wouldn't you help Bill Clark load the body in a wagon?" Beidler demanded.

"Don't know nothin' about it!"

"Tbolt lay dead near your place for several days. Why didn't you say something?" Reno demanded. "You'll hang, Frank!" He had no thought that Frank was guilty, but he knew there was a good chance he knew who the killer was. He had Frank picked as a weak sister, and he grabbed him by the arm, saying, "Come on, Beidler, we'll string him and Hildebrand up right now!"

"No—wait!" Frank began to tremble in his long limbs. "I didn't do it!"

Beidler caught Reno's drift. He grabbed Frank's other arm, saying, "I've got a rope."

"Wait! Wait!" Frank began to plead. "I won't take the blame for anybody! Ives did it—George Ives!"

"What's Ives doing here? What's that bunch here for?"

"I don't know. They just drifted in."

Reno shoved him back toward the cabin, and when they got inside, he said at once, "We want you, Ives—for the murder of Tbolt."

Ives gave a contemptuous look at the posse.

"You'll never prove it!"

"Let's hold court right here, Jim!" Jukes said.

But Reno and Beidler both shook their heads. "No," Beidler said at once. "We'll try 'em in Virginia City. We're going to clean the vipers out, but we'll do it according to justice." He gave Ives a steady look and said, "I'll see you hang, Ives."

Ives merely laughed, but when he turned his glance on Reno, he said under his breath, "Have your fun, Reno, but you'll be dead in a day or two!"

When the posse got back to Virginia City the next day, the whole town was alive, the news of the capture of Ives drawing the miners from their claims. Ives, Frank, and Hildebrand were put under guard. Beidler said, "They'll have every lawyer in town to defend Ives, but Wilbur Sanders is here. He'll prosecute for us." He paused, then added, "The toughs will try to take over, like they did with Stinson and Lyons."

"They won't do it!" Creighton said firmly. "We're going to hang these men, then we'll smash the rest of the Innocents!"

"It better work, John," Sam Bible said, rubbing his cheek with his steel hook. "Every man of us will be shot down if they get off. It's convict or die."

Beidler spoke up, "I dug two graves for Stinson and Lyons. All for nothing. But this time we'll have some bodies!"

"It all depends on the miners," Creighton said slowly.

"What do you say, Jim?" Bible asked.

Reno turned his face toward the crowd, a cold anger in his wedge-shaped face. "The crowd can do it's crying, but I've been thinking of Nick—and

Charley Rixie and Link McKeever. Somebody's got to go down for them."

Creighton stared at him, then nodded. "All right, we're going to organize like they did in San Francisco. It'll be hard, but we can make it work."

"The tough part will be after the verdict. That's when the Innocents will try to control the crowd. I want a ring of guns thrown around Ives to see he doesn't get off."

They made plans to join forces with others at Bannack and Nevada City to form a compact body of vigilantes, then they broke up.

Reno found Dooley waiting for him at the stable, worry on her face.

"Jim, I've been worried!" She waited until he put his horse up, then pulled at his arm. "Have you eaten?"

"No."

"I'll fix you some eggs and bacon."

As he ate, he told her the story of Ives's capture, but his mind was not on it. He finished the meal, pulled his pipe out, and then put it back suddenly.

"Been worried about you, Dooley," he said directly. She was sitting across the table sipping coffee, but at once she put the cup down.

"You've heard about Zane and me?"

He nodded, and his face was totally serious as he said, "Dooley, you made a mistake about me, didn't you?"

She knew instantly that he meant her infatuation with him, and though her cheeks grew pinker, she kept her head high. "Yes, I was silly."

"No harm in that, Dooley." Reno smiled and reached across to put his hand on her arm. "I knew you'd outgrow it." Then he shook his head and added, "But this business with Logan—"

"Jim!" she broke in, and she took his hand in both of hers. Her eyes were pleading for understanding as she said with trembling lips, "I was wrong about you. But you don't know Zane!"

"Neither do you, Dooley. How long have you known him? A few weeks? And you know what he is—a gunfighter."

"So are you, Jim," she countered.

He sat there unable to answer that, and he saw that nothing he could say would make any difference. He said heavily, "You're right. Maybe that's why I know what he's like, since I've been in the game myself. I want the best for you, Dooley, and you're moving in the wrong track."

She sat there, tears in her eyes. She loved Jim Reno, but it was not the kind of love she'd thought. He was the brother she'd never had, her friend. She hated the idea of disappointing him, of hurting him. Finally she said quietly, "Jim, try to get to know Zane. Will you do that?"

He nodded, "Sure." He had the wisdom to see that her mind was made up, so all he could do was try to make it easier. "Where's he staying now that he's not a deputy?"

Dooley's eyes grew warm, and she said, "You'd never guess! Ivo Morgan offered him a share of his claim!"

"Morgan did that?" Reno asked in surprise.

"Yes! Oh, of course Zane won't be able to work much until he gets well, but Ivo says he'd have lost the whole thing if it hadn't been for Zane, so they're partners."

"Ivo's a pretty shrewd fellow," Reno said with a smile. "He wouldn't go partners with a bad one, would he now?"

She saw that he was trying to help, so she jumped up and ran around the table, throwing herself in his lap and her arms around his neck.

"Jim Reno, you are just the sweetest thing in the whole world!"

"Whoa! You Southern gals are the worst flirts in the world! You let me alone, now, you hear?"

He left her room and made his way along Front Street, finding Ivo Morgan and Zane Logan in a crowd of men.

"Zane, like to see you."

The crowd moved to let Zane Logan pass through, curiously eyeing the two men as Reno led the other to a quiet corner outside the blacksmith shop.

Reno said at once, "I think Dooley's making a mistake with you, Zane."

"In that, you'd be right, Reno."

The straightforward admission caught Reno off guard. He looked up at the serious face of the tall man and took a moment to consider.

"Want to spell it out, Reno?" Zane asked. "I've been a gunman. Been in prison. Spent most of my life in trouble. Got no skills. Never stuck to anything very long. My prospects are pitiful and my history is sad. No decent young girl should have anything to do with me. That about sum it up?"

Reno's lips suddenly curled in a smile, then he laughed outright. "Sounds like my biography, Zane. You been reading my mail?"

He suddenly liked the man. The free admission

and the frank confession lightened his mood. And what the tall man said next did even more.

"Dooley deserves the best there is, Jim," he said, and an intense soberness filled his craggy face. "And I'm not it—not now. I ask one thing of you. Give me a year. If I don't cut it, shoot me. If I do, you give the bride away to me. What do you say?"

Reno took the hand that Logan put out and clamped down on it. "That's a bargain, Zane. You'll make it, too."

Zane Logan asked suddenly, "You a religious man, Jim?"

"Well, I'm on my way, Zane," Reno answered. "Why you asking?"

"Been on my mind a lot. Guess that preacher got to me when I was at his house." He shrugged and then smiled. "Guess I'm sayin' that only the Lord God could pull a fellow like me up out of the pit! Anyway, I'm thinkin' on it."

"So am I, Zane," Reno murmured.

SEVENTEEN
The Trial

Virginia City turned out for the trial of George Ives.
Hildebrand and Frank were minor figures, but Ives
was the pivotal factor. The monotonous grinding
labor of mining offered little relief, and the stark
drama of the thing fed the hunger of the mob for
excitement.

Judge Byam presided, Wilbur Sanders acted as
prosecutor, and James Thurmond defended Ives.
Judge Byam wrote the names of twelve miners, one
from each mining district, and Judge Wilson, his
associate, wrote the names of twelve townspeople,
the twenty-four constituting the jury.

The excitement of the crowd grew as the numbers swelled the town. From eight to ten miles up
the Gulch, and two to three miles below, the miners,
mostly armed, arrived in great numbers, until at
least fifteen hundred had assembled around a wagon
set in the middle of Front Street. They milled
around, and there were several strange faces,

Creighton pointed out. "The Innocents from the other camps will be busy. Watch out for them."

Although the process of picking the jury was slow, few of the spectators left, and when after dinner the scene of the event was changed to a big Schuttler wagon drawn up in front of a two-story building, the crowd simply followed. A semicircle of benches from an adjacent hurdy-gurdy house was placed around a fire built in the center for the accommodation of the twenty-four jurors, and behind them a place was reserved for a cordon of guards. Nearby stood over a thousand miners, teamsters, mechanics, merchants, gamblers—all sorts and conditions of men, all caught up in the drama. It was, at first, a good-natured crowd quick to obey the instructions of the judge to observe the order of the court.

Bill Clark was the first witness. In a loud, confident voice he told of finding Nick Tbolt's body and of the behavior of Frank and Hildebrand. The testimony of Long John Frank told heavily and was a clear indictment of George Ives. His testimony was seconded by Wiley Hildebrand.

During their testimony, there were cries from the crowd—"You'll die for that, Frank!" and the like, obviously from the friends of Ives.

Reno paid little heed to the legal proceedings. "That's not our worry," he murmured to Beidler as they watched the crowd. He found himself the object of attention, for his fights with the roughs had not been forgotten.

When Wilbur Sanders made his summation, a quiet fell over the crowd. Sanders, a polished man in rough surroundings, spoke well and with great feeling. He spoke of the murdered Tbolt, what a fine young man he was, honest and faithful. Then he stirred the people by telling in graphic details of the murders that darkened the history of Virginia City, including the brutal deaths of Link McKeever, Beans Melton, Charlie Rixie, Jay Dillingham, and many others. The list had a visible effect on the crowd, and Reno saw many grow restless under the address. Growing eloquent, Sanders pointed out that no honest man with a dollar in his pocket would be safe if human wolves were allowed to range abroad.

"You must find George Ives guilty, for he *is* guilty!" he cried at last, and the crowd moved like wheat in a high wind.

The defense lawyer, James Thurmond, got up on the wagon, and it was obvious that he had been drinking. "The evidence is not clear. Who knows who did the foul deed?" he said in a thick voice. Then he meandered into a long, rambling talk about the good deeds of his client until the judge finally asked him to sit down.

The jury left and in less than thirty minutes came out from Creighton's Store.

"Have you reached your verdict?"

The jury foreman handed a slip to Judge Byam. "We all signed this verdict except one man. Guilty!"

At once a series of loud cries went up from various places in the crowd. "It's a frame-up!" "Let's have another trial!"

Sanders ignored them and said, "I move that George Ives be hanged."

Judge Byam nodded his head. "I direct that the arrangements be made for the verdict to be carried out."

As several men moved to obey the order, the

roughs raised their cries louder. "What's the hurry?" "Give him a chance!"

Ives had been quiet during the trial, not appearing concerned. Now, however, he was pale. He rose up suddenly and the crowd grew quiet as he spoke to Byam.

"Your honor, I am a gentleman, and I believe you are. I want to ask a favor that you alone can grant. If our places were changed, I know I would grant it to you, and I believe you will to me. I've got a mother and sisters, and I want you to get this execution put off till tomorrow morning so I can write them. I will give you my word and honor as a gentleman that I will not undertake to escape, nor permit my friends to try to change the matter."

Byam was moved by the plea. He stood there, thinking deeply, and there was a thick silence over the packed street. It was a strange moment, and he was a man of intense sensitivity. He said slowly, "I can understand your position, Ives. . . ."

It was clear that he meant to grant Ives's request. X. Beidler had gone from the crowd and climbed upon the dirt roof of a cabin where, from upon the ridgepole, he was surveying the crowd surrounding the prisoner. Then X. spoke in a voice that boomed up and down the street.

"Byam, ask Ives how much time he gave Tbolt!"

He had said the right thing, and a roar went up from Tbolt's friends. Byam said, "You can write your letter while the rope is being rigged."

Ives glared at Beidler and made no attempt to write on the paper furnished by an officer of the court. The men sent to find a place for the hanging returned, saying, "Can't find a suitable place."

The indomitable Beidler called out, "That will do!" pointing at a log house under construction. The walls were up, but the house was not yet covered by a roof. One of the officers mounted the wall and threw down a log. With assistance it was placed at an angle of forty-five degrees, so that the upper end of it protruded into the street. A rope was tied around the end of the log. A box was placed under it, and Ives's hands were tied behind his back. He was lifted up on the box and stood there, his face white.

The toughs began making their last stand. Gallagher pushed forward and was followed by a large number of men.

"You can't hang a man like Ives!"

"I'll kill the man who touches that box!"

"Let's have another trial!"

Ives stood on the small box, holding himself rigid for fear of falling. He was pale as paper and seemed to be looking to the crowd for help. His eyes were wild, and he looked suddenly right into Reno's eyes and the fear changed to hate. "I wish I'd killed you!" he groaned. Then he shouted so that everybody could hear, "I am innocent!"

"That's the password!" Beidler said.

The Innocents pressed in, yelling and waving weapons. This was the final test, and it was Judge Byam who saw it clearly and shouted, "Men, do your duty!"

Suddenly there was a stir, and the sun glinted on the rifles of the men stationed around Ives. Two men dashed forward and knocked the box from under Ives's feet. Reno, his back turned, heard a strange whining thump of the rope and heard Ives's choking gasp. Then Beidler said with satisfaction, "He's dead!"

A roar went up from the crowd, followed by a silence, then Judge Byam said loudly, "This court is adjourned." The crowd began to fade, headed for the saloons to drink and talk about the event and what it meant. "We'll meet tonight and organize," Creighton said.

The vigilantes were organized at Creighton's Store that evening. Ten men met to sign the vigilante oath. Creighton was chosen president, Jim Williams the executive officer. These men were given authority to pass sentence. The only sentence was death, although they could banish a man if they saw fit.

"We've got to work fast," Beidler urged. "The Innocents are talking big, and they'll pick us off one by one if we don't get them. Speed is essential!"

Williams had asked Reno to lead the first foray, and he agreed, stipulating only one matter: "I want Zane Logan in on this." A murmur went up, but Williams looked at him shrewdly and agreed.

Two days later, a party of men rode into the yard of Ivo Morgan, and when Ivo and Zane came outside, Reno looked at them and said quietly, "We want you to come along, Logan."

Zane Logan stared at Reno, knowing there was more in this than he understood. He finally said, "All right, Jim. I'll get my gun."

They moved out as soon as Morgan and Zane were mounted, and Reno said to Williams, "You think you've got a lead, Jim?"

"Ed Rachaner says they've been holed up at Dempsey's ranch. He thinks it's most of the bunch that hangs out at Virginia City. Maybe we can stamp them all out at once!"

They rode hard and by noon came to Dempsey's ranch. "Not a big bunch here," Williams said. "Guess they've scattered."

"Let's see to it," Reno said. They rode right into the yard and found only Red Yeager and Thad Hilderman.

They separated the two men, questioned them, and found no trouble tying them in with the Innocents. After the questioning, Williams said, "All right. All for hanging, step this way. All against, the other way."

The verdict was unanimous: all the vigilantes moving to the hanging side.

Williams hesitated, then said, "I'd like to know what Creighton and Bible think of this. Ringo, you go see them; tell them what we've got."

They stayed that night, and the next morning Ringo returned, saying, "They say go ahead. You're doin' right."

Williams said to Hilderman and Yeager, "Guess you know what's coming. I'm sorry for it."

As they were standing under the cottonwoods, Beidler said, "Who are the others, Red?"

Yeager thought about that, then said, "Get Plummer. He's the worst!"

"Plummer!" Williams was surprised. "This is no time to lie, Red."

"Think I don't know? He's the ringleader." The rope touched his ear and he turned to look at it, then said, "Got a pencil?" He gave a list: Steve Marshland, Alec Carter, Buck Stinson, Jack Gallagher, Haze Lyons, and Ned Ray, all deputies.

Charley Forbes, Bill Hunter, Clubfoot George, Joe Pizanthia, Sam and Bill Brunton, Jen Romaine, and Boone Helm.

"That the list, Red?" Williams asked.

"That's most of them—the main ones, anyway."

There was a stillness, and then the chairs that had been brought out were knocked from beneath the two men. They fell with a twanging sound of the ropes.

The trip back to town was gloomy. "I'll be glad when this is over," Williams said.

"Red's list will help," Beidler responded. "Some of them will run, but we'll get most of them."

"We'd better, or they'll get us!" Williams said.

Beidler was not a man given to fear, and he spoke only what he felt to be true. He turned to Reno and said quietly, "Why'd you want Zane Logan to come on this trip, Jim? He's not one of us. Matter of fact, up until recent, I'd have said he'd be one of the ones we're looking for."

Reno said at once, "No, he's never been mixed up with the Innocents, Beidler. We both know men well enough to know he's cut from a different pattern than men like Ives and Yeager."

"He's Saul Logan's brother," Beidler insisted.

"Sure, but he cut loose from him when he stood up with us at Ivo Morgan's claim." Reno shook his head, adding, "Don't know what's between Saul and Zane. Maybe nobody does. But they're two different breeds of cats, X."

"That's so, but I still don't see why you asked him along on this trip."

"I wanted him, X.," was the only reply Beidler got, and he shrugged and put the matter aside.

"You got any more ideas about how to move, Jim?" Williams asked.

"Have to play it as it falls, I guess. But it'll have to be quick."

They got back to Virginia City and met with Creighton and Bible, giving them the details of their business. Then Reno made his way to the livery stable. He climbed the stairs, and Dooley opened the door before he knocked.

"Jim, is everything all right?"

He looked at her with a weary smile and said, "I guess so. Came by to tell you that I asked Zane to go with the vigilantes on business."

She stared at him with her eyes watchful. "Why, Jim?"

He shrugged his shoulders and leaned against the wall, letting the fatigue run through him. "Couple of reasons, Dooley. For one thing, I wanted to get him included so he'd be thought of as one of us. It's going to be pretty hard to convince folks he's changed after being Saul's hired gun."

"What else?"

He gave her a direct stare and said slowly, "I'm thinking that sooner or later Zane's going to have to make a choice, Dooley—and he may not be able to do it."

"What sort of choice, Jim?"

"This vigilante business is going to get mean." He shook his head sadly, and his lips tightened as he went on. "We hanged two men today, and they won't be the last. Before this is over there's going to be quite a few men dangling at the end of a rope. I wanted Zane along so he could see the way things are going to go." He paused and said without emphasis, "One day Saul Logan might be one of those hanging from a cottonwood, and I'm not sure how Zane would take it."

Dooley bit her lip and said, "He's been tied to his brother for a long time, Jim. I can't tell you why he's done his dirty work because it's not my secret. But I can tell you he won't do any more killing for Saul!"

"Maybe not, but could he stand by and see his brother hang?" Reno laid a direct glance on Dooley and added, "That's what's on my mind. He's quit the old life, but Saul's his brother, and if Zane sees him about to hang, I'm not sure he'll just stand by. And if he does try to help Saul, there's nothing I can do, Dooley. He'd be treated by the vigilante committee as one of the Innocents. They'd hang him on the same limb with Saul!"

"Jim! We can't let that happen!" Dooley caught at his arm, and begged, "You've got to help him!"

Reno shook his head. "I'll do what I can, Dooley, but every man gets to a place where he has to make his own choice. For Zane, I think, that'll be when he sees Saul about to go down."

"I'll talk to him, tell him he mustn't get involved with Saul!"

Reno smiled, and there was a world of sad experience in his dark eyes. He pulled free from her grasp, turned to go, but paused at the door, looked back and gave one final judgment.

"You might love Zane, Dooley, but you can't live his life for him. He'll have to play his own hand, just like the rest of us."

EIGHTEEN
Vigilante Justice

The trial and formal execution of George Ives and
the banishment of Wiley Hildebrand and Long John
Frank did not put an end to the activities of the
Innocents. The stage was robbed the next day, two
passengers being killed and the driver badly
wounded. Even the quick justice dealt out to Yeager
and Hilderman seemed to have had little effect. In
fact, it seemed to have stirred the Innocents to more
violence.

On his way to Nevada City, Jim Williams narrowly
escaped death when a bushwhacker threw a shot
that missed his head by inches. He managed to get
away, but he spread the word to the rest of the vigilantes that the toughs would whittle them down if
they could.

Merritt was getting his buggy from Easy early
one morning, and as usual he said, "Like to see you
in church next Sunday, Easy."

Easy pulled his high-crowned hat off, scratched

his head, and gave a faint grin that did not conceal the worry in his eyes.

"Wal, you may get yore wish, Reverend. This here vigilante business is enough to drive a man to religion."

"Been bad, has it?"

"I ain't never seen Jim Reno like he is now." Easy shook his head. "I've seen him mad and I've seen him in a fight, but this is different. We caught up with Steve Marshland and Jen Romaine over at Keyhole Mountain, and after a vote, we hung 'em. Wasn't neither one of them worth pig tracks—but hangin' a man is kinda final. I don't like the job, and it's eatin' on Jim somethin' awful."

"I'm praying it'll be over soon," Merritt said as he lifted the reins.

"Be lots more cottonwoods bearin' strange fruit 'fore that happens, Parson," Easy said. "And the toughs are out to get Jim any way they can."

While Merritt was talking to Easy, his daughter was sitting in the parlor with the subject of their conversation. Reno had stopped by to return a book, and Rachel said, "Come in for a minute, Jim. I've got another one that you ought to study."

Going inside, she found the book, and handed it to him. "You're looking tired, Jim—and worried."

"Guess my sins are catching up with me." He smiled, took the book, and would have left, but she took his arm.

"It's this vigilante business that's pulling you down, isn't it?"

He paused, and there was an intense sadness in his eyes as he shrugged and said, "Guess that's right. It's worse than the war, Rachel. I could live with that. Facing men who had guns, I'd take my chances." He shook his head slowly, and distaste for the whole thing was revealed in the lines around his eyes. "Can't get used to sending men out on the end of a rope!"

She found nothing to say, no formula that would make the thing any easier, so she said quietly, "You're worried about Dooley, too? About her and Zane?"

"Yes. Don't see any good ending to it." Then he forced himself to smile and said in a lighter tone, "Zane's too much like me. Guess that's why I don't like it."

"That's not bad, Jim," she answered at once.

He was caught off guard by her words. There was something about her that was different from every other woman he had known—something deep inside that was reflected in her violet eyes. He knew that beneath her placid beauty there was a rich passion. It was that quality, along with her absolute trust in God, that drew him to her.

"You're a charitable woman, Rachel," he murmured, and as the silence ran on, he knew that if he put his arms out, she would come to him. There was a willingness in her eyes, and he almost did so.

Then the thoughts of where such a thing might lead caught at him. He knew that she had been badly hurt, and while he was not completely certain of the nature of his own feelings for her, one thing was clear—he would do nothing to bring more pain into her life.

"I'll be going back to work now," he said, putting his hat on. "Lee and I will be in later in the week."

"All right, Jim." She did not move, but he did not

miss the disappointment in her eyes, and he knew he had been right. She had wanted him to kiss her.

He rode back to the claim, and for the next three days he drove himself and Lee, trying to ignore the urge to pull out of it all. Lee knew him well enough to read the signs, but he said nothing. *Guess we'll be pulling out of here pretty soon,* Lee thought, and it saddened him, for despite the rough side of the Gulch, he had come to like it.

They were getting ready for bed on Thursday night when Ringo Jukes came through the door, his face serious. "Jim, I got a message for you from Creighton."

"What's going on, Ringo?"

"He says that he's got word about a meeting of the toughs. Wouldn't say where he heard it, but the word is some of the wild bunch is holed up over at Bob Zachary's cabin. You know it?"

"Over by the Owlhorn diggings—close to Abe Dennison's place?"

"Yeah, that's it," Jukes said. "Now the problem is that Jim Williams is off with most of the vigilantes. Creighton wants to know if you can get some help and go to Zachary's place and hold 'em until I can find Williams and get the bunch over there."

Reno studied it, then said slowly, "Be pretty hard to find help, but I've got a feeling these meetings are pretty short. The birds might fly if we don't move quick."

"That's what Creighton said," Jukes agreed. "You want me to go with you, Jim?"

"No, you light out and find Williams. I'll take care of this end. Be quick as you can."

"Jim, don't do nothin' foolish, you hear?" Jukes had

a worried expression on his face, and he shook his head adding, "Don't try to hold 'em if there's too many. There'll be other times."

"We'll see how it goes." Reno frowned, and a streak of anger flashed in his eyes. "But we've got to take a few chances if we want to end this thing. Get moving, Ringo, and make it fast!"

As soon as he had left, Lee asked, "Can I go with you, Jim?"

"No." A bleak look on Reno's face told Lee that discussion would be useless. Lee had seen that look before and knew it meant that Reno was not to be changed.

"Be careful," the boy said. "I don't want anything to happen to you!"

Reno stopped, gave a sudden smile, and punched Lee on the arm, saying, "I'm too ornery to die, Lee. Now you saddle up my horse while I get a few things."

He threw a few supplies into his saddlebags, added ammunition for his .44, then plucked up his rifle. He mounted swiftly and threw a wave at the boy. "Be careful yourself, Lee!" Then he rode out at a fast clip.

He pulled his mount down to a gallop and turned her around the curve of the creek toward Ivo Morgan's claim. Zane was at the sluice box working, but there was no sign of Morgan.

"Ivo around, Zane?" Reno asked when he drew near.

"Gone to town. What's up, Jim?"

Reno gave Zane a direct look. "The usual, I guess."

Zane put his shovel down and said at once, "I'll get my gun."

He was back almost at once, mounted on a black

gelding, and Reno said, "This will be just you and me, Zane. And we'll have to make a quick trip."

As they rode along he explained the situation, and when he was finished Zane was silent for several miles. He was filled with a soberness that made him look older than usual. Finally he said, "This is bad business, Jim. I don't like it!" Then he gave Reno a quick look and added, "You don't either."

"No. Guess none of us do. But if we're going to live, looks like we'll have to fight for the right." He thought about it, then said, "It's a bad world, isn't it, Zane? Seems like all I've wanted to do is just be left alone. And mostly I've had to fight just to be allowed to do that."

Zane gave a short laugh. "Guess that's my story too, Jim. Reckon there's any hope of a fellow ever just *living?*"

"Man's got to hope, Zane. Otherwise he might just as well crawl in a hole and pull it in after him."

"Like to think that when the smoke clears away, things will be different," Zane said. They had slowed their horses down to save them, and he added quietly, "Never believed much in good things happening."

Turning to look at the other man, Reno had a strange look on his face. He said, "Guess you and me had the same kind of education, Zane—brought up the hard way. But I'd say you got a pretty good chance lying in the road in front of you."

"Dooley?" Zane lifted his head and glanced around the broken timber they were riding through before he murmured, "Well, like Easy says, Jim, it ain't over till it's over. Guess I want to do the right thing with that girl more than I ever wanted anything in my life."

"I think you'll make it, Zane," Reno said, and a smile broke the sobriety of his dark face. Then he said, "We better get moving."

By three o'clock they were approaching the foothills of a small mountain range that curled around like a fishhook, surrounding a small lake and several acres of flatland. "Zachary's place is just around the bend of those pines, Zane," Reno said, pulling up to a halt. "We'll leave the horses here and make a stalk through this brush."

Zane followed Reno as he moved quickly through the undergrowth, marveling at how little sound the smaller man made as he went across the broken ground. He tried to be quiet, but he did not have the art of it, and finally just kept up as best he could.

"There it is," Reno whispered, pulling a branch aside and peering through the opening. Zane saw a dogtrot cabin with several horses tied to a hitching rail.

"How we going to work this thing?" he asked. "Looks like about eight or nine horses there. We goin' to wait for Williams?"

Reno studied the house, then said, "I reckon we better make our play, Zane. If we don't get the whole bunch while they're together like this, we'll have to hunt 'em down one at a time, and that'll be hard." He pulled his gun and checked the loads, then nodded toward the house. "They're all inside, so I'll take the front and you take the back. We'll go in and throw down on 'em at the same time."

"How'll we time it?"

"I'll give you plenty of time to make it to the back door. Then I'll jump in and give a big war whoop and

I'll slam the door behind me. When you hear that, you jump right in. We'll have 'em flanked."

"Let's do it, then!"

Zane made his way around the broken edge of timber that lay fifty yards away from the side of the cabin, and Reno waited until he saw the tall form break from the timber and cross the open space, making it to the back porch in long running strides. Then he moved toward the east side of the cabin. There was no window in that side, and he reached the wall and edged his way toward the front.

He could hear voices inside, and he bent down and crawled underneath the window in the front. Getting to his feet, he took the handle of the door in hand. Then, taking a deep breath, he shoved it open and stepped inside. Clearing the door, he slammed it hard and shouted, "Hold it, you jaybirds!" at the top of his lungs.

He caught sight of Bill Hunter and Boone Helm sitting at a table playing cards. Bob Zachary was standing beside the stove, a plate in his hand. Clubfoot George was at a kitchen table, his fork raised and his eyes wide with shock.

Zachary went for the gun at his side, but suddenly the door behind him slammed open against the wall, and Zane shouted, "Don't do it, Zachary!" Zachary got completely still.

Reno knew he had to move fast, so he moved to take the guns from Hunter and Helm.

The shock of the entrance had paralyzed the men in the cabin, and they sat there as Reno and Zane disarmed them. "Get over against that wall, all of you," Reno ordered, and he stood side by side with

Zane, both of them keeping their guns trained on the men as they moved against the wall.

"What's going on here, Reno?" Zachary demanded.

"You've probably got a pretty good idea, Bob," Reno said. "You should have been expecting a visit."

"You goin' to rob us?" Clubfoot George asked. He was a small man with muttonchop whiskers. "You won't get much from me."

"Not what we're here for, George," Reno stated. He checked to see that Zane had all the guns, then said, "We'll have a little wait until the others come."

Instantly the faces of the men against the wall changed, and Zachary began protesting loudly. He was talking so loudly in fact, that Reno was puzzled. He was about to tell Zachary to shut up, when a voice right behind him ran like a shock along his nerves.

"All right, you two! Hold it right there and don't move. There's two shotguns pointed right at your spines!"

Reno saw a smile run over the faces of the men, and he knew that he and Zane had been suckered.

"Just get the guns from them, Bob," the voice said, and Reno knew it was Jack Gallagher.

"He can't get both of us, Jim," Zane said, and made a slight movement to turn.

"He's got help!" another voice said, and that froze Zane into place. He stood there until Zachary took his gun, then he turned to find himself looking into the eyes of his brother. Saul had a sawed-off shotgun pointed right at him, and Gallagher had another aimed at Reno.

Gallagher reached over and pulled the gun from Reno's hand, then gave him a slicing blow with it that caught him on the left shoulder. Reno staggered and was shoved by the burly deputy against the front wall, where he stood with his arm paralyzed from the blow.

"Well, now, guess this is the time I been waitin' for, Reno," Gallagher grunted. "You been top dog, but that ends right now."

"We better get movin', Jack," Boone Helm said nervously. "You heard what he said about company comin'."

"Yeah, that's right. But this won't take long." Gallagher gave Reno a malevolent look, then laughed out loud. "Don't take too long to hang a man, does it, Reno?"

Reno looked at him, then said, "You'll find out soon enough, Jack. Your number's coming up."

Angered by Reno's lack of fear, Gallagher shouted, "Hunter, get a rope and put it over the limb on that cottonwood outside!"

"Make that two ropes, Hunter!" Saul Logan said.

He leaned his shotgun against the wall and came to stand before Zane. He made a strange figure, like an alien from another world, as he waited, looking up into Zane's eyes. His dress was immaculate, in the latest fashion, in violent contrast to the rough dress of the other men. He had a thin face, intellectual and sharp-featured, and out of the hooded eyes that nobody in town had ever been able to penetrate, a tremendous hatred flashed forth. He said almost in a whisper, "You were always the best, weren't you, Zane? Always better than me?"

Zane looked down at the smaller man, and there was no anger in him at all. Rather, a profound sense of regret marred the even tenor of his eyes as he shook his head. "There's always been something wrong inside your head, Saul. All your life you've hated me, and there was never any reason." Zane's face changed then, and he said quietly, "I always wanted to help you, Saul, but you never wanted it."

"Help me!" Saul Logan flushed, and he raised his cane and shook it in the air. "You crippled me, then you throw it up to me how *strong* you are! Now you want to *help* me!" There was a look in the face of the dapper man that was not quite sane. He whirled and shouted, "Put those ropes up, Hunter, and *I'll* drive the horses out from under them!"

Gallagher stepped forward and waved his gun at Zane. "Get out there, both of you!"

Zane and Reno went through the front door, and Hunter stepped to his horse and got a rope. "Have to use yours, Boone," he said.

"Best use it's ever had!" Helm said with a grin. "Lemme help you make them loops."

Helm made a hangman's knot in each of the ropes, then led the way to a tall cottonwood tree near the cabin. Boone threw one rope over, and Hunter the other, and they knotted the free ends tightly on the trunk.

"Get two horses," Gallagher snapped, and he waited while Zachary brought the two animals forward under the swaying nooses. "Tie their hands, Bob," he said.

Zachary got his own rope, cut two pieces out, and tied Zane's hands behind his back, them moved to Reno. Saul Logan said suddenly, "Wait a minute." He came to stand in front of Reno and asked softly, "You remember how you dumped the chili on my head in front of the whole town?" He waited, but Reno did not answer, so he said, "I always collect my debts, Reno, so I'm calling this one." He said to Zachary, "Don't tie his hands, Bob."

Zachary looked at him in surprise. "But he'll grab the rope, Saul!"

"Let him!" An unholy smile was pasted on Saul Logan's pale face, and he was rubbing his hands together as if they were cold. "Let him climb up like a monkey on a string! Let him climb until his arms give out! Boone, you can give him a pull, can't you? I want to see his face turn black and his tongue fill his mouth!"

Bob Zachary was a hard man, but he made a sour face, saying, "That ain't no way to kill a man, Saul!"

Saul Logan lost his calm and shouted angrily, "Do what I tell you!"

Reno and Zane were hoisted into the saddles, and Gallagher saw that someone would have to get mounted to put the nooses on. "Clubfoot George, get mounted and put the rope on Reno."

As he turned to go, Zane Logan said in a croaking voice not at all like his own, "Don't—don't kill me—please don't kill me!"

Reno turned and saw that Zane's face was working, his mouth going open and shut like a fish out of water. He was swaying in the saddle, and his whole body was heaving in a jerking motion. *Can't take it*, Reno thought, and looked away, not wanting to see it.

"Please, *Saul!*" Zane cried out, and he fixed his eyes on his brother. "I'll—I'll do anything you say, Saul! I'll lick your boots—*anything!* Don't let them hang me! Please!"

The cry went on and on, and all the men in the

yard felt queasy. "Man ought not to die like that!" Gallagher muttered. "Hurry up, George!"

George had mounted his horse, but the animal was spooked by the screams coming from Zane, and he could not get the animal under control.

Reno looked down at Saul Logan. There was a look of pleasure on his face. His lips were open and his eyes half-closed as he listened to Zane's pitiful screams. He swayed slightly, and once he nodded to himself. Then as Clubfoot George got his horse under control and came up beside Reno, Saul opened his eyes and stared at Zane, who was reduced to a trembling heap of flesh, his face turned into that of an idiot.

"Cut him loose, George!" Saul called out.

"Wait a minute, Saul," Gallagher protested. "You can't trust him!"

"He'll be all right now," Saul said. He smiled as he looked at his brother. "You see, he's never been broken before, Jack. No matter what I did, or what anybody did, he never cried! But he's crying now! Look at him! He'll never have any guts, not after this." And he called out, "You heard me, George; I said cut Zane loose!"

"What about it, Jack?" George asked.

"All right, cut him down!" Gallagher snapped. "We can always take care of him later! But the other one goes!"

"Yes, the other one goes," Saul agreed with a searching look at Reno. "Put that noose on him, George!"

"Can't do but one thing at a time!" Clubfoot George said. He had already drawn his knife and was reaching around Reno, and he sliced the ropes binding Zane's hands, then clicked the knife shut. He put it in his pocket, then reached up to take the noose, but he never made it.

As soon as Zane felt the ropes holding his hands drop away, he turned in the saddle, twisting and lunging. Throwing himself across behind Reno's saddle, he made a quick stab at George's gun, and the effort sent pain along the nerves in his chest and shoulder, but he ignored it. If he missed, it was all over, but his hand closed on the gun, and he pulled it free. He was off-balance, and he heard Gallagher yell, "Get him!" as he fought to straighten up.

A shot plucked his hat off, then he swiveled around and threw a shot at Boone Helm that drove the big man backward. His horse reared, and Zane fell heavily, his leg pinned down by the bulk of the animal.

Reno grasped what Zane had done, and instantly drove his spurs into the horse. The animal, maddened by the sudden gunfire and the savage jab of the spurs, shot forward. As he went by the men who were firing, Reno dropped off, falling on Bob Zachary who was firing wildly at Zane.

Zachary gave a shout and tried to lunge free, but Reno reached out and locked his hands behind Zachary's face. Reno lowered his head and jerked the man forward with all his strength. Zachary went limp, and Reno snatched up his gun and came to his feet.

Clubfoot George had yanked his rifle from his saddle boot and was firing on Zane Logan, who was carrying on a fire fight with Hunter. Reno leveled his gun and got off a shot just as the rifle came to bear. The slug caught George in the chest, and the dying pull of his finger set the rifle off, but the slug went into the dead horse instead of Zane.

Hunter saw Reno whirl, and he at once threw his gun down, crying out, "I'm finished! Don't shoot!"

Reno quickly surveyed the scene. Zachary was getting to his feet, his face bleeding profusely, and Hunter had thrown his gun down. Boone Helm was climbing to his feet, holding his side, which was bleeding. Saul Logan stood slightly apart from the action, staring with unbelieving eyes at what had taken place.

"Watch it, Jim!"

Zane's call made Reno throw himself to one side, and he missed death by inches as a bullet that Gallagher fired at him hissed by his ear. Gallagher had his arm leveled and got off another shot, but he missed again. Zane had a clear shot, but his weapon clicked on an empty chamber.

Gallagher tried the third time, and it raked along Reno's side. Reno brought his weapon up and was ready to fire when Gallagher's weapon clicked on a spent shell.

The huge deputy stood there, looking into the muzzle of Reno's Colt, and he dropped his gun, crying out, "Don't shoot!"

Seeing that Gallagher was helpless, Reno lowered his gun.

A strange quiet reigned over the yard. Far off a bird was singing a plaintive song, and a cricket was making music somewhere.

"Guess that's it," Reno said. He came to stand over Zane, then motioned at Gallagher and Hunter, "Get that animal off him!"

Zane gave a yank as they heaved at the bulk of the

horse. He went at once and got some shells from the dead man's belt. He reloaded his weapon, then said, "Pretty close squeak, Jim. What'll we do with them?"

Reno said wearily, "Wait for Williams, I guess. Let's get 'em tied up."

"What about this bullet hole?" Helm demanded sullenly. "I'm going to bleed to death if it's not plugged up."

Reno stared at him and said without a trace of emotion, "Don't worry about it, Helm. You won't have time enough for that."

The reply turned Helm's face a pasty color, and he took a quick glance at the twin nooses swaying in the breeze, then quickly looked away.

Zane took a look at the slight wound on Reno's side, but it was merely a graze. Helm's wound was painful, but the bullet had passed through, so they put a couple of pads on the wound and then sat down to wait inside the cabin.

Saul Logan had not said a word for over an hour as they sat there waiting, then he stood up. Reno said, "Sit down, Logan."

Saul did not even look at him. He came to stand in front of Zane, his cane making a tapping sound on the wooden floor. He stood there and looked at Zane, then he said, "Get me out of this, Zane!"

Zane stared at him. "You've always had me when you went smash, haven't you? I had to take on all the fights you caused, even when we were kids."

"Zane, you were right," Saul said quickly. "I've been wrong, my thinking. I must have been insane to do what I did."

"You've always put me down, Saul."

"No more!" the small man cried out. "No more,

Zane, I swear it. I can see what a mess I've made of everything! But it's not too late." His face lit up, and he leaned forward saying in a whisper, "I've got fifty thousand dollars, Zane—fifty thousand! We can take it and go anywhere you like. It's all yours!"

"Too late, Saul."

Saul Logan glanced at Reno, who was watching carefully. "You worried about him?" Saul motioned with his cane. "He's nothing to you. I'm your *brother*, Zane—your brother!"

"No, I don't think so." Zane looked across into Saul's feverish eyes. "I don't think I've ever been your brother, Saul."

"Is it him?" Saul looked at Reno. "You can take him with your left hand, Zane, then we can have the world!"

Reno turned to look at Zane. The tall man was sitting in a chair, his head bowed, and there was a desperate look on his face. As Saul continued to whisper, Reno saw a tremble come to Zane's hands, and his face grew pale.

This is where we find out, Reno thought. *He's never been able to say no to Saul. Doubt if he can cut it now.*

Zane got to his feet, his hands at his side, and Saul smiled. "Sure, you can take him! Just one shot— that's all we need, Zane. Then it'll be me and you with all the money in the world!"

Zane looked into Reno's eyes, and there was a tingling in Reno's right hand. Then Zane deliberately sat down again, saying in a low voice, "I've always picked up your tab, Saul. But this is one time you've got to answer for what you've done."

Saul Logan's mouth dropped open, and a wild

light came into his eyes. He began to beg in a high-pitched voice, but Gallagher shouted, "Shut your mouth, Logan! You'll take what the rest of us get!"

Logan slowly turned and walked back to his chair, his back bent, and he sat there until Jim Williams pulled up in the yard three hours later with ten men.

"Got 'em, did you, Reno?"

"Zane mostly," Reno said, and he took one look at Zane. Never had he seen such pain in a man's eyes, and he said, "Maybe you ought to ride on back to Virginia City, Zane."

The tall man flashed him a look of anger. "I'll stay, Jim!"

The routine was established by this time, and the vote came quickly. Every man voted for death, and Williams said, "I'm sorry for you, but it's the end of the line. Get three more ropes on that limb, Beidler!"

It was a matter of minutes until the five men were seated on horses, nooses around their necks. Gallagher was cursing and shouting. Zachary, his bloody face white, said nothing. Helm had asked for a drink and had finished off a pint of whiskey before he was hoisted onto his horse. Hunter seemed to be saying a prayer of some kind.

Saul Logan looked across the yard, his eyes meeting those of his brother, and he said clearly, "Get me out of this, Zane!"

Then three men whipped up the horses, and the ropes went taut. Reno felt sick as he always did at such times.

X. Beidler said, "They're dead."

Zane went to his brother, cut him down, and picked up the frail body. He looked down into the still face, and then after a long pause he looked at Reno and said, "He could have been anything— anything at all, Jim!" Then he turned and said, "I'll bury him out in the meadow. He always liked spring flowers."

Watching Zane go across the yard, Beidler said, "I was wrong about that one."

Reno said, "I guess he's going to make it, X. But he's got a heavy load of memory over this day."

"My boy, we all have to eat our peck of dirt," the stocky Beidler said. "But he is a good man, and that makes up for everything."

The news of the execution of the five came to Virginia City on the heels of a word from Bannack. The vigilantes there had rounded up Buck Stinson and Henry Plummer and had hung them side by side at a shed on the edge of town. Before the hanging, Plummer had fallen to his knees, crying in terror, and had to be held on a box until it was kicked out from beneath him.

All sentimental pity vanished from the camps. All the accumulated memories of the murders and cold-blooded villainy came back, and the vigilantes hunted down their men one by one in canyons and remote settlements and isolated cabins. They pulled them out, passed sentence on them, and hung them from any tree or rafter available. So died, finally, the last of the Innocents.

"We can stop trembling at last," Reverend Merritt said from his pulpit one sunny Sunday morning. He looked over the congregation, noting Dooley and Zane sitting in the back, and he gave a nod of approval.

After the service he talked with Easy, who was

making his first visit to church. "Looks like a bride, don't she now?" the bandy-legged rider asked with a fond look at Dooley.

"Probably will be one soon," Merritt said. "You and Reno and Lee are taking dinner with us."

"About which I ain't gonna argue!"

After a dinner that staggered Easy, he groaned, "Miz Rachel, I was gonna beat your dad at horseshoes. Now I don't think I can pick one up!"

"Then I'll take you on now, Easy," Merritt laughed. Pulling the small rider to his feet, the two went outside. While Reno and Lee helped Rachel with the dishes, they smiled at the outraged yelps of Easy as he got badly trimmed by the minister.

"Dad's a professional," Rachel said as she watched them out the window. Then she asked, "You want to work on your English this afternoon, Lee?"

Lee shook his head gloomily. "Reckon no. Looks like we might not get to do much more anyway."

Rachel stared at him. "Why is that?"

Lee dipped his head, then lifted his head with an accusing look at Reno. "Aw, Jim's goin' to get itchy feet. I've seen it lots of times. Now that Dooley's all right, we'll be movin' on."

He went to the door and said, "That was a real good dinner, Miss Rachel. And I've really enjoyed the teachin'!"

He left, and Rachel's face was sober as she hung the dishcloth on a rack and said, "You want me to show you how to work that problem, Jim?"

"Sure."

She led him into the dining room, and they sat down close together while she went through a problem that had given him difficulties. Her mind was not on it, and she made several careless mistakes, which made him smile.

Finally she put her pencil down and looked directly at him. "Why will you leave here, Jim?"

He was disturbed by his reply, for he did not have any answers. Always before when it was time to move on, to see the other side of the hill, he was happy, anxious to be on the road. Now he was dejected, and he could only say, "Don't ask me that, Rachel. I'm just a roving man, I guess."

He grew warm under her close inspection. As always her beauty swayed him, and he got up quickly, saying, "I'll not leave without coming to say good-bye, Rachel."

He went through the door feeling completely drained and as unhappy as he could remember. He got to the end of the walk and turned, but as he walked rapidly away, he heard her call, "Jim!" and he turned to see her come running out the front door. She ran down the steps, to the front, her face tense and strained.

"Rachel! What's the matter?" he asked.

She threw herself into his arms, and he had to catch her to keep her from falling. He was aware that her father and Easy had come around the house and had stopped to stare at them.

Tears were glistening in her huge violet eyes like diamonds. Her soft lips trembled, and she said in a rush, as if she had to get it all out at once, "I'm in love with you, Jim Reno—*that's* what's the matter!"

"Rachel—!"

"No! You listen to me!" Her breath came in short gasps. "I wanted a storybook courtship, Jim. I wanted you to come calling and after a long time ask me to marry you. But that'll never happen! So I could be a lady and let you walk away—and lose you!"

She was crying in earnest now, the tears rolling down her flushed cheeks. She looked up at him and pressed her lips together, then said defiantly. "So I'm not going to be a lady, Jim! I'm going to fight for what I want, just like you do. And what I want is you!"

She buried her face against his chest, her soft body shaking with deep sobs.

Reno stood there and thought, *What's over the next hill that's half as good as what I've got right here?*

He began to smile, and then he reached down and pulled her face up, and he said gently, "I'm glad you're not a lady, because I wouldn't let a lady marry a bad bargain like me." Then he kissed her, and she came to him, and there was nothing but her in his world.

She pulled her head back and said softly but with a laugh in her voice, "I'll take the chance, Jim!"

Merritt and Easy watched in amazement as the two went back into the house, and then Easy said sadly but with delight in his blue eyes, "Never was a horse couldn't be rode, never was a rider couldn't be throwed. And I guess James has met his match." Then he shot a humorous glance at Merritt and asked, "You got a Bible verse that might fit this here leetle situation, Reverend?"

Merritt gave a fond look at the house, then turned to face Easy. "Well, I guess like the Book says, Easy, he was a stranger, and she took him in!"

OTHER WESTERNS
from Living Books

Westerns in the Living Books series feature the action and excitement you expect from Westerns—plus a concern for moral choices and personal integrity. In the great tradition of American Western novels, Living Books offers you quality stories that show—with realism and compassion—the age-old conflict between good and evil.

THE DRIFTER by Gilbert Morris. War-weary drifter Jim Reno finds himself caught in the conflict between the greedy Carrs of Skull Ranch and a group of small ranchers. Though tired of violence, Reno is determined to free the rancher from Skull's exploitation. Number 1 in the Reno Westerns Series.

TREACHERY AT CIMARRON by Jim Ross. Ruthless killers and a beautiful scheming woman haunt the Cimarron range, seeking a rancher's gold. Marks Dunlee learns of the plot and plans a daring rescue. Number 1 in the Dunlee Westerns Series.

AMBUSH AT VERMEJO by Jim Ross. Lonan Dunlee sees a rancher ambushed and vows to find the killers. In the search he unravels an elaborate scheme involving a false burial, a conniving brother, a corrupt lawman, and the vicious Gaster brothers. Number 2 in the Dunlee Westerns Series.

BRECK'S CHOICE by Bernard Palmer. Former gunman John Breck had sworn never to use a gun again. But when his gold is stolen and his wife and child murdered, he must find the killers. And his only clue is a broken hoofprint. Number 1 in the Breck Westerns Series.

HUNTED GUN by Bernard Palmer. Colorado rancher John Breck encounters an ambush, suspicious townspeople, and deceit spawned by gold fever as he searches for the killers of a rancher who just found gold. Number 2 in the Breck Westerns Series.

KID BRECKINRIDGE by Bernard Palmer. This tale introduces young John Breckinridge (the John Breck of *Breck's Choice* and *Hunted Gun*). John, a runaway, learns a lot about the Old West as he experiences an Indian ambush, a cattle drive, and a bank robbery. Number 3 in the Breck Westerns Series.